CELTIC

MAIDENS

CERI NORMAN

Published by

MELROSE BOOKS

An Imprint of Melrose Press Limited
St Thomas Place, Ely
Cambridgeshire
CB7 4GG, UK
www.melrosebooks.com

SECOND EDITION

Copyright © Ceri Norman 2010, 2011

The Author asserts her moral right to
be identified as the author of this work

Cover designed by Catherine McIntyre

ISBN 978 1 907732 39 3

Printed and bound in Great Britain by:
CPI Group (UK) Ltd, Croydon, CR0 4YY

www.cerinorman.com

Visit Ceri's website to find out more about Ceri, her work and her love of mystery, history and mythology. Discover the places that have inspired this novel.

Dedication
For my dearest husband.

Acknowledgements
A huge thank you to my husband, for all his love and support.

My thanks to all those who have taught and inspired me over the years
in classrooms, workplaces or out in nature.

Thank you to all at Pemberton's Chocolate Farm
for their kindness and the delicious hot chocolates.

Thank you to all the team at Melrose Books for their encouragement and
support.

PROLOGUE

The winds whirled wildly around the ancient stones, howling as the black storm clouds rolled in across the mountains. Darkness was approaching but not complete, not yet. The thick clouds were obliterating the divisions between night and day; this was a time of the in-between. A powerful time when the veil between worlds is as light and transparent as gossamer.

A solitary figure slowly approached the circle of stones. His footsteps were uneven as he fought frantically with the soggy marshland beneath his feet. With each step the marsh tried to suck him down, to deter him from his purpose and to prevent him from reaching the sacred stones. The Heavens opened and hail poured down, hail so small and hard that it stung on contact with his body. The figure wrapped himself ever more tightly in his coat, determined to continue. The ache, the pain and desire welled up within him, he could wait no longer. He wanted her more than life itself. It had to be done now, while the portents and planets were powerful, or he would have to wait for another lifetime. A bolt of lightning streaked across the sky, adding to the urgency.

Finally, he reached the first of the outlying stones. Leaning against it, he paused to get his breath, as the wind whipped the very air from his lungs. He swore at the elements trying to defeat him; not this time. He needed to be whole. The words of his incantation were lost as thunder roared overhead and echoed around the valley. Falling to his knees in the lee of the stone, into a small depression in the ground, he reached into his pocket and pulled out the items he had brought for this task. With his bare hands he scraped away at the waterlogged soil. The grass cut at his hands, making them bleed, and the mud stuck painfully under his fingernails. Within the small hole he placed the offerings and, as he pushed them down, the marsh responded, sucking them deeper. Leaning back on his heels, the figure raised his head, looking, searching, for something or someone.

More lightning flickered against the top of Carn Siân. By its light, shadows formed around the stones; the shadows moved and swirled with each strike. The thunder roared in anger. A second figure appeared behind the first, formed as if out of the stone itself, shadowy, dark and ghostly. It stepped forwards into the other, merging with him, forcefully, mercilessly filling his emptiness. The mortal man shuddered and twisted in torment as his muscles contorted, threatening to tear skin from bone. His eyes flickered madly under his closed lids. His breathing ceased as his heart raced on and on. Pangs of fiery pain shot through his every nerve, his brain felt aflame and then an eerie cloud swept over his mind. His thoughts became slow and muddled. Someone else was at the controls now. The man opened his new eyes for the first time and inhaled a deep, cool breath of air. Slowly he raised his arms and howled his triumph to the elements, a howl of hate, of anguish and of evil. The wind carried his cry out across the mountains and through the aeons.

CHAPTER ONE

The first warm rays of sunlight flooded over the mountains. The storm of the night before had cleared the air and the tang of tin from the electricity was still evident. The birds were in the mood for celebration; spring was coming gradually to the Preseli Mountains.

Siân Derwyn had a spring in her step as she rushed around the house, getting ready for work. She always left it until the very last moment; to her it was an act of defiance. It was not that she disliked her job, far from it, but the job had only meant to be temporary and here she still was, over two years later. In the shower she washed away her frustrations and the last of her tears, not just from the shampoo in her eyes. Hurriedly she pulled on her clothes and ran a brush through her fine jet-black hair; it crackled with static. As she grabbed for her keys, Siân cast a glance around the cottage and sighed deeply. She had lived here for most of her life with her Mamgu, her beloved grandmother, and now she lived in it all alone. It had been three months now since the cancer had defeated Branwen Ellis. Three months, yet still she expected to hear her Mamgu Branwen's voice, or see her coming to wish her off.

Siân pulled the door closed behind her and gently placed her hand on the elegant Dragon Gargoyle above the door, which had earned the cottage the nickname of 'Dragon's Cottage', or, more simply, the lair. "Ddraig fach, wela i ti, please take care of the cottage and me." It had become as part of her morning ritual as cleaning her teeth, as it had been for Mamgu before her. Mamgu Branwen had told her the tale so many times, how Tadcu Dai had carved him from a fallen yew from the Chapel grounds to protect the house and all who dwelt within. Turning away from the cottage, with sad and serious eyes, Siân gazed out at her namesake, the mountain she had been named after. It looked to be a beautiful day, and Siân found herself smiling broadly to welcome it, before hurrying down the road to the shop.

"Siân, where did you put the little Easter eggs?" called a muffled female voice from the stockroom.

"In my stomach, where else?" Siân giggled.

"You never, not that many anyway. Come on, it's freezing in here."

Siân sighed. "They're with the other sweets, opposite the soups, as always." She carried on tidying up the magazines.

"Nope, I still can't find them. Can you come and have a peek, please?"

Siân stood up, paced around the counter, and into the stockroom. It took her eyes a moment to adjust to the dark gloom that seemed to lie like thick fog in this room. She shuddered and felt her energy levels fall as always.

"Please tell me I'm not just being thick." The other, older, woman looked worried.

Siân scanned the shelves with her big blue eyes and frowned, "No, Mandy, you're not being thick, they're not there. I swear I put them there, next to the bigger ones. Hang on." Siân tied her hair back in one deft movement. She clambered down on all fours, put her head almost to the ground and inspected behind the unit. "Poop, they've fallen down the back. Have we got a stick or something?"

"Erm, yeah, I've got a brolly somewhere." Mandy disappeared for a moment and came back with a pink, child's umbrella. "Will this do? Alice left it here."

"Perfect." Using the handle of the umbrella, Siân sought to get a hold on the box. After several attempts, it finally worked, and slowly Siân retrieved the box of Easter eggs. She put them on the shelf marked 'Not For Sale'. "Ugh, they're all broken. I'd better order some more."

"Yeah, but you know Lloyd will just put them out when you're not around."

"That's because Lloyd's a skank."

Mandy laughed, a warm laugh. It made her dark eyes sparkle. "Oh my, you do know that my darling daughter has picked that word up."

"Really? I am sorry." Siân had the grace to appear to be embarrassed.

"It's better than the latest word she's got from her dad. At least skank only sounds like a swear word without actually being one."

The shop bell interrupted them, and the two women wandered back out to the counter. One of the regulars stood before them, dressed as usual in jeans and a T-shirt; no matter how good or how awful the weather, that was always what he wore. The man was young, but how young was hard to tell. His dark hair was a mess, some of it spiky, some of it flat. It always looked slept on, though once, when Siân had asked him about this, he had been very pleased; apparently that was the image he had been going for. He had earphones in each ear and an MP3 player in his pocket. Siân smiled to herself. Huw West had hardly changed since school, apart from in height. He was that odd creature that every school had at least one of. He was painfully shy and had often been bullied for it. Quiet, thoughtful, with serious eyes hidden under a glazed expression that made everyone think he was either sullen or dim, when in fact he was pretty bright. When he noticed the two ladies, he quickly pulled out one of his earphones.

"Bore da, may I have a pack of triple A batteries, please?"

"Sure, Huw." Siân bent down and grabbed the box of batteries from under the counter. She sifted through them. "That's £1.99, please."

Huw handed her a two pound coin and wandered away, happy in a world of his own.

Mandy watched him go. "He's always been sweet on you; I don't know why you two aren't together."

Siân shuffled the papers on the counter, trying to appear far too busy to hear her friend.

"Would you like a cuppa?" asked Mandy instead.

That got a response. "Please."

Sipping her hot tea slowly and noisily was one of Mandy's little pleasures. It was a moment for her, a moment of peace and quiet, the likes of which she did not often get at home. The shop bell rang again and Mandy rolled her eyes in annoyance. Both women eyed the visitor up and down. He wore dark jeans and a dark navy ribbed jumper, underneath his open coats, both of which suited his winter complexion perfectly. Young, handsome and obviously lost. Undoubtedly a tourist, they knew he would be English before he even opened his mouth.

Siân stood up and set her funky coloured mug down on the countertop. "Good morning, can I help you?"

"Err, yeah," the tourist shuffled awkwardly. "I'm looking for the Ring of Maidens, the stone circle."

Siân nodded. "I can show you on the map, just don't ask me for directions."

Mandy snorted with laughter. "They never did find the last tourist she gave directions to."

Siân glared at her as she pulled out an OS map from the stand and unfurled it across the remainder of the morning papers, moving her tea to hold it down. "See, you're here in Maenddu. This is us; there's the Chapel. Take this road, go over the crossroads. Carry on until you find the little lay-by and from there you'll need to take the footpath. Make sure you keep the big gorse bushes to your left, otherwise you'll miss it." She pointed to the cluster of black dots on the map and looked up to make sure he was following. Her eyes met his and for the first time she truly studied him. His green eyes were soft and sparkling, with the clarity of the western coastal waters, and a huge contrast to his dark brown hair.

Mandy viewed their awkwardness with great amusement; she shook her head. The movement broke their concentration and they both glanced away, a little embarrassed.

"So, why are you looking for Cylch Morwynion?" asked Mandy, trying to be polite. He did not seem like the usual megalith hunters; he was too well dressed for starters.

"Cylch...? What?"

"The Maidens."

"Yeah, I'm interested in Megaliths."

"There are hundreds around here, you know. Most of them only known to the locals. Siân here would be happy to show you some of them, I'm sure. She knows lots about them." She elbowed the reddening Siân in the ribs.

"Er, thanks. How much for the map?"

"Ten pounds, please."

The tourist fiddled with his wallet as he sought for a ten-pound note. He gave it to Mandy while Siân refolded the map. He flashed a smile at her as she handed it over to him and then bolted out of the shop.

"Why did you have to go and do that?" Siân asked her colleague through gritted teeth.

"Aw, come on, he was gorgeous." Mandy grinned cheekily.

"I beg your pardon."

"It's been a while now since your Gran died, time for you to start moving on. I think he liked the look of you." Mandy's voice was filled with genuine concern, despite her mile-wide grin.

Siân gave up the argument. She knew better than to argue with Mandy when she got an idea in her head. "He did have lovely eyes."

"Hell, I didn't see that! I was too busy inspecting his body. I wish my husband had a bum like that."

"Mandy, you're obsessed! I didn't think married women were supposed to look."

"Oh, we can look all right, look all we like, we just can't touch," Mandy said seriously, and they both erupted into laughter.

The bell rang again and the tourist stuck his head around the door. This time it was his turn to blush.

"Sorry to bother you again. Is there a B&B around here, somewhere I can stay?"

Mandy opened her mouth to speak, but Siân cut across her. "Try the 'Merry Maidens Pub'. They have rooms sometimes."

"Thanks, Siân. I'm Ryan, by the way." He ducked back out of the shop and headed off to his car, grinning like an idiot.

CHAPTER TWO

The figure huddled further back into the prickly leaves of the yew by the old Chapel, not wanting to be seen. He calmly exhaled one long breath and tried to mould himself into the tree, physically and spiritually. The yew refused and attacked him more, pushing its prickles through his clothes and into his skin. He watched the newcomer with interest and curiosity. Who was he and what was he doing here? More importantly, would he interfere? The figure observed how the young man walked with a bounce in his step, with a keenness and energy that smacked of city life, or at least life in the fast lane when it was still being enjoyed, before it gnawed away at the soul. He was dressed for the outdoors in that way that city folk do; huge cagoule over fleece and expensive walking boots. He climbed into a shabby old four by four and drove off out of the village. Something did not quite fit in the eyes of the watcher; it felt wrong that he had turned up now, out of tourist season, and when he had set his plan in motion. He had, much to his own horror, already got rid of one obstacle and he knew that, if he had to, he would do so again.

Ryan pulled into the lay-by and studied the map; it only seemed about a mile or so to the circle, maybe less. After working out which direction to head in, he pulled out his camera and tripod from behind the passenger seat. Slinging the camera around his neck, he opened the door and headed off into the unknown. The warm sun was a blessing; it would make for a great shot. The grey of the megaliths matched with the green of the land, and the blue of a bright day would be perfect, just the kind of shot he had been asked to get. He pushed open the gate and observed the moorland laid out in front of him. He squinted in the low sun, seeking out a pathway, but could see only a faint green line ahead. Ryan had not gone far before he realised how muddy and marshy the ground was. With each step a puddle arose, as well as a squelching noise. Using his tripod as an impromptu walking stick, he ploughed on. It took him a while to reach the circle, but it was well worth it.

As he approached, Ryan was struck by the wild beauty of the place. He had, on his travels, seen many such monuments, each with its own story to tell, its own unique presence, but this one, this place, blew him away. The circle was set in a cauldron of hills, almost in the lowest point of the valley. The stones were low, much smaller than he had expected. The tallest was only a couple of feet high. There was no uniformity of shape or size; each one was totally unique. Ryan wondered if each of these stones represented a maiden in some way, each as individual as they were. As he studied the arrangement of the stones, something slowly dawned on him. This was neither a stone circle, nor an oval or egg as he had seen in Devon and Cornwall. It was not quite one, nor quite the other; the ring seemed unable to quite make up its mind what it wanted to be. How intriguing, it had been clearly laid out in this way. He smiled to himself; perhaps this had been what the professor meant when he had said many of the megalithic structures of the Preseli Mountains were not going to be quite what Ryan expected. Five larger stones, as tall as Ryan, stood outside of the circle, like sentinels guarding, watching through eternity. They dwarfed the small stones of the oval itself, yet leant slightly in towards them, as though supportive.

Peering out further to the horizon, he noticed more and more small stones just lying about, many with tufts of gorse or scrub almost, but not quite, concealing them. They did not look like a part of the main circle; more like someone had dropped them haphazardly. An old tale told by his Scottish great-grandfather sprang to mind; that the mountains had once been rocks, and the monoliths had been pebbles dropped from the apron of the Cailleach Bheur, the hag of winter.

Pacing slowly, purposefully, around the circle, he took in the variety of angles of the mountains around it. Some were soft and undulating, others rugged with fierce escarpments. Each was illuminated by the sun, highlighting every crag, tree and slope. The trees made him laugh aloud; they were comical. Here the wind blew in mostly from one direction and as the trees had grown they had bowed down to the wind accordingly. The atmosphere was phenomenal. Ryan felt strangely invigorated and energised. The hairs rose on the back of his neck and his hands began to prickle with energy. The scene seemed to clear, as though his eyes had focused beyond their usual capabilities. From here, no houses, no road, no sign of the Twenty-First Century was visible. Here it was just Ryan, the stones, the gorse and perhaps the echoes of times past. Forcing himself to remember to breathe, he felt weighed down by his awe, by the timelessness of the place. Would it have looked like this when the circle was erected thousands of years ago? How many people since then had come here and stood where he now stood, surveying the wild beauty of this valley and the Ring of Maidens? Why had they come here? What had their purposes been?

Why was this place called the Maidens? Who had those Maidens once been, before they had become immortalised in stone? Why did people so often name stone structures after maidens? Ryan recalled the Merry Maidens and Nine Maidens in Cornwall, where he had been the week before. In the last few weeks he had heard many tales from all over the British Isles of people being turned to stone for some misdeed or wickedness. So many questions raced through his mind to ask the professor when he got back to Cardiff.

Happy that he had got some sense of the Ring of Maidens, Ryan turned on his digital camera. He took shot after shot, wide angle shots, trying to show the Maidens against the mountains; shots of the circle from all around; close-up shots of the intricate markings of the lichen on the stones. Even some pictures of the gorse, flowering fiercely. The sun moved across the sky as he worked, changing the shadows and light subtly. He tried to capture the scene as best he could, for the old professor was no longer as able as he had once been to visit these sites in person. Finally, Ryan thought he had found his perfect shot; the circle from the east framed behind it by the mountains, and, in the foreground, a gnarled and twisted gorse bush in some half-hearted attempt at flowering. The image was loaded with the power of the place, its aura and timelessness. Ryan could see it now, printed up in black and white to highlight the otherworldliness. He surveyed the other shots; none was as perfect as his last one.

Something caught his attention; a mark or shadow in several of the shots. Always in a different place, always within the circle. Perhaps it was some odd effect of all these stones and bushes? Turning the camera around and into the light, Ryan peered intently at the lens. Pulling a white cloth from his pocket, he wiped down the lens.

Ryan turned his attention to the outlying stones; they must have been once part of an avenue leading up to and away from the main circle. These stones were heavier, chunkier and much more squared-off than the hotchpotch of the circle's stones. They had clearly been dressed, so why had the others not? The rest of the avenue was presumably gone; he explored the moorland for a while, looking for others, possibly fallen or sunk partway in this marshy land. How long had the avenue once been, and where had it led from and to? All these questions, but no answers. All he found were more of the smaller, stubbier stones; it appeared the other larger avenue stones had been looted away, like so many others. Making his way back across the scrub, Ryan stopped to take some more pictures, trying to get one or more of the outlying stones in the foreground, with others and the circle in the background. It showed the contrast in their style very effectively.

Within the image displayed on the back of the camera, Ryan thought he saw movement. A shadow of some kind within the circle ahead, a person moving, a jogger or dog walker perhaps. That must have been what appeared in the other pictures. His brain kicked in; he had not noticed anyone else here; surely he would have seen another person approach? Man, this place was mysterious. He took a step forward to say hello; his foot slipped on the wet grass and his legs went out from under him. He knocked the tripod over and, in leaning over to stop it, Ryan plunged headfirst into the stone before him and crumpled into a heap at its base. The camera bounced as it hit the ground and a shadow moved across the lens.

CHAPTER THREE

The old Druid was sleeping by his fireside; he looked wan and pale, his skin and hair as white as bone. Despite this, his personal power was still there, still singing like the shriek of the hawk. The visitor did not bother to announce himself as he pushed open the wicker door, for he knew he did not have to.

Still with his eyes closed, the Druid began to speak, with a warning in his tone. "Badden, you are not welcome here."

"A shame, when I have come all this way to greet you, teacher." The last word was emphasised coldly.

"As I recall, it was you who severed that kinship when you decided you knew everything, precisely two years into training. You never did have any patience."

"Oh, I have plenty when it matters, Gwalchwen."

Gwalchwen was already bored with the conversation; he had little enough time left and did not wish to spend it with the prideful, unpleasant Badden. "What are you doing here? Last I heard you were in the tin trade in Kernow."

"Where you had me sent, I might add. I've done well for myself, as you can see." Badden spread his arms wide, indicating his fine clothes, thick, checked cloak and the fine pin which held it around his shoulders with two boars' heads moulded in bronze. "I've come back for Morwyna, as I told you I would."

"You will not have her. She is promised to another, willingly and wholeheartedly. They are a good match and they care for each other deeply. We have completed the negotiations; the terms of the union have been arranged and witnessed. "

"Unions can be broken, with persuasion." Glee shone wildly in his eyes.

"No, the honourable do not break their oaths. You would do well to remember that."

"I will take her, by force if I must, and you cannot stop me."

Gwalchwen smiled weakly. "That is a union in its own right, not a wise one, and one that neither her family nor his would stand for. Still you have not learnt. You cannot control the heart of another."

"You mean *you* can't, you always were weak."

"You were weaker, Badden." The tone was matter-of-fact.

"Then I will kill you for your insolence, old man," Badden spat with fury.

Gwalchwen laughed. "No, you cannot kill me, only the husk that is my old body, and I would be rid of it now. Life goes on and on, as the seasons do."

* * *

"P'nawn da, ladies."

"Prynhawn da," Siân and Mandy echoed in unison, almost sarcastically.

The burly bloke pushed past them into the stockroom. "Tea, now."

Siân was not impressed. "Bloody typical, what time does he call this, he's over an hour late."

"Ooh, an hour late to sit on his backside, like we'd notice if he didn't come in."

"Sometimes I wish he didn't bother."

"Amen to that. I'll make him his blasted cuppa, then I'd better be off to pick up Alice. We've got to go hunting for a birthday present."

"Ah, the sleepover."

"Yup, she's so excited. It'll be her first night away from home."

The man appeared at the doorway, brandishing the box of Easter eggs like a weapon. His face was like thunder, his voice laced with irritation. "Mandy, what the hell happened here?"

"They'd fallen down the back of the shelves." Mandy defiantly held his cold grey-eyed gaze; she had nothing to hide. "They're broken; we can't sell them like that."

"Yes, we can. They ain't broken, they're fine. Put them out before you go home." He pushed them out at Mandy, who took them obediently. "Yes, Lloyd. I'll do it now."

Pleased with himself, Lloyd Cullen disappeared again, probably until closing time.

Siân found herself wishing he would disappear for good. He was a useless boss, never there, and if he did bother to come to work it was to play games out the back. It allowed her a degree of freedom, which she liked, but it did mean that Mandy and Siân each dreaded when the other was not there. As for holidays, she shuddered; they were a nightmare. She reached for the box. "I'll do it, you need to go."

"Oh my God, something's bitten him on the backside. Cheers, m'dear." Mandy grabbed her coat and scarf in a flurry of red wool and was out of the door before Siân could say, "Hwyl".

Her attention shifted back to the box of Easter eggs. The rhythmic action of putting them out lulled her into a daydream. She was running fast, gasping for breath, her long hair streaming out behind her. Her hands were fists at her side, grabbing on to the material of her soaked and muddy dress, holding it away from her feet so she did not trip up. The horse was getting closer, its hooves thundering, echoing her racing heart. Soon she would feel its hot breath on her back and she would have lost. Ahead of her lay the Maidens; she had to reach them before the horse caught her. Within them she would be safe, protected. She pushed harder, through the pain, her heart and lungs aching, wanting to give up. "Owein!" she screamed.

Siân shook herself from the daydream. It was not her; when did she ever wear a dress, except for weddings and funerals? Who was Owein anyway? Was he some character from the latest romance novel that Mandy had been going on about? Probably, it was all so fanciful. The dream had been so vivid, so bright and clear, not like the usual blurry, half-remembered dreams that were the norm. She pinched the bridge of her nose. It was turning out to be a long day and a sharp headache was brewing behind her eyes.

Aware that someone was watching her, Siân shifted around. "Yes?"

Lloyd crept closer. "Tomorrow, I'd like you two to have a move around; I think the card display needs to be nearer the door and move those tins and things nearer the back of the shop. The cards need re-pricing, add twenty pence to each. Tell Mandy she's staying as long as it takes to help you."

"OK, but you'd better ask Mandy if she can…"

"The stockroom also needs a damn good clean, when did you last clean it?" Lloyd interrupted. "I don't pay you two to sit around gossiping like a pepper mill all day."

Siân frowned; they cleaned the stockroom every week, every Tuesday, regularly, yet it always looked horrid. They had come to the conclusion it was like some storehouse for dust and darkness, some hole of doom and the damned.

Breaking up the Easter egg box and stuffing it into the recycling, Siân watched Lloyd retreat, off for an afternoon nap no doubt. What had put him in such a foul mood today? Digging into her coat pocket, she found her clunky mobile and slowly but surely texted Mandy.

An hour later, the phone vibrated with Mandy's response: 'nly if u n me go out 4 dina afta'. Siân read the message to herself phonetically; she knew she should be more familiar with the language of texting – she was only twenty-four for goodness' sake – but somehow she had never got the hang of this peculiar way of twisting the words. Siân mouthed every letter as her thumbs moved slowly to type her response.

CHAPTER FOUR

Ryan blinked slowly; the world turned from black to grey. His eyes gradually focused and he realised that he was lying on his side, facing one of the grey rocks. He shivered; the water from the ground had seeped through his clothes and on to his skin. The cold chilled him to the bone. Rolling on to his back, he stared at the sky above. Like the stone, it was grey overhead; the sun had retreated behind the darkening clouds. Dusk was fast approaching and the warmth of the day had gone. Ryan checked his watch; he had been out cold for hours.

Shakily, he got to his knees. His head was throbbing with pain, making it hard to concentrate. Every movement made him want to retch. He put his hand to his head, where he felt a bump and something sticky. Bringing his hand down to eye level, he noticed a small blurred pattern of blood, mixed with rain on his fingers. He let his hand fall to his side, keeping the other firmly against the stone. He looked around; the tripod lay at his feet where it had fallen. Where was his camera? It must be here somewhere. Working on his hands and knees, Ryan searched the tufts of grass until his fingers wrapped around the cold plastic that they knew so well. Breathing a sigh of relief, Ryan pulled the camera towards him. The switch was still in the on position, but the camera was lifeless. Ryan hoped that it was only that the battery was flat. He did not want to think of anything else right now, apart from finding warmth and some dry clothes. Climbing uneasily to his feet, with the aid of the tripod, he slung the camera around his neck, determined not to let it meet the mud again.

'The Merry Maidens' was a sizeable tavern, built from local grey stone and topped with a grey slate roof. Someone had painted the door and window surrounds in a warm, rich red, which toned down the austere grey and gave it a cosier appearance. The sign swung in the wind; it was colourful and bright, not what Ryan had expected at all. The sign depicted a few of the Maiden stones, crowned with circlets of wild flowers against heather-covered mountains and a clear blue sky. From the brush marks, it appeared to have been hand painted with a flourish. Pushing open the door, Ryan was met with silence and stares. The conversation halted mid-word as lips stopped moving and heads stopped bobbing. The air of stony silence would have given the stones up at the circle a run for their money. Glasses were left halfway between table and mouth. The regulars were rather amused by this bedraggled city boy. He scanned the room; the colour scheme inside was once again the warm red, with dark oak furniture.

"Come in, what can I get you?" the village's resident Mother Hen clucked around him.

"Have you any rooms available?"

"Yes, come with me, away from these nosy buggers." She cast them a fierce glare that no man dared argue with. "Get back to putting the world to rights; you know it won't do it by itself."

The plump, middle-aged woman led Ryan through behind the bar. A plait of incredibly long hair ran down her back and to her backside. Once it had been dark blonde or brown, the colour now faded with grey hairs, leaving it mousy. Her long, strangely coloured, velvet dress dragged on the floor behind her like a small bridal train. Ryan tried not to glance at it; the combination of swathes of bright red, maroon, green and brown were doing nothing for his poor head. At the bottom of the stairs, an overly friendly golden retriever welcomed him with a big slobbery lick.

"Don't mind him, he's a soppy sod. Back to bed, Bryn, good boy." She led Ryan up the stairs as the thrum of conversation resumed in the bar, undoubtedly all about him, for the next five minutes anyway.

"Now dear, how many nights?"

"Four nights, maybe more."

"Stay as long as you like, the tourist season doesn't get going for a few weeks, we've plenty of space. Shall we say forty pounds a night?"

Ryan nodded, too exhausted to think. He would have said yes to anything, as long as there was a warm bed.

"I'm Ffion, everyone calls me Ffi. What's your name, dear?"

"Ryan Ackley."

"I hope you'll be very comfortable here." Ffi pushed open the slightly battered green door at the top of the stairs, revealing a cosy and warm room. The decoration was a little old-fashioned, the wallpaper, curtains and duvet cover all a similar shade of peach. It complemented the warm hues of the pine furniture. The room was much better than many of the other places he had stayed at so far on his journey, and much nicer than his dingy, cramped studio flat.

"Thanks!" said Ryan appreciatively.

"Bathroom is through there, you'll be wanting a hot shower. Leave those muddy clothes outside your door when you're done with them and I'll stick them through the washing machine for you."

"That's very kind of you."

"No bother," Ffi squeezed his arm. "I know it's none of my business, dear, but are you all right?"

Ryan smiled with exhaustion. "I fell over in the marsh, that's all." Ffi checked his eyes, seeking the little telltale signs of untruths she knew so well in her regulars. She knew that was not the whole truth, but the poor lad looked so awful she did not think now was the time to push him.

"Oh dear, well, you be more careful. We're down the hall, see that red door," she pointed. "That's ours if you need anything." She fussed some more. "We leave the things for breakfast in the conservatory; will you be wanting a cooked breakfast?"

"No, cereal will be enough."

"What about dinner?" Ffi sniffed; this lad needed feeding up. Well, for the next four nights he would be her new project.

"Nah, I'm fine thanks." Ryan wanted some sleep and soon, he was starting to sway. Ffi opened her mouth to insist but changed her mind. "All right then, you sleep well." She closed the door soundlessly behind her.

Ryan chucked his backpack unceremoniously on the bed and placed his camera carefully on the dressing table. Grabbing some tissues, he began to wipe down the outside, then he took as much of the rest of it apart as he dared, laying it out to dry overnight. He removed the battery and fiddled in his backpack for the charger. He plugged it in and was pleased to see the little light turn on. Inwardly he prayed that the damp had not got too far into the camera and that all would be well with it come the morning.

Ryan caught a whiff of himself; the mire had made him filthy and stinky. What a great first impression he had made, he thought sarcastically. He pulled off his clothes and climbed into the shower, complete with peach shower curtain, and turned it on. The power shower whooshed as it kicked in, warm and fierce, chasing the chill from his bones. Ryan ducked his head under the showerhead and let the water wash all over him, clearing the dirt from his body and the fog from his brain.

The shadow, he remembered. That had been what made him fall. Had it been a person? Surely not; a person would not have been so cruel as to leave another out on the moors, would they? Perhaps a trick of the light? As he poured the little complimentary bottle of shampoo on to his hands, he saw how grey and pale they were. The light and shadows swirled in the shampoo, the rainbows playing and dancing. Ryan rubbed it vigorously into his hair, trying to clear his brain as well as his hair. He had heard too many ghost stories in the last few weeks. Yes, that was it; being on the road like this had made him over-tired, and so many people telling him tales of ghosts, fairies, black cats and dogs at the places he was photographing had finally got to him. A good night's sleep, that was what he needed.

He dried himself off, pulled on his nightclothes, and placed his muddy clothes outside the door as requested. He got the distinct impression that if Ffi told you to do something, you did it; she was the kind of woman that you did not want to upset. She might tell you off, and she would not care who was watching. Ryan smiled sadly; he wished he had had a mother like that, growing up.

Collapsing on to the bed, Ryan fell asleep almost at once, his head resting in the crook of his arm. The bed was soft, enveloping, as the marsh had been, but this was warm and snug. Perfect! Within minutes he was asleep, asleep and dreaming.

* * *

Smoke spiralled upwards from the fire, turning and twisting as though glad to be free of the flames. Someone to the side threw a handful of herbs into the fire. They scattered in the flames, spluttered for a moment, and the flame changed hue. Owein sat, staring into the flames.

"Seek deeper, my son. Let it speak to you." The old man's voice was gentle, full of calm and wisdom.

He searched frantically in the flames for an answer, for an image of what he must do. Nothing came and he was getting uncomfortable. A cramp was starting in his knee and an itch on his foot was driving him crazy.

"Yes, Gwalchwen."

"Feel the flame within, let two become one," the older man encouraged.

Owein exhaled, feeling the heat of his own breath, the heat of his own blood and body. He felt his inner flame flicker and reach out to the flame before him. Carefully, as he had been taught, he allowed the two flames to blend, to join and dance in ecstasy. The trance was upon him now.

The old man tried not to cough in the thickening smoke. The tickle in his throat became too much and he coughed uncontrollably, the action and pain racking his frail body. He spluttered, "Tell me what you see".

"I see... a radiant gorse bush. Also a yew tree. The Holly King is trying to cut down the yew; there is an axe blade set in his club. His crown falls from his head to the ground. He does not stop but redoubles his efforts, hacking away at the yew, which falls into an open grave. The Oak King has come. He is angry with his rival, the Holly King. Oak draws his magical lightning sword and attacks. The Holly turns to face the Oak, raising high his holly club. They fight and the year turns. In the winter months, when snow falls around them, Holly is winning. In the summer months, when the sun shines bright, the Oak King is winning…" His voice faltered into silence.

"Keep going, what else do you see?"

"The Wild Hunt emerging from the Carn, coming to take souls. They ride on white horses with red ears with their hounds, the Cŵn Annwn. They ride out across the skies, bringing the storms. I see Arawn… He beckons to me... No, not to me, to you, Father." Owein shook himself out of the trance.

"Do not look so worried, Owein, I am ready…" The rest of the sentence was lost in more coughing. Owein filled a goblet and passed it to his father. Observing the face he knew so well, now lined with wrinkles, the sharp eyes like the waters of the pool, Owein nodded sadly.

CHAPTER FIVE

The chinking of pots and pans from downstairs woke Ryan; he rolled over but a few moments later his watch alarm joined in. Giving in, he got out of bed and put on some clothes. Opening the curtains, he was greeted by bright sunshine; it was going to be a beautiful day, and a busy one. He opened the door and was greeted by the smell of eggs and bacon, much to the appreciation of his stomach. As he made his way to the conservatory, Ryan spotted lots of pictures on the walls; most of them seemed rather out of keeping with a pub, rather like its own sign. There were several rich silk paintings and raw canvasses of ancient sites, but most of them were of animals, horses, kites, swans and even dragons. Each painting was fluid and vibrant, and as he peered closer at a particular image of a stag, he noticed each one was also tagged very subtly with a price.

A voice broke his concentration. "Morning, dear, did you sleep well?"

"Yes, I did, thanks. These paintings are wonderful, whose are they?"

"Thank you, they're mine." Ffi beamed with pride. "A little hobby of mine, left over from my hippie stage, not that I've ever grown out of it. See this one, the bear, one very like that was used for the cover of a book on Shamanism."

Ryan nodded, genuinely impressed. These were not fine art, or picture quality, but something far more soulful. The colours were rich, vivid, more like dream images than paintings. The bold, curved, rounded style of her paintings matched those of her figure. They touched something within him, they reminded him of something, maybe someone he should know or remember.

"Come through and have some breakfast. Help yourself to drinks." She led the way into the conservatory, her long, deep purple and blue striped velvet dress swishing out behind her.

Ryan's legs started to follow Ffi, but he found it difficult to take his eyes from the picture of the stag. The more he studied it, the more he saw. Other, smaller, animals were hidden in it, such as a little wren in the corner, and oak leaves too. Was that a word, distorted, behind the stag's left ear? 'Protect', maybe?

The conservatory was bathed in soft morning light, dappled by the branches of the massive oak trees outside. The room had a clean feel, with slick pine furniture and a pale stone-effect floor. A well built, sturdy man, in tatty jeans and a faded T-shirt, was busy laying the table in the conservatory. As they entered he stopped midway and turned to face them. Ryan guessed he was Ffi's other half, as Ffi planted a little kiss on the man's cheek before heading off into the kitchen.

"Good morning. You must be Ryan; I hope everything is to your satisfaction?"

"Yes, thanks."

The man put down the fork he was carrying and held out his hand to shake Ryan's. "I'm Alun, Ffi's husband." His handshake was firm, the guy clearly was into working out; it was also friendly and genuine.

Ffi popped her head through the small hatch between the kitchen and conservatory. "What would you like? You'll be wanting something to keep you going, so you won't have to worry about lunch. I've got all the usual ingredients for a good Welsh breakfast, all local and all organic."

Ryan opened his mouth to ask what the difference was between a Welsh breakfast and an English one, but decided that could be dangerous territory.

Alun mistook Ryan's actions for an imminent refusal. "Say yes, to everything," he whispered. "Trust me, it'll make life much easier, then just leave anything you don't like. She'll figure it out."

Ffi was still going, disregarding her husband's comments. "There's bacon, sausage, cockles, tomato, mushrooms, beans, fried bread or laverbread and egg – anyway you like it."

His question now answered, Ryan gave in to the pressure. He had no intention of upsetting his hosts on the first morning, and he did not know how long he would need to be staying yet. "Oh, go on then, the whole lot. Fried bread and scrambled eggs." He rubbed his hands together. "Sounds great."

Both Ffi and Alun seemed oddly pleased with his request, as though he was some child who had done them proud in a school play. Then Ffi's attention turned to her husband, "Your usual, dear?" Alun nodded enthusiastically.

"So, Ryan," asked Alun, "What brings you to this part of the world?"

Ryan took a deep breath, unsure of the reaction he would get. "I'm here to take photos of various megalithic sites for a book."

Alun beamed. "Well, you've certainly come to the best place for that, there are hundreds around here, most of them unrecorded, some are even unphotographed. You've come at the right time as well; by summer, most of them are covered in such thick undergrowth that they almost disappear. Makes them a bugger to find. Ffi hates that."

"Oh," said Ryan, unsure of what to say.

"Yeah, her and Lowri, that's our daughter, and sometimes another girl, Siân, do tours of some of the more accessible sites. Gives the tourists what they want and keeps an eye on them, makes sure they don't get stuck in the marsh, wander off on to private land, or get any stupid ideas about taking bits home. That reminds me." Alun shuffled awkwardly in his seat. "Don't take this the wrong way, but would you mind paying for a few nights up front, or giving us a card number? Only, the last bloke we had staying packed his bags and buggered off without paying his bill, completely disappeared; very rude."

"I'll get some cash out today for you." Ryan was not even sure that the other man had heard him, he was already starting again before Ryan had finished his sentence.

"To be honest, it was all a bit odd; he came by taxi but never called a taxi to leave, at least the local taxi firm never got a call." Alun tapped the side of his nose.

"Did you report it?"

"Nah. Weather was bloody awful though last week; he probably got fed up with all the rain and decided to go home. Can't blame him really, but he should have paid, we can't control the weather."

Ffi chose that moment to come bustling in with three loaded plates of breakfast. She laid one in front of each of the men and the third she laid before her own seat. "Dyna ti, eat up. Now, Alun, darling, as I've told you before, don't bore the guests."

"Alun was just telling me that you and your daughter do tours sometimes of the megaliths. I could do with a guide; if you have any time this week, I'd be very interested."

Alun nodded, his mouth too full of sausage to speak.

"Sorry, dear, I'm a bit busy this week. I've been asked to exhibit at a gallery in Swansea for a charity thing next week, all a bit short notice…"

"Your daughter perhaps…"

"Ha! She's up in Aberystwyth, an apprentice jewellery designer, that's her latest thing. Only comes home when she wants something. I'll tell you what, why don't you ask Siân at the shop. I'm sure she'd be only too glad to help you out. I can ask her for you if you like…"

"I've already met her," Ryan said shyly, feeling his face go hot. He tucked into his breakfast, lowering his face to hide his flushing cheeks. Alun and Ffi exchanged glances and then knowing smiles over the top of his head.

In the next room, the washing machine launched into overdrive, rattling whatever it was that was on the worktops. "That's your muddy clothes, dear, almost done. I'll have them back dry to you this evening," Ffi offered as way of an explanation.

Ryan swallowed; this was the best and biggest breakfast he had eaten in ages. "Thanks. Is there a laundrette around here, I've been travelling for a while…"

Ffi interrupted, "You don't want to fork out for a laundrette, they can be ever so expensive, besides there's not one for miles. No, just load the machine with your stuff when that wash is done."

"That'd be great."

Alun paused from his eating. "So, where are you planning to go today?"

"Funnily enough, up near Aberystwyth, to the circles of Hirnant and Ysbyty Cynfyn." He saw his hosts try not to grimace at his pronunciations.

"If, on your travels, you see a young Goth girl with black and red hair, and lots of those weird pewter pendants round her neck, that'll be our Lowri. Remind her she has parents who might like to see her occasionally." Mid-flow he changed tack; Alun really liked to talk. "Hirnant is a funny little circle, has the most stunning views. Try not to come back as muddy as you did yesterday though, eh?"

"I'll try not to." He was not going to live that down.

"Where were you, anyway?"

"The Ring of Maidens. I've never seen anywhere like it before. Beautiful, but a bit creepy."

Alun chased the last few baked beans around his plate with some bread. "That's not a bad way to put it. Strange old place. Defies the laws of everything. Must be some old magic still at work."

"What do you mean?"

"You've been there, you've seen and felt how marshy and boggy the place is, right?"

"Yes?" Ryan was curious, and hoped he was not about to be mocked or spun some local yarn.

"Well, in all that marsh and soggy mud, didn't you think it was odd that those stones hadn't been sucked down into the marsh years ago?"

It was a good point, an eerily good point. A cold, icy, tingling sensation ran over Ryan's scalp and down his spine.

CHAPTER SIX

Ryan unloaded more of his stuff into his room, via filling the washing machine. He plugged his laptop into the mains and flicked the switch, then plugged in the camera. This was going to be the moment of truth. Again, he found himself praying that it would all be OK. Alternate black and white lines scrolled across the screen. Ryan closed his eyes, hardly daring to open them again in case he had lost the whole day's work and that magnificent shot that he had taken. He counted to twenty, then opened one eye very slowly to check the screen. "Yes!" he screamed aloud, absolutely ecstatic. His camera and all the pictures were fine. Usually at this point he deleted all the pictures from the camera to make way for more, but something made him hesitate.

He clicked off the camera, to reserve as much of its power as possible for the trip ahead. Curiosity got the better of him. Remembering which pictures he had noticed the odd shadow in, Ryan scrolled through them on his computer. He zoomed in closely, using the arrow keys to navigate around the image, trying to find those same shadows again, but this time in greater detail. There was nothing, no sign of them. Ryan was confused and annoyed. There had been something there; he would have sworn his life on it. He had seen it on the pictures as he had played them back on the camera, seen it from the corner of his eye before he fell; that had been what made him fall. It made no sense. Perhaps the shadows would still be there on the originals on the camera; he played them back. Again, the shadow had vanished. He deleted all but those that he was sure the shadow should have been on, his mind set on taking them back to Cardiff for further investigation. Glancing at his battered steel watch, he realised that the morning was already starting to pass him by, and he had a long way to go and two circles to find. Turning off the laptop and seizing his beloved camera, Ryan raced out of his room and off to face the challenges of the day.

* * *

Bryn padded quietly through the door and made his way straight into his bed. "What's the matter with you?" asked Ffi as she went to give him a good fuss, his short fur coarse beneath her hands. He gazed up at her with his big brown eyes; he was not a happy chap.

Alun hung the dog's leash on the coat rack. "Someone's been up at Cylch Morwynion and it's not for anything good this time. Bryn wouldn't go anywhere near it."

"What did it feel like?" Ffi's voice was strained with concern.

"Something dark; you know I'm not much use at picking up the vibes. All I know is that it felt dark and horrible, a bad cloud sitting over the old avenue. Made it hard to breathe."

"Damn. I can't get up there 'til Sunday, what with this exhibition to sort out."

Alun clenched and unclenched his fists. "You don't think it was Ryan, do you? He did say he was up there yesterday."

"No, I'd have picked something like that up from him. He's lonely, I'll grant you that, but he's a nice lad. He has the stag as his totem; did you see the way he could not take his eyes off that painting? The stag is strength, wisdom, majesty and regeneration. It's not a bad combination; no, he's a good lad. Now, come on, my darling, come and help me pack this first lot of paintings. The quicker I get this organised, the quicker I can get up to y Morwynion to sort things out."

* * *

The dry dust was getting in their throats; no matter how hard they tried, or how damp the dusters, all they seemed to be doing was moving the stuff around.

"Ugh, I'm filthy. I swear he's put a load of dust in here, just so we could clean it up."

"Nah," Siân giggled. "I mean, that would mean he'd actually have had to do something, and that's not like Lloyd at all."

Mandy paused thoughtfully. "I guess not then. Pass me one of those little Easter eggs."

"They're going to be horrible."

"Yep, totally unfit for selling to our customers. Not unfit for eating though."

"Mandy, you can't, Lloyd will go mad. Besides, you'll ruin your dinner!" Siân berated her.

"Yes, Mother. Come on, we've earned it, cleaning all this twice in one week. Besides, I feel like I could eat two of Ffi's dinners."

"What?" exclaimed Siân. "Are you pregnant?"

"Fat chance. Pete and I haven't had any 'us' time for ages. I was really hoping we'd get tonight together, as Alice is at a sleepover, but he's had to go off to some boring accountants' dinner or awards thing, something like that anyway. I wasn't really listening after I heard the word 'accountant'."

"Oh, so I'm the alternative?"

"Yep, I need a girls' night out, even if it is only down the pub for a chat."

"So, what exactly do you think we do all day then?" Siân asked with mock innocence.

"Work bloody hard for bugger all money, actually. Lloyd only pays us minimum wage because he has to, without that we'd be on nothing. You can move on to better things now if you want; you only took this job so you could care for Branwen, and she's gone now. I don't think she'd want you wasting your life away in this God awful shop."

Siân simply sighed.

CHAPTER SEVEN

By evening, the pub was bustling with activity, the locals wedged firmly into their favourite seats with their favourite tipples. The place thrummed with noise, the hum of voices, the chinking of glasses, the crackling of the fire and the odd guffaw of laughter.

Ryan sat at the table in the corner, the local map and several dozen pages of white paper spread out before him. Some pages were as new, others crumpled and dog-eared. Many had hand-written notes scrawled all over them in two distinct hands; one small, controlled and fine, and the other larger and bolder. A large glass of fruit juice stood on the edge of the table, the condensation running leisurely down the glass, forming a small puddle and soaking the edge of the map. He held his head in his hands, reading through the notes, mouthing the words to himself, trying to familiarise himself with the details of the next few days' worth of sites. These notes were the most complicated by far. Practically every site said it was of a certain type, but then underneath mentioned that maybe it was not after all; perhaps it was something else, or something unique.

Siân and Mandy sat at the bar; Siân was already halfway through her first lemonade whilst Mandy was still studying the menu intently. "Mmh, choices, choices… Oh sod it, I'll have what you're having." Mandy took a sip of white wine. "Ffi, can we have two veggie lasagnes please, with garlic bread, no chips – we might want dessert later." She turned to Siân. "It's nice not to have to do the cooking or the washing up for once."

"I should be so lucky. Oh, Siân, I've got to tell you, Lowri is planning to come back for Easter." Ffi was so pleased.

"Great, I want to hear everything about how she's getting on. Nice that she's found something that she really loves at last."

As Mandy and Siân slid awkwardly off the stools and plonked themselves at one of the tables, Siân asked, "How about one Sunday I take Alice out for the day, give you and Pete some quality time together?"

"That would be great."

"I'll take her to a wildlife park, or the chocolate farm, or something like that."

"Now, is that for you or for her, Siân?"

"It beats going on my own."

Mandy looked sideways at her friend; she was getting worried. Siân had always been subdued and a bit of a loner, especially when compared to her own gregarious nature, but in these last few months Siân had become even more introverted.

"Do you want another lemonade?"

"Please."

"Back in a minute." Mandy left her friend staring at the wood grain of the table.

"Ffi, another round, please?" As Ffi poured the drinks, Mandy nonchalantly scanned around the pub and caught a glimpse of Siân. She was casting the odd peek at Ryan, and then, if she thought anyone was observing her, she reverted to studying the surface of the table.

"What's all that about?" Ffi presented Mandy with the two drinks. "He went bright red at breakfast when I mentioned her name."

"Oh my God! Ffion Phillips, do you have eyes in the back of your head?"

"I know people, that's all. Siân could do with a bit of romance, even if it is only for a few days. I did say I'd ask Siân to take him on a tour."

Mandy took the drinks and sat down by Siân. "He's only here for a little while, so you'd better be quick to ask him out."

"It's not a leap year," she mumbled into her glass.

"Come on, girl, this is the Twenty-First Century. I don't think anyone worries about that anymore," Mandy said, louder than she anticipated. The whole pub heard, except Ryan, who was far too engrossed in his paperwork.

"That's not the point."

"Siân, listen to me. He's gorgeous and he likes you. As your friend, I am begging you, ask him out."

"No."

"All right, then I will." Mandy rose to stand, a little unsteady on her party stilettos, but Siân lunged for her arm and pulled her back down hastily. Mandy landed in her seat with an indelicate thud.

"Don't you dare! Stop trying to match me up with every single male you come across. This is real life, not one of your romance novels. Not everyone in the world has to be paired up and paired off. I still remember the last time you set me up with a date. Trouble was, as I recall, you asked me for Huw and Huw for me, but neither of us had actually asked you to! It was the worst date ever. Three hours of awkwardness and even the film was complete poop."

"What film was it?"

"Some weird sci-fi. I don't remember the name, it was so poopy. Leave it well alone."

"All right, I will," Mandy said sulkily, as Ffi approached with their meals. She would leave well alone, but only as Ffi was already hatching her own plot.

Straight from serving the two women, Ffi made her way to Ryan's table. The fruit juice was still untouched. She coughed politely. "Ryan, can I get you something to eat, dear?"

"Huh?" Ryan only picked up at the end of the sentence that anyone was speaking to him.

"What can I get you? Alun makes a mean steak and ale pie…"

His stomach growled in response, much to their joint amusement. "Yes, steak and ale is just what's called for."

Ffi leant in closer and could not help but notice the subject of the mountain of paperwork. "Siân's in tonight, don't forget to ask her about a tour."

"No, I won't."

As Ffi strolled away, pleased with herself, Ryan went back to re-reading the notes. The focus had gone; the words seemed to swim in front of his eyes. He started the same paragraph on the peculiarities of the Cerrig Y Gof chambered mound five times before he finally gave up. Without even trying, he found himself listening in to the conversation two tables over. Mandy and Siân were both laughing; Mandy's laugh was loud, harsh and shrill, whilst Siân's was softer and more of a giggle. The two women seemed an odd combination for such close friends; one was clearly very extroverted, confident and the kind of woman he, and many other men, normally hid from in social situations, whilst the other was so quiet, sweet and timid even. One was buxom, well-built and proud to be so, her tight black dress showing off all her curves and her rich dark brown hair twisted into a posh up-do of some kind, with flashy costume jewellery. She was probably in her late thirties or early forties; Ryan knew himself to be pretty awful at judging women's ages. The other was much younger, only in her twenties. Taller, thinner, but not overly thin, with silky black hair that ran free. Her skin was incredibly pale, almost translucent, only given life by her natural luminescence. She was not dressed for an evening out, he noticed, more for comfort, and if anything it served to summarise the differences between the two women. He did not think it mattered what Siân wore; she had the natural ability to appear beautiful, graceful even, no matter what. He caught Ffi scrutinising him from behind the bar and, aware that he was gawking impolitely, he turned back to study the map. He picked up a pencil and began to circle the sites he was looking for, and noticed how many were not even marked on the map. It was no good; all that did was remind him of who he had bought the map from.

Taking a deep breath for courage, Ryan got up and walked quickly over to Siân's table. "Sorry to interrupt you, ladies, I hear you do tours of the Megaliths. I could really do with a guide. There are so many around here and I'm not sure how to get to most of them, they seem to be in the middle of nowhere…" His voice faded away as he ran out of both breath and courage.

Siân looked up with her big blue eyes and smiled. "OK, we only open for a couple of hours in the morning on Saturdays; how about tomorrow morning at ten a.m. I charge ten pounds an hour. Meet me outside the shop and be ready for a long day and lots of walking." Mandy poked her under the table and her concentration wavered. "Is there anywhere in particular you want to see?"

"Quite a few places, actually."

"Make me a list, and I'll see what I can do."

Strolling the short distance between the pub and home helped to clear Siân's head. Getting Mandy packed off in the taxi home had been a bit of a nightmare; she had overdone the white wine a little bit. She was looking forward to tomorrow. She enjoyed going up into the mountains, visiting the old sites, educating the tourists about them, watching their jaws drop with awe at the sight of the ancient monuments. The burial chambers, the stones and the cairns; they connected her to this place, this wonderful place she called her home. There was nowhere else like it in the world, this place had history like no other. Siân felt honoured to be a part of it. The stones appeared to live forever, monuments to those now long forgotten in the mists of time, perhaps even her own ancestors, as one day she knew she would be forgotten. Siân was so engrossed in her own thoughts that she failed to hear the footsteps of the man who was following her.

CHAPTER EIGHT

Ryan hung around the outside of the village shop, waiting for his guide for the day. As Siân moved to shut the door, Lloyd shouted something at her from inside. Pretending not to notice, she closed it behind her and approached Ryan. "Hiya," he said.

"Hiya, have you made that list for me?" Her hair was tied roughly back in a bun, but most of it was already escaping into the breeze.

Ryan produced a crumpled piece of lined paper, torn from his notepad. She scanned the places briskly, nodding and shaking her head as she worked her way down the list. "There's an awful lot here, a few days' worth at least. How about I take you to the more remote ones, the ones that are harder to get to by road? Then the rest should be easier for you to find on your own."

"Whatever you think is best."

"Even then, I can't take you to all of them." Ryan appeared crestfallen so Siân went on. "Only a couple of the old monuments are in the hands of public bodies; most of them are on private land and while some landowners are kind enough to allow visitors access, not all do. You can't blame them in this day and age; some of the monuments have suffered in recent years."

"That's understandable."

Siân narrowed her eyes as she set off hiking. "Why do you want to go to all these places anyway?"

Ryan set his pace in line with hers. "I'm taking photographs for a new book on Megaliths of the West. There will be about three chapters solely on the Megaliths of the Preseli Mountains. There are so many here, I think it will need three chapters at least."

"It is very unusual; Preseli must have been a place of enormous religious significance. We have all kinds of monuments all over the mountains, from monoliths to complex burial chambers. There's also a fair few Iron Age hill forts dotted all over the mountain tops."

"Why was this place so special then?"

"No one quite knows; it could have been trade with Ireland and the continent coming through here. Preseli could have been a major religious centre, like Anglesey was later on, with the Druids. Or it could be the rocks or geology around here; it may have had some significance. It could be that this land was seen as particularly sacred, perhaps the embodiment of a specific Goddess, like the River Severn is said to be the Goddess Sabrina. We may never know, wouldn't it be great if we did?"

Ryan nodded; this was going to be an educational day.

"Do you know about the whole Stonehenge thing?" she asked.

"Yeah, don't some of the stones at Stonehenge come from near here?"

"Some say that they were taken to Wiltshire by glaciers, but I've seen no evidence that makes me think that the glaciers got that far. I reckon they were quarried and transported via the Bristol Channel. It's 250 miles from here to Stonehenge; our ancestors were much more skilled than we give them credit for."

"There's going to be a chapter on that as well," said Ryan.

"This book sounds interesting; I don't suppose you have any of the work that's been written so far with you?"

"Not yet, Professor Trevivian is still working on it."

Siân laughed. "Do you mean Professor Gavan Trevivian, Senior Lecturer at Cardiff University?"

"Yeah, why? Do you know him?"

"Yup, he was one of my lecturers. One of the best. Gets really fired up over anything even vaguely related to history and archaeology. He's like a steam train once he gets going. How is he?"

"Not great anymore, he's been fighting cancer for a couple of years now, then last year he contracted pneumonia and he's been very ill ever since. What a small world we live in."

"That's a pity; I thought he'd go on forever, strong as an ox and a mean marker if ever there was one."

Then it was Ryan's turn to laugh. "Yeah, you should see the amount of red ink that I get all over everything; he thinks nothing of scrawling all over my photographs."

They walked in silence for a while, their steps in unison.

"So, how long have you been a photographer then?"

"I started taking pictures with my dad's camera when I was young and never stopped. I was lucky my local college did an A level in photography and after that I did my degree in Photographic Art at Newport. I've done a couple of shows; one was in Cardiff, which was how Trev found my work. This is the second book we're on to now. Most of the time, though, it's babes and bells that are my bread and butter."

"Always the photographer and never the groom, huh?" Siân regretted her words instantly. They were too forward.

"I rather like weddings; it's the kids I mind. Horrible, noisy, stinky creatures; it's enough to put me off them for life."

"Mandy tells me it's different once you have one; your own is always sweetness and light, even when everyone else says they're a little shit."

"Is Mandy the woman I saw you with last night, the one who laughs like a hyena?"

"Yes, bless her. Not the quiet sort."

"Not like you then?"

"She makes more than enough noise for the both of us." She opened the gate into the field and Ryan closed it behind him. A serious expression crossed her face. "Now, be careful here, this whole area is a bog. Walk where I walk." Siân took a huge step forward and then another, using the tufts of long grass as stepping stones. She tilted her head around to make sure Ryan was following her exactly. "Having fun?"

"It certainly livens things up a bit. You look silly walking like that."

"I know, but it beats getting a soggy arse. If there's one thing I hate, it's getting wet."

They continued on, striding with overlong steps, until the stones came into view.

"What is that?" asked Ryan.

"Bedd Yr Afanc – the Grave of the Water Monster," Siân said in her best spooky voice.

"Is that why this place is so wet and boggy?"

"Could be. That grave is on an island of dry land in the midst of the Brynberian bog; I reckon someone didn't want the Afanc's spirit to use the bog to get home. He used to live under a bridge in the Brynberian River before he was killed and dragged up here."

"Is the Afanc like Nessie?"

"A bit. Some say he's reptilian like Nessie, but others say he looks like some overgrown beaver or a combination of both, like a giant crocodile with the head of a beaver. He's not got quite the same celebrity status as Nessie; I don't think he likes the publicity."

Ryan manoeuvred his camera and took some shots. "This is unlike anything I've seen before. It looks like two rows of jagged teeth, the monster's maybe?"

"It's down in some books as a stone circle, but, as you can see, it's rectangular. Could be a gallery grave; if so it's the only one in Wales. Ireland has several and there were close ties between this area and Ireland; it's only a short boat trip away. See here, you can see the two lines of paired stones in parallel, and once there was a rectangular mound covering it and a cairn of rocks; some of them are still lying around. It's Neolithic – New Stone Age, around 6,000 years old."

As he carried on clicking away, Ryan continued to listen to Siân's speech on the history of the site. He was interested to hear it, and he loved the sound of her gentle voice with its soft Welsh lilt. He worked his way towards the stones and leant out to touch one. Siân placed her hand lightly on his arm. "Please don't touch them."

"Why not?" His heartbeat quickened and he hoped she would not notice.

She turned his hand over, enjoying the warmth of his skin. "I don't mean to be rude, but do you have any idea how damaging the oils and bacteria of the skin can be? It can be very bad for all that beautiful lichen and even for the stones underneath."

"I'm sorry, I had no idea."

"Most people don't," she said, forgiving him immediately. "If you want to feel them, try sensing them instead. I picked this up off Ffi." She held her hands out to the stone, about an inch or two above them, and closed her eyes. Ryan copied her closely. "This way you do no damage. First sense the lichen beneath your hands, its life and energy, then move down to the stone underneath and then you can even move on to feel the energy of the land if you want to; that's for the more advanced." Ryan felt the palms of his hands tingle with energy; his rational mind told him it was the power of suggestion, while his intuition told him it was the power of this place. "That feels really weird," he said after a while.

Siân tipped her head. "Ffi's lovely but a bit unorthodox; she spouts some weird stuff sometimes but that one works. Have you seen her paintings?"

"They're beautiful."

"She did one of here once, complete with the Afanc rearing up from his grave."

"Is she a witch? All the velvet dresses?"

Siân was thoughtful. "She calls herself a Neo-Druid; I don't really know what the difference is. You'd have to ask her about it. Let's get on; we've a lot of ground to cover."

The figure on the distant horizon watched them. The sun was out, all around was warm, but he was still cold, as cold as he had been that night on the moor. Things were not going according to plan. A dark thought crossed his mind but he tried to dismiss it. "No, I won't do that again. You can't make me."

"I can and I will. You know the stories, you knew the deal."

The figure shivered as he felt the icy shadow move over his heart.

Near to the next site, the young couple paused for lunch. The gorse and heather danced to the breeze and the music of the moors, their sweet vanilla-coconut scents wafting over them. Ryan carefully unwrapped the lunch his hostess had packed for him. There were sandwiches stuffed full, biscuits, cheese, fruit and a yoghurt. Siân carefully unwrapped her own, more meagre, meal. "Is that Ffi's handiwork?"

"She practically forced it on me this morning and that's after a cooked breakfast!"

"She probably thinks you need feeding up." Siân poked him playfully in the stomach and wondered why she did it.

"I couldn't have wished for better hosts really."

"Ffi's great; ever since my parents died she's always been a sort of surrogate Mam to me."

Ryan opened and closed his mouth a few times, doing an impression of a goldfish. He wanted to ask about Siân's parents, but he did not want to upset her. Besides, was that not more of a third date sort of thing, and this was not even a date, was it? Siân figured out what he was thinking and waited a few extra seconds, amused by his exasperation. "My parents were killed in a car crash when I was four."

"I'm so sorry," he blurted out.

"Why? Wasn't your fault. Ffi took it hard; Mam and her were best friends since the year dot. She and Mamgu, Granny, raised me between them. Lowri is kind of my little sister. So, come on, spill the beans on your family... only fair."

Ryan shifted position, partly because his leg was going to sleep and partly because he was uncomfortable with the topic.

"There's not much to tell. My mum left when I was little, ran off with some bloke. Dad raised me and my two brothers and did a good job of it."

"Now it's my turn to be sorry."

Siân leant back in the dry grass, letting the warm sun fall on her skin. Ryan watched her. "Do you want some of this, I'm stuffed?"

"You'd better eat the yoghurt; it won't be fit for anything by the time we get back."

Ryan sighed deeply, expelling air to try and make room in his stomach.

"Where do you come from? I can't place your accent."

"Essex," Ryan spoke calmly. People tended to react to that snippet of information and not in a positive manner.

"Oh, right, that's the opposite end of the country, isn't it? What's it like?"

Ryan nodded and swallowed his mouthful. "It's flat, incredibly flat, we've nothing like this." He cast a hand at the mountains around them. "The sea is much calmer and there's almost an invisible join between the land, sea and sky. Whereas here, you know where the join is, it's all so dramatic and photogenic."

"Do you have any megalithic sites over that way?"

"Nothing as spectacular as here. A few odd stones and one circle, but they plonked a church in the middle of it."

"Do you ever miss it there?"

He packed his rubbish neatly back in his bag. "Not really, I only go back to see my dad. I'm ready when you are."

"Great, next stop is Bedd Arthur, the Grave of Arthur. There are dozens of places called Arthur's this or Arthur's that. Sorry to disappoint you, but I don't reckon it's King Arthur's grave. 'Not wise the thought – a grave for Arthur', as one ancient poem says. King Arthur can't have a grave, he's not dead, he's still sleeping." Siân swung her backpack back on to her shoulders and led the way.

CHAPTER NINE

The light of the day was fading, from bright yellow to a richer orange. "I can either take you back that way, back to the road, or we can go down that way..." Siân pointed to the valley bottom, "and you can experience Cylch Morwynion by sunset."

The answer was obvious; "The Maidens, please".

"We're going to need to be quick then." Siân raced off down the mountain path, the backpack bouncing up and down on her shoulders. Ryan followed; he was not used to all these mountains, all this altitude, he was out of breath after only a small way. He kept going, pushing through the stitch that crept upon him, gnawing at his side, eager to impress his tour guide.

Two dry days had made a huge difference to the marsh around the Ring of Maidens. The ground was drier, firmer and easier to navigate. The slowly setting sun cast a warm glow over the lichen on the stones and the gorse bushes. Ryan seized the opportunity to get some fabulous shots, as Siân explained the history of the site. They walked around the circle clockwise before entering it. "Most of these are dolerites, or other local rocks, it's a real mix. Some are like the smaller ones they have at Stonehenge. Ceridwen's cauldron, possibly the original Welsh Grail, was s'posed to have been carved out of this stuff. Did you know one name for her magic potion was grael? The Maidens are far more like the more westerly, smaller monuments, than Stonehenge though. At Stonehenge the huge trilithons act as a barrier, keeping events within the circle private and out of view for anyone outside it. Whereas here is very open, allowing everyone, inside or outside the stones, to see what's going on. I think that's a big part of the appeal of the more open circles."

"I can agree with that. Are there any old tales about the Maidens?"

"Plenty. Over the years it's been called many things. Some of the older folk still call it Cylch Morwyna; that means the Ring of Morwyna, rather than Morwynion or Maidens. Supposedly named after a young woman called Morwyna who was sucked to her death into the marsh. Her name means maiden anyway. The Merry Maidens or the Ring of Maidens are its usual names and what's on the maps because of the usual Sabbath Day tale. Five musicians struck up a song on the Sabbath Day and sixteen local maidens danced to their tune. God saw them blaspheming against his Holy Day of Rest and turned them all to stone as a punishment; hence the five musicians are the larger outlying stones, and the sixteen maidens, dancing in a ring, became the sixteen smaller stones of the circle. It's also meant to explain why so many different types of rock were used."

"I heard a few like that down in Devon and Cornwall."

"It's a pretty common one, to be honest. There were strong links between Kernow and here, trades in ore and such. Several other stories describe this place as a place of healing. It's also recommended for couples who are having trouble getting pregnant. Another local tale is that there is a Druid buried within the circle, but that doesn't really make a lot of sense to me, what with all the burial chambers around here."

"Has anyone ever excavated it?"

Siân was careful to stay behind Ryan at all times, to avoid getting in the way, and partly to admire him as he stood backside-out in the classic photographer's position as he tried to get down low. "Nope, I hope they never do. I'd hate to see this place disturbed. It's so important, not only back then but also even today. The whole area is a National Park, a Special Area of Conservation. It's a European Protected Area, so it's even internationally important. Many of these monuments are scheduled, rightly so. The Preseli Mountains are a place like no other on earth."

Ryan removed a filter from the lens. "Go and stand in front of that stone."

"Why?" Siân was suspicious.

"Why do you think? Let me take your picture."

She tightened her jaw and shook her head energetically. "No, thanks."

"Please…" Ryan begged.

"OK…" Siân agreed begrudgingly. "But this is hardly my best gear."

"Doesn't matter to me."

'No, I bet it doesn't', Siân thought. She untied the bun and shook her hair out, the colours of the setting sun making it gleam. She made her way to the largest of the standing stones as Ryan had asked. She stood close to it for a moment. A feeling of unpleasantness crept over her, from her feet up to her hair. This was odd, she had never felt anything so negative here before; normally this entire site was wonderful, invigorating even, to visit. A cold, oppressive feeling of greyness, as you get before the rain comes pouring down. She shivered in the cooling air and coughed, finding it hard to breathe. Sensing her discomfort, Ryan called over to her. "Are you all right? Come and stand in the circle instead and I'll try and get one of you and the stones in front of the dying sun."

Gladly, Siân moved away from the stone. With each step she felt the sense of greyness lift. Her breathing became easier and more relaxed.

"That's it; now move to your left about a foot and a half. Right, shake your hair out again for me."

She obliged; head forward, she brushed through her long hair with her fingers and flipped her head back with one swift movement.

Ryan took the shot, his breath stopped, his heart in his mouth. The last golden rays of sun were coming through from the clouds, past the mountains and on to Siân's shiny black hair, making it shine like a halo around her delicate face.

"You're beautiful."

Siân's face blossomed like a wild dog rose. Ryan strode straight up to her; nothing in the world could have stopped him. He took her face in his hands and leant in towards her. Their lips met as the sun withdrew behind the mountain. They kissed passionately, sensuously, each savouring the taste and scent of the other, feeling the warmth of their close bodies. This did not feel new, as a first kiss should; it felt like coming home.

The air became increasingly cool as the night set in. Siân broke off their kiss. "We'd better get back to civilisation before it gets much darker." She placed her hand around his, feeling his thin, soft fingers beneath her own. As they left the confines of the circle, the mist rolled in as if from nowhere. It arrived in swathes of wet cloud and went straight through their clothes, soaking them with tiny droplets of moisture. "Damn, the weather can turn fast around here." The words came out as frosted breath.

"Not usually this fast. I think we'd better hurry."

The silver vapour thickened until the two of them were trapped in a small island of visibility within a sea of opaque grey. The sound of footsteps came into earshot, in the distance running towards them.

"Hello?" they called in unison. "Anyone there?" The footsteps grew nearer but they heard no response. Siân yelled, "Make your way to my voice, I can guide you". The footsteps continued, they could hear the person gasping for breath, but still they could see nothing. They could hear a horse approaching, galloping in the night towards them. "Are you lost?" called Siân into the ether, her voice cracking with anxiety.

"Owein…" It was a woman's voice, it sounded so close, perhaps right next to them, yet it also sounded faint and distant. "Morwyna, stop," a male voice demanded harshly. He sounded further away from them.

"Don't be such a pillock, Huw!" Siân shouted angrily. She squeezed Ryan's hand affectionately. "Sorry, it's probably just some of the local idiots trying to mess with your head. There's a bridleway runs close to here. I reckon they heard us talking and thought they'd try and spook us in this fog."

"Will they be all right?"

"Oh, that lot? They know their way around here, and if they don't, that'll teach them for pratting around…" Suddenly she recalled her daydream of a few days before; how could they have known about that? How could anyone have known? Poor Morwyna, drowned centuries ago out on the moor; everyone knew of her sad story, but who was Owein?

CHAPTER TEN

The orange glow of the street lamps in the gloom told them they were almost home. Neither wanted this day to be over, but both wanted to get in the warm and dry as soon as possible. They reached the 'Merry Maidens' a few minutes later. Ryan ran his hand through his dank, sodden hair. "Thank you for a wonderful day," he said, unsure of what he should be saying. He had never been any good with women. "May I treat you to dinner as a thank you?"

"What, now?" Siân squeezed some of the water from the corner of her fleece to make her point, playing a little hard to get.

"Maybe not now, half an hour then?" Ryan used the side of the pavement to scrape off some of the mud from his walking boots.

"Good grief," Siân gawped at him. "I can't get ready in half an hour; I don't think any woman can. Give me an hour and I'll say yes."

"An hour then?"

"Yes, I'd love to." She checked her watch. "I'll see you in there, don't be late." Ryan watched her disappear into the veil of quicksilver. He realised too late how ungracious he had been; he should have offered to accompany her back home.

Fifty minutes later, Siân was washed, dried and in the midst of chaos and crisis. Her wardrobe was empty; her clothes lay strewn over her bed and the chair in the corner of the room; still she had not found anything that she wanted to wear tonight. She sat heavily on the edge of the bed and fiddled with the cord of her dull-coloured dressing-gown. Tears welled up in her eyes and cascaded down her pale cheeks as rain began to fall outside. How had it got to this? She had enjoyed socialising at university, going out with friends, going to the cinema, the coffee shop, just going out. She had studied hard but she had also enjoyed herself. Since coming back to Maenddu to care for her Mamgu, who was already very ill by the time Siân had finished her degree, life had become very dull and plain. For a while she had managed to maintain contact, and of course Lowri had been around. Lowri had been her good friend since the day she was born, her surrogate little sister. Then friends had drifted away, even those who promised faithfully to stay in touch; going out had become difficult, nigh on impossible. Even Lowri had moved away for her apprenticeship. Where was there to go around here anyway? She bit her lip; that was a lie to make herself feel better; there were places to go; Mandy certainly found plenty. More tears glided heavily from her sore eyes. She was lonely. Lonely now that Mamgu was gone, but she had been lonely long before that as well if she was truthful.

She turned her head to observe the pile of clothes. All were clothes for comfort and work; cardigans, long-sleeved T-shirts and jeans; there was nothing elegant, nothing glitzy, nothing nice. Almost every piece was black or dark grey. The dreary colours depressed her even more. Nothing for a date here at all, and she was pretty sure that this was a date. The kiss had been wonderful, caring, and loving. There had not been the wild, untamed passion that she had half expected, but it had felt deeper than that, a deeper, older, more perfect love, not lust. A joining of souls as well as bodies. In that moment, everything else had faded away, and there had only been the two of them on the moor, in an embrace that lasted both seconds and aeons. Her heart grew warm and leapt to her throat, just thinking of that wonderful kiss, and thinking of him.

Roughly rubbing the tears from her eyes, Siân psyched herself up for the task ahead; she began to ruthlessly attack the clothes in earnest. Black trousers, she remembered; she had some really nice smart black trousers somewhere; she had got them for graduation and she could not remember having got rid of them. She grabbed handfuls of clothing, throwing them out behind her. "Yes," she exclaimed as she finally found them buried under an old and tatty pair of jeans. 'OK, that's one half done, now what about a top?' Siân drew a complete blank. Right, she would come back to that in a minute. She scrambled over the clothes lying on the floor to the dressing table and sifted through her underwear until she found a small, battered, old wooden box. She gently stroked the lid engraved with her Mamgu's initials – B. E. – Branwen Ellis. Would Mamgu have approved of Ryan, she wondered. Shaking herself from her reverie, she opened the box. Inside the box were some pretty silver earrings that Lowri had made for her last birthday; they would have to do. Siân held them up to her ears and scrutinised her reflection in the dressing mirror. The earrings were long, sinuous swirls of silver in a subtle chandelier style; they elongated her neck and suited her perfectly. Siân wondered why she had not worn them before. For the first time in ages she was happy with her reflection; this was more like it for a date. Hang on, what was that behind her, sprawled half over the pillow. A plain black v-neck top, hardly the most chic top in the whole world, but it might just do, combined with the smart trousers and the earrings. Siân donned the outfit and smoothed out the odd crease with her hands. Perfect, the effect was exactly what she had hoped for. She looked elegant, pretty, but not like she had made too much of an effort.

Pulling the metal toothed brush through her hair, Siân wondered what to do with it. Twisting it up into an up-do was too much, a ponytail was too cold. The chime of the clock downstairs told her she was running late. Not knowing what else to do with her hair, she left it down, hanging loosely past her shoulders.

As she skidded into the front room, she ran her hand across her black fleece, hanging over the main radiator. It was still sopping wet and a small puddle was forming underneath it. She could hardly go out in that again and still look nice by the time she got there. Although it was not far to the pub, in this rain it would have been far enough to be transformed from almost chic woman into drowned rat. Raiding the under-stairs cupboard, Siân found her black woollen hat. She twisted her hair under it and then reached into the darker recess. To her surprise, her fingers encountered a sheet of plastic; she lifted the plastic and felt wool, lots more wool. Reaching deeper, so that her arm was almost coming out of its socket, she pulled out the item. A woollen black and white checked coat; very retro! She removed the plastic cover and turned it around and around before her. A thought or memory was clamouring at her brain, trying to get her attention. She knew this coat, she remembered this coat. She very vaguely recalled her mother, Elain, wearing it. A sense of numbness crept over her. Mamgu had kept so little of Elain's stuff after the accident; she had found it hard enough to be reminded constantly of her lost daughter through her granddaughter, Siân, let alone through Elain's possessions. The tears welled up again in her eyes, but she tried to blink them back; red eyes were not appropriate for a date. Tentatively, she put her arms through the arms of the coat and pulled it close around her. It fitted her as though it had been made for her. Grabbing her keys from the sideboard, and feeling wonderfully warm on the inside, Siân paid her respects to the house Dragon and headed off for her first real date in years. As she walked along past the grey stone chapel to the main road, she realised that she had been so worried about what to wear, that she had not had any time to worry about the date itself. Well, there was no time now, she was already late.

Precisely an hour after they had parted, Ryan was waiting in the bar, showered, dried and very snug as he had managed to sneak a table next to the old fireplace. Each time the door opened, Ryan had glanced up, hopeful, but so far each time he had been disappointed. The clock told him that she was late, but that was to be expected on a night like this. He worried that he had been too forward in kissing her; after all, he had to go back in a few days and it was not really fair to her. Oh, but what he would give to come back here to get to know her. The more he stared at the clock on the wall, the more worried he became. The dancing flames of the fire caught his attention, their merry dance leading him in, mesmerising him. A voice that he barely heard told him to seek within the flames. He obliged willingly. The warmth of the fire on his skin, the fire of his heart and the warmth of his breath intensified. His soul blazed as the fire before him blazed. The two flames reached out to each other, and for a moment they danced around each other as a pair, like two strands of life force and DNA, joining and spiralling together. Within the flame, images appeared, distorted and then disappeared. A distant voice coached him further; Ryan barely heard it against the roar and crackle of the flames. "Tell me what you see."

A curling flame became a gorse bush, brilliantly shining like the summer sun, its flowers like a thousand tiny flames burning brightly. Within one of those flames a new vision formed, that of an ancient and magnificent yew tree, its bark and berries reflecting the deep red of the flames. A man stepped forward. Ryan noticed he was not a normal man; he was dressed from top to toe in holly leaves. No, not dressed in holly leaves, but made of holly leaves. He wore a flaming crown upon his head and carried a pale wooden club with a bronze axe head embedded within it. He glowered directly at Ryan; the face was filled with resentment, spite and hatred. The Holly King took a swing at the yew tree with his club. The trunk bled, rich dark red blood, as the axe club made contact. The crown fell from his head and landed at the foot of the yew. Again and again, the

Holly King struck the yew; the attack was ferocious. Ryan wanted to call out to him to stop, but no words came; this was not real, this was a dream. A grave opened up before the yew tree, an enormous hole in the ground. The yew tree creaked and splintered under the blows; it gave way with an almighty crack that threatened to break the world in two and fell into the gaping void of the grave.

Ryan tried to close his eyes, but he could not drag himself away. Part of Ryan stayed as he was, staring into the flames, while another part, a spirit form of himself, stepped forward. Ryan saw that he was made entirely from the lobed leaves of the Oak. He too wore a flaming crown. There was a lightning sword hanging from his waist; it was on the right-hand-side, which Ryan thought was odd. He grabbed the sword and pulled it from its oak leaf sheath in one expert sweep. The moment the sword was drawn, it crackled with electricity. He ran forward to slay the Holly King, to exact revenge for the yew. The Holly King saw him coming and raised his club to strike. They exchanged blows, each trying to dodge the other's blows while still striking hard their own.

"Penny for them?" Siân asked, as she hung her damp coat on the back of the chair. Ryan coughed, trying to clear the burning sensation in his throat and lungs. "Sorry, I was miles away."

"So I could see. What was so interesting?"

"The flames, they really are quite hypnotic." They reflected still in Ryan's green eyes.

Siân nodded. "I know what to get you for Christmas then. Sorry I'm late, turns out I can't get ready in an hour." She cast him her best apologetic expression and prayed that it did not come off as appearing dim or desperate.

"You're here now, and you look great."

"Thank you, so do you." Siân blushed as hot as the fire, as much with relief as anything. It was not an empty compliment; he looked incredibly handsome in navy chinos and a smart blue and black checked shirt. She picked up a menu and started to pretend to read it. She already knew the menu by heart, and it gave her cover as she watched Ryan go through his menu.

Ffi was overjoyed to see these two young things together like this. She could barely contain her excitement. She lifted the bar hatch, but Alun blocked her path. "No, you stay here. They don't need you interfering, sweetheart." Ffi stuck her tongue out at her husband who guffawed. "I'll go."

"What can I get you?" Alun asked, his deep voice warm and kind as always.

"I'll have a jacket potato, please, with tuna, sweetcorn and salad, no onions," Siân replied. "Oh, and a large glass of lemonade, please."

"What about you then, Ryan?"

"Jacket potato with chilli and salad, and a pint of beer, please."

"Coming right up." Alun rambled back to his wife, who was bobbing up and down on her toes behind the bar, champing at the bit for gossip.

Siân leaned in across the table and whispered to Ryan, "I don't think I can cope with another full meal. Ffi's portions are a bit too generous for me. Don't tell her I said so."

Ryan could not take his eyes off the ring hanging on a black cord around Siân's neck. It had fallen forward and free of her top as she had leaned forward. He tried to avert his eyes, as he did not want her to misinterpret his interest in that particular area of her anatomy. He was too late; he caught her clear blue eyes intently regarding him.

"You're looking at the ring, aren't you?"

"Sorry, yes."

Siân pulled the cord to extend it to its maximum; he noted that she did not remove it. She let Ryan hold it as he peered at it, her heart racing with his proximity. "My mother's wedding ring. For most of my life it's been the only thing of hers that I was allowed to keep."

Ryan studied the outside of the ring; it was clearly well used and well loved. It glinted in the firelight, the rich reds and golds of the flames adding to the deep hue of the old gold. Small scratches and dents covered the surface. He was about to say something but then he remembered how Siân's mother had died, and decided it was best to remain silent.

"Read the inscription," she encouraged.

"Is this real?" he asked in awe. "Real Welsh gold, from Wales."

"Yes, back from the days when it was still mined. They gave up mining it a few years ago, no longer economically viable or something. A real shame."

"What's this, in the middle of the words?" Ryan squinted at a tiny image. The light in there was not very good for detailed work, but it did give everything a warm, cosy tint.

"Y Forwyn Gymreig. A little Welsh Maiden in National Dress. The big skirt and tall black hat outfit, I'm sure you've seen it."

"This is very special."

"To me it's priceless." Siân re-adjusted the cord so that the ring hung back in its previous position.

"So, all those gold torcs and armbands and things I've seen in Cardiff Museum; are they made of Welsh gold?"

"Welsh, Irish, perhaps even English."

"Wait, are you telling me that there is gold in England?" Ryan almost choked on his beer.

Siân was greatly amused as he coughed to clear the beer from his airway. He made her smile, he made her laugh, he made her feel happy, happier than she had felt in a very long time. "It used to be mined in Derbyshire, Cornwall, Cumbria, and there's the site of an old gold mine in the Malvern Hills."

Ryan was genuinely impressed. "I never knew that…"

"Gold and other ores were a part of why the Romans were so interested in coming to Britain." She paused uncomfortably. "Sorry," continued Siân apologetically. "I'm one of those people who is a mine, no pun intended, of useless, totally unusable, information."

Ryan put his hand over hers; her skin was soft, smooth and a little cool. "I think you're very interesting and very knowledgeable. I'd love to know half as much as you do."

Dinner arrived and they tucked in merrily.

"Tell me all about your work, Ryan."

"There's not much to tell, really. I set up a small business, straight after Uni. It's just me, it's so small."

"So, what's the best photo shoot you've done then?"

"There was this beautiful wedding at Castell Coch that I did last summer. Have you ever been there?"

"It's a fabulous place."

"Well, in that case, you'll know what a bizarre, funny-looking place it is, more like a German fairy tale castle on the side of a mountain. You couldn't get anything more suitable for a fairy tale wedding. It was a big show, top hats and tails all round, expensive marshmallow dress, attendants and guests galore. So many that less than half of them fitted in the chapel in the end. Even the cake was in the shape of the castle. The photo opportunities were fantastical;

the album came out like a fairy tale book." Ryan's face was animated when he talked; he was so passionate about his work.

"Sounds lovely. One day perhaps you'll show me some of your pictures."

"Yes, I would like that too. Mind you, it's probably just as bad as being forced to sit through people's holiday pictures."

"I'm sure it's not!"

Ryan looked bashful. "Are you doing anything tomorrow?"

"Erm, let me see, there's the washing, some reading and quite a bit of lazing around that I had planned. Why?"

"I have some of my pictures with me, if you'd really like to see them. Let me take you out somewhere to say thank you for today."

Siân hesitated. She really liked this guy, but should she let herself fall for him? He was going back to Cardiff soon enough. Would he ever come back here, would they be able to meet up in Cardiff, was this that serious or was it fun for just a couple of days? In her heart this felt serious, the most serious she had ever been, but what of him? He was open, kind, but a little reserved, which made him difficult to read. Oh, what the hell, why not? "This time, I choose where we go."

"Agreed."

CHAPTER ELEVEN

Siân headed home in an aura of happiness, but even that warm aura failed to keep the rain away. There was a bounce in her step and a swelling heart in her chest. Was this what it was like to fall in love? She had loved every single moment of the day with Ryan; she felt as though she had known him for years, despite the fact that they had only met a couple of days before. She felt at home in his company, like she belonged there; it was hard to describe the myriad of feelings that she was experiencing, most of which she had never felt before today, except to say that they felt good. Ryan had offered to accompany her home. He was very old-fashioned in that way; how charming was that? Siân had insisted that he stay in the dry and warm, there was no point in both of them getting soaked again. Besides, it was only a couple of minutes' walk down the road to her place, and if she had allowed him, who knows what could have happened? She was not ready for all that yet.

Uneven-sounding footsteps on the gravel behind her disturbed her from replaying the date in her mind. She put her hand into her trouser pocket, feeling the reassuring cold metal of her house keys. She was almost home, not much further now. Damn, the lane was dark tonight; her neighbours must have already retired for the night, as their lights were off and, despite the tall windows of St Ffraid's Chapel, it was in darkness. The mist was obscuring most of the moonlight; there was barely enough to see by. She quickened her pace. The footsteps kept up with her and moved nearer. She could hear the person's breathing. "Who's there?" she called out, as she wrapped her coat tighter against the chill of the night and the chill of her own fear. Who else was crazy enough to be out on a night like this?

"You little tart." The voice was quiet, threatening and eerily calm.

Siân turned to face the shadow. Huw stood there, swaying, dripping with the rain and shivering with anger. His hair was matted to his forehead and the underlying veins stuck out, throbbing as his racing heart pumped blood to them.

"I beg your pardon?" Siân had never seen him like this before.

"You slebog, don't you realise he has a slut like you in every town or village he visits? He's a city boy, only after you for one thing. He'll use you and throw you away like the piece of rubbish that you are. You make me so angry." Huw's breath stank of alcohol, be must have been drinking at home. Siân had not seen him in the pub earlier, and Ffi did not allow her patrons to get this far over the mark.

"Go home and sleep it off." She tried to add an authoritative tone to her voice, but it shook with nerves.

Huw leaned in and Siân backed away. "You're throwing yourself at him; you're making a fool of yourself in front of the whole village. I saw you today."

"Were you following me? You freak! You have no right to do that. And your silly little stunt at the Maidens didn't frighten us; it pissed me off. Now, go home." Anger crept into Siân's voice. What right had he to speak to her like this? She backed off and continued towards home.

Huw grabbed her roughly, clumsily by the arm. "I saw you making big eyes at him, flashing your eyelashes and God only knows what else."

Siân bashed his arm away; she tried to be gentle but forceful enough to break free. "Leave me alone!" she shouted as loudly as she could, hoping someone would hear her.

"He's not the one for you, Siân, he never will be."

"Who should I be with; not you, surely?" Was it a droplet of icy rain or fear that ran down her spine at that moment? Oh God, was that what all this was about? Had Huw really liked her? Had it not just been Mandy's insane need to try and pair people up?

"You should have been mine, Siân. Everyone says so." Huw grabbed at her coat, trying to open it. Siân fought him off, slapping his hands away. He relented and began to shake violently as the anger became sadness and tears poured forth.

She tried to let him down gently as she had done last year. "I'm sorry, Huw, really I am, but I don't love you, I never have. Did you not get that? Dates are not meant to be that awkward. They're meant to flow, to be fun, exciting. There was never any spark there with us, not for me anyway. I don't feel that way about you."

"But Mandy…"

"I never asked Mandy to ask you out for me. She was interfering; you know what she can be like. I never fancied you; I'm sorry, I never have."

"Why not, what's wrong with me? Why don't you love me? I know I'm not great looking like him, but I'm a nice guy." Huw was wailing now. "What's wrong with me?"

Siân bit back her initial response; she was not seeing the best of him tonight. "It's not as simple as that, is it, Huw? Love is very complicated; you can't fake it, you have to feel it. It's not fair otherwise, not fair on anyone. Please, go home and stop watching me."

He nodded sadly and turned to walk away.

Siân practically ran the rest of the way home; relief washed over her as she closed and locked the front door. She sank to the floor against the sturdy wooden door and rested her elbows on her knees and her head in her hands. What a night!

CHAPTER TWELVE

Ryan bounded up the stairs to his room, taking them two at a time. That was the best date ever! Everything felt so right; it was the first time he had actually enjoyed himself on a date, rather than worrying about what to say and what not to say the whole time. He felt comfortable in her presence, as though she understood him for all his quietness, gentleness and complexities. They had talked late into the night about anything and everything, and she had seemed so genuinely interested in what he had to say. Ffi had practically had to kick Siân out before closing. How he wished that she had permitted him to accompany her home; she had been quite insistent that he stay in the dry. He would not have minded getting wet in order to see her safely home. He leapt, still fully clothed, on to his soft bed, putting his hands behind his head. He bounced twice and felt like a kid again. His mind was excited, racing with exhilaration, but his body was aching, exhausted from all the hiking of the day.

* * *

The roundhouse was thick with smoke, the heat and scents of cooking, ale and so many bodies crammed in together. People came from far and wide to gather at this time of year, to resolve disputes, make claims and marriages. Cadog was doing his best to work through them, fairly and lawfully. He felt lost, alone, despite the dozens of faces watching his every move, every expression. There were many people to speak to and catch up with.

Squished on the wooden seats by the fire, the noise and smell was becoming too much for the young couple. Owein squeezed Morwyna's slight fingers tenderly. "Let's get out of here." Morwyna nodded in agreement and slowly prised herself from between Owein and her well-proportioned neighbour, a woman from the next village who was bringing a dispute over wandering sheep. Everyone was so busy, only one person noticed as the couple stole away.

The fresh air blowing in from the bay was a welcome change to the smell of hot bodies and smoke. Owein and Morwyna walked and talked over their future plans. Owein talked of how he would like to finish his training, which could mean having to travel, to live elsewhere. Morwyna loved the idea. The world seemed full of possibilities now that their marriage was witnessed and official. Morwyna held Owein's hand, never wanting to let go, her other hand tracing, stroking the vivid blue spirals on his wrists and forearms. They reached the cairn on the mountaintop and sat for a while on the stones, gazing out at the landscape, their family lands, the land of their ancestors and possibly their descendants too one day. The sky clouded over as they talked, as though formed from their breath, and Owein pointed out to the north-west. "The sea fog is coming in; let's get home before we are missed."

"Must we?" asked Morwyna. She hugged her new husband close, nestling her face in his neck. "This is the only place that I want to be. Right here, in your arms, forever." Owein wrapped his wife tighter in her checked shawl and held her tight against him. He kissed her soft hair.

"Well, isn't this nice?" remarked Badden sarcastically. "Now, take your hands off *my* wife." He was mounted on a magnificent brown mare, which seemed edgy; she was pacing and stamping. Badden was having trouble keeping her in one place. His bronze sword was drawn and already aimed at Owein.

Morwyna gazed up at Owein with horror as Owein waved the other man away. "She is my wife, as she chose to be." With one hand he pushed Morwyna behind him and the other rested on the hilt of his sword.

"Morwyna, come to me." Badden concentrated his personal power into his words, to call her to him. He tried to command her with the power of his soul. He reached out his other hand, channelling his energy to a silver coloured chain to seize her, as the mad old man he had met and then killed in Kernow had taught him.

"Leave us alone, Badden." Her words stung Badden. How could she resist his magic, the spells he had made on her over so many years? "Come to me, now."

"Go back to Kernow and find yourself a woman there, one who wants you. I never will. I love Owein."

Badden leapt from the horse, bowing as he hit the ground. "I can make you happy and rich. Isn't that what you want? Isn't that why you and your family had Gwalchwen send me away all those years ago, so I could make something of myself and come back to you, worthy and wealthy?"

Owein drew his sword; the sound was silken as though it was cutting the air itself. "No, you were sent away because you are a liar and a coward. You are an evil man, Badden."

"No one speaks to me like that, especially not Gwalchwen's whelp." Badden plunged forward with his sword, aiming a low blow. Owein stepped back, dodging it easily.

"Did you not think it odd that I came back and, within days, Gwalchwen, the man who ruined my life and forced me from my true love, was dead?"

Owein had suspected as much. Despite Gwalchwen's illness, something had not been right with his death. Anger swelled within him; this time there would be no sending away, no banishment for Badden. For the killing of his dear teacher, Gwalchwen; for this to end; for him to live peacefully with Morwyna, Badden must die. He pushed Morwyna further back; she resisted, trying to get close to him again. "Run home, raise the alarm and tell them what has been said here. I will deal with this."

Morwyna knew better than to argue. She ran off down the mountain, towards the circle and towards home. Owein took one quick glance at her in full sprint, her dress and shawl billowing out behind her. He prayed silently to the gods of his people that he would see her again soon. His heart ached already from their parting.

"Run along, my love, I will come for you soon enough," shouted Badden after her, spit flying from his mouth. Still facing away, he lunged a second blow at his opponent; it was met by a strong defence as Owein raised his own sword high. Owein swung on to the attack, raining heavy blow after blow at Badden. Each blow was skilfully deflected; both men had learnt their sword skills from Cadog, whose skill with a sword was legendary in these parts. They had fought before as children, both had experienced victory and loss at the other's hands. "So, you've been practising then," goaded Badden. Owein kept silent, concentrating on the fight. He knew that Badden liked to talk when fighting, his whining, nasal voice a deliberate distraction. He struck a downward blow at Badden's neck, but an upswing caught it, brushing it away. Badden used his blade to twist his opponent's sword around and down towards the ground, and, in a lightning second, drew his dagger. He lunged both sword and dagger at Owein, who leapt backwards. Owein was slightly too late. The sword nicked the skin of his stomach; a thin red line oozed blood. Now Badden was on the attack; he rained down a quick succession of mighty blows, some with the sword, others with both the sword and dagger. He let forth his rage and obsession in a frenzied attack. He knew that Owein would be a true fighter and be true to the skills he had learnt; he, on the other hand, had picked up a few dirty tricks. Owein staggered back under the repeated clashes of bronze; he was sweating with the strain, and the sweat was stinging on his skin and in his eyes. The veins in his neck stretched against the bronze torc. Thunder crashed in the distance, or was it the clash of their swords that echoed around them for miles?

* * *

The noise awoke Ryan with a sudden jolt. He was sweating profusely, his heart hammering wildly against his ribcage. His dreaminess went in an instant. He wondered where he was, until he saw the peach curtains. This was not where he had expected to wake up, but this was where he was staying, so where else could he have woken up? The noise continued. 'What the hell is that?' he thought. The noise was angry, unrelenting. It sounded like swords clashing, like thunder, or metal on overdrive. The frequency of the alien noise began to die down and the pitch became lower, throbbing in ever-decreasing cycles. Ryan realised that it had to be the washing machine, in the room below his. 'A bit early for doing the washing,' he thought. He rolled over on his side and fell back to sleep.

CHAPTER THIRTEEN

Ffi rose well before first light, keen to greet the new sun from within the Ring of Maidens, determined to work with the dawn to bring the light back to the area, to undo whatever darker deed some fool had been up to. She climbed out of bed and said farewell to Alun; he responded with a thunderous snore as he rolled on to his back. Ffi left him to it, pulling on her clothes, the multi-coloured velvet top and the more practical faded brown velvet trousers that she wore for outdoor work. Tucking the hems into her wellington boots, she removed the cloak from her staff, swirled it around her shoulders, and fixed it with a pewter clasp in the shape of a wolf's head. She checked the pockets for her bramble wand. It made perfect sense to Ffi to have a wand made from the plant she was named for, only vine was not easy to find in this area so she had settled on bramble; similar enough, she thought. The wand worked wonderfully for her, it had felt right the moment she collected it. Next, she armed herself with her alder staff, slim, pale and a foot taller than she was. The staff always gave her a sense of protection from its energies, as well as the fact that only an idiot would mess with a rotund woman with a bloody great stick. Feeling that everything was ready, she headed off into the remainder of the night.

The darkness loomed around the circle like a fog, thick, dark and sinister. The light of her torch was sucked away into the gloom. Alun's description of this feeling had been accurate; the air felt dense and cold. As deep as Ffi breathed, very little of the air seemed to be light enough to enter her lungs; it was like trying to breathe underwater. Her palms were sweating, though her skin tingled with iciness. Ffi paced around the circle; the closer she was to the circle, the better she felt. This had always been one of her very favourite places; its energy was sunny, bright and optimistic, even in winter. Anger rose within, anger at whoever had done something bad here, something that angered not only her but also the spirit of the place. She could feel it now; the anger was not hers alone; it came from within the circle too. She paced to the very centre of the circle and, facing east, she called aloud her intentions and began her rite. "I honour the Spirits of this Place; know that I come in Peace. Peace be in the East, Peace be in the South, Peace be in the West and Peace be in the North. May there be Peace in the whole world and may there be Peace here." Once again, she turned to face the east, as the first sliver of the golden sun rose above the horizon.

"Hail to the rising Sun, the bringer of light and of life, who reminds us that darkness and light need to be in balance." A goshawk, soaring in the distance, caught her attention. "Hail, hawk of the dawn, who soars high and free in the currents of the air, I seek your inspiration. Hail to the stag of the woods, he of the antlers, who walks upon the earth and between worlds; I seek your protection. Hail to the salmon of the flowing waters; I seek your wisdom. Hail to the ancestors, those who have been born, have lived, loved and died on this blessed land. I ask you for your guidance and assistance."

Ffi paused, watching the hawk swoop closer, and planned what to say next. "Spirit of this place, help me to help you. Let us together undo whatever negative act has been done here and bring blessings and peace once more."

She paced around the whole site, within the circle and without, clapping her hands occasionally to clear away the negative energies. The hawk continued to swoop high above, watching this human woman with curiosity. Back within the sanctuary of the circle, Ffi was troubled. Someone was watching her, the same someone she had felt many times before here; could he be the Druid said to be interred here? Before, his aura had been one of kindness, of care and of love, but now there was only his fear.

"Beth sy'n bod? Speak to me, friend, I will help you if I can. As once you helped me…" Her heart ached as she remembered the anguish of all those childless years, the endless humiliating tests and jabs and the endless longing. The jealousy and misery, as her friends all had their own, but she and Alun remained without. Then they had come together in the circle as a last ditch attempt, and they had been blessed with Lowri. "Please let me help you."

Ffi put her hand into her pouch and pulled out four small wooden cubes. They were of pale wood, the same alder as her staff, all carved from the same tree. Closing her brown eyes, she rattled them in both hands, fell to her knees and cast them before her. Opening her eyes, she read the signs before her. Closest to her, face up, was the bird footprint carved into the wood, representing the hawk. The other three had landed awkwardly; two seemed to be squashing the third. She poked at them; there were the antlers of the stag at an angle, but touching the boar tooth; she flicked them out of the way, revealing the hoof print of the deer underneath. The modern-day Druid put her hand to her mouth. She knew only one deer alive today. Siân, like her mother before her, had a deer spirit guardian. Elain had even been named for the deer, albeit unintentionally, and Siân bore her mother's name as her own middle name. By her reasoning, the stag must surely be Ryan, with the way he had been so drawn to the stag picture. Stag and boar seemed to be fighting over deer, so who was boar? Who else was interested in Siân's affections and why was hawk watching them and watching her? What did this have to do with the circle and the negativity? She rubbed her eyes, hoping to obtain a clearer level of focus.

The hawk landed on the closest of the outlying stones, bobbing its head up and down. Very slowly, so as not to disturb the creature, Ffi crept towards the stone. The hawk bobbed more vigorously. "Keep your feathers on, boy, I get the hint," she whispered, as she settled her ample frame into the lee of the stone. Beneath her, the ground had been disturbed; someone had dug here by hand, the grass was in clumps and there were deep lines from their fingers in the mud. Ffi held her own hand over the marks. They were larger than her own, so most likely a man's; the same man who was after Siân? She began to dig herself to see what was buried here, to see what had disturbed the energies so drastically. The rain had made the soil so soggy, she was digging up water and mud; whatever had been buried there was long gone down into the marsh. "I'm sorry, I can't get to it," she said aloud to the hawk. "What can I do?" She watched the hawk, seeking for an answer as he watched her. "Any ideas, Gwalchcyfddydd, hawk of the dawn?" The hawk screeched in response; Ffi felt he rather liked that name.

Ffi felt lost. If she could dig up whatever was buried, she could break the magic by breaking and burning them, but without them what could she do? She pulled a bottle of water and a small sachet of salt from her crane bag, the special pouch that contained the tools of her Druidry. Ripping the sachet with her teeth, she opened it and added the salt to the water and held her potion high to the rising sun. "Hail, Oh Sun, Day, Summer, Light and Life, fill this water with your warmth and light. Balance this darkness that is here." She turned to the darker half of the sky. "Hail, Oh Moon, Night, Dark and Death; do not allow your powers to be used for harm and ill will. You are neutral powers, energies opposed and balanced. As we are coming to Alban Eiler, the Spring Equinox, Ostara that is now Easter, I welcome and ask for your balance between night and day, light and dark, Sun and Moon. By these powers I ask you to bless this salt and water, fill it with your powers and may the salt wash away the negativity, Mother Earth transform it into positive energies for healing your body on which we all live."

She opened the bottle again and poured the contents into the hole in the ground. She felt the negativity drain away a little, but it was not enough; nowhere near enough. From within her pouch she pulled a bundle of dried herbs; sage and rosemary for blessing and purification. There was no doubt in her mind, this place needed it. Lighting the bundle with matches, blowing on it to get the smoke wafting, Ffi paced around the circle anti-clockwise, wafting the bundle in circles. Once she had completed her circuit, she turned on her heel and went back the way she had come, clockwise around the circle, wafting the smoke in circles. She visualised light as well as the smoke purifying and cleansing the energies. Next she left the herbs, still smouldering, over the muddy hole. She waited as the herbs continued to shrivel and singe, the smoke wafting into the air above. To her horror, the smoke darkened, casting shadows and eerie shapes. A boar, a holly leaf and a blade. This was not going well. The herbs were spreading the negativity, not negating it. With her foot she hurriedly stomped on the bundle to put it out. Ffi was out of her depth; she placed her hand over her mouth and chin in worry. She would have to speak to others with more experience of neutralising bad energies, maybe get more people together for a ritual to cleanse this horrid negativity away. What could she do in the meantime to protect Siân? Was her only option to find out who was doing this and stop him? But how? So much to do and so little time, so many more pictures still left to paint for the exhibition and a talk on her work to prepare for the opening day. She was contracted into it. Ffi closed the rite; what else could she do right now?

"I thank the God and the Goddess. I thank the Stag and Earth, the Salmon and Water, Hawk – Gwalchcyfddydd – and Air, I thank you, shining Sun, Fire and ancient ones. I thank you all for witnessing and blessing this rite. This rite ends in Peace as in Peace it began. May the world be filled with Love, Peace and Balance, especially Maenddu and the Maidens... Please... Awen!"

CHAPTER FOURTEEN

The shadow sat, crouched in the gorse. The body he occupied screamed in torment; he enjoyed it, watching him squirm, hearing him beg for his freedom. What a simpering, pathetic fool! He had invited him in, open, willingly and foolishly. Had he really considered that this connection would be anything else? Badden was hardly going to refuse an offer like that, the man was driven by the same lust for power and for her that drove him. The two bitter souls were a perfect match, if the fool would only shut up and let him get on with what he had been waiting centuries to do. The waiting had been torture, pure merciless agony. However, now the ecstasy that had kept him going was nearly his, he was so very close to obtaining all that he had desired.

The woman prancing around before him was entertaining; she knew some of the old words, the old ways, but in a diluted form. She had no real power, despite her very great magical potential. He could see it flowing around her and in her aura; he could have taught her if she was not such a do-gooder. He watched in silence as the hawk had tried to tell her what to do, guided by the spirit of Gwalchwen. Still the old Druid tried to interfere. How typical of the old man; still he would not let go and let Badden have his victory. Hardly anyone told the old tales, and no one seemed to truly understand their message anymore. The old wisdom was lost now; no one in this odd world would know how to defeat him or undo his spells and charms, unless some idiot showed them how to on the television, and that was not likely to happen. Even this sad soul within him had no idea how to fight back. "Hush now," he warned the subdued, moaning voice. "Hush now, or I will snuff you out like a candle, for I am the darkness." The screams within faded to silence. Badden smiled in triumph.

He waited patiently until the woman had finished and gone, then he stepped out from his hiding place amidst the prickly bushes. The body was stiff and took a few seconds to get going; it ached with cramp and the damp in its bones. This body had not been well cared for; he was doing it a favour. The hawk grew agitated by his presence. Badden wondered why the animals hated him so when he was named after one of them, Badden – the boar. Setting his feet firmly on the ground, he squatted down by the stone. Hesitantly, he placed his left hand over the hole in the ground that she had widened and deepened. She had scrabbled around in vain. Through the palm of his hand he sensed the energy of her interference, feeling a dim light dissipating into the ground, negated with ease by his earlier handiwork. Silly woman, what good did she think that the light would do against his dark spell? Instinctively he knew that the charms, the bones and carved talismans, were all still intact, deep within the dark solidity of the earth. Ah, they were working, he could feel the shift in the air and almost taste his victory. However, this was all happening too slowly. He desired her, he hungered for her, and he wanted her now. Seeing the two of them, Owein and Morwyna, together again, had enraged him; this time he would not allow it to continue. No one was going to come between him and his love.

Water was seeping into the hole, muddy and murky. With his index finger, he began to trace a spiral in the sludge, working inwards then outwards until the motion of the water took over from the motion of his finger. "I have a request, White Phantom, a present for you. A young soul eager for love, eager to please."

Within the waters appeared a face, a white, ghoulish face. A skull barely covered by flesh, with black holes for eyes. Even Badden shivered in its presence. The dark eyes searched his soul, cutting through it like lasers. "I am lonely, so lonely. It is no fun to dance alone on the moors. Will you dance with me, sir?" The phantom spoke mildly, her delicate voice filled with sad sorrows.

"Not I, White Phantom." Badden was uncomfortable, he regretted having to call the Pwca, to call to the Fairy Folk in this way.

"Then why do you call me here?"

"Tell me your name."

"I will not give you power over me; you may call me Gwynhwyfar, for you address me as White Phantom. I will not give up my powers or my dancing for you, weak mortal."

"There is one who is in my way. I need him gone."

The Pwca tilted her skull to one side, watching this one closely; he had magic of his own, so why did he need her? "Will he dance with me?"

"Yes. Call to him, Gwynhwyfar, and he shall keep you company for all time. You know that no man can resist your call."

She shrieked with laughter. For all his magic, how very little he truly knew. It took more than a call, more than her song to enchant a man; otherwise, she would have plenty of company in the long, lonely nights. "Tell me, what is the name of the one you wish me to call to?"

"In this life he is Ryan." Badden was sweating with discomfort.

"Is he handsome?"

"Yes."

The ghoulish apparition smiled, the white flesh creeping back to reveal a black mouth and rotten teeth. "Are you prepared to pay the price for this little favour?"

"What is the price?"

Gwynhwyfar shook her head, and her pale, matted, rat tail hair swung with the action. "I will tell you when I am ready, when the man is mine."

Badden narrowed his eyes and mouth. "I cannot agree to a price I do not know!"

"Then you have wasted my time. We folk do not look kindly on mortals who waste our time." The words were spat out with venom. The Pwca's image began to melt away from the puddle.

"Wait," he called after her. "Yes, fine. I agree."

"Good." She faded from view and the swirling water grew calm and still once more. Badden was left with an inner sense of dread. He quivered with revulsion at his own actions. He hated dealing with the wretched Fairy creatures of the night, they never quite did as they were asked and the price was always so damn high, but oh, what he would give for her to be his. Let Ryan pay the price; let his soul be the payment and the favour.

There was only one thing left to do now, to spread the macabre magic, to increase its power by feeding off the latent magic of the land. Placing both hands against the cold, hard rock, he pushed hard into it, pouring his desire, his desperation and his dark soul into the very being of the stone, until it began to throb with his dark power. The stone cracked with the intensity, the earth shook beneath his feet. The sonorous noise, a vocalisation of centuries of sorrows, resonated to the other stones and roared off into the distance. A short while later, when the vibrations had died down, Badden walked around the circle to the outlying stone on the opposite side. When he was last free to roam around here, all those years ago, there had been many more outlying stones, standing guard. Once these had been two avenues leading up to or away from the circle. They were pathways, conduits of energy as well as people. Again, he placed his hands to the stone, and deluged it with his negativity. He turned towards the circle and bowed down low in mock courtesy to his old adversary, the hawk, which shrieked in grief and pain and flew off high into the sky above. The web began to form, stretching like black silk across the land, ensnaring and holding swathes within its grasp. Shadowy energy pulsed along the old avenues, and the old energy lines in towards the circle and out towards the other ancient monuments of the area.

The circle's own rainbow of light deflected most of the shadows, though not all of them. There were cracks in the light where the gloom began to creep in, eating up some of the light, dimming it into darkness, and weakening the warding and protection of the circle.

CHAPTER FIFTEEN

A shrill, incessant ringing woke Ryan. Groaning with annoyance, he put the pillow over his ears. Things were conspiring against him getting much sleep this morning. The ringing continued. He sat up and reached for his mobile phone on the bedside table. Squinting, he checked the time; 7.50 on a Sunday morning was not a time he was used to. Professor Trevivian's name was flashing at him; he thought he had better answer it. Pressing the green button, he cleared his throat huskily. "Hello, Trev."

"Good morning, lad, hope I didn't wake you." Trevivian's voice was upbeat and abhorrently gleeful for this time of day.

"Erm, yeah, you and a few other things."

"Sorry. Well, how are you, how are things going?" The enthusiasm grated on Ryan's nerves.

"Good, I'm still in Pembrokeshire. Got some more assignments to do around here, I should be back in a few days." Ryan rubbed the sleep from his eyes with his free hand.

Trevivian paused. "I hate to do this to you, Ryan, only I could do with those pictures that you've got sooner rather than later."

"Is everything all right, Trev?"

"Sure, sure. I've reached a bit of a full stop and I could do with some of the pictures to get me going again. A bit of inspiration, reminding me what's what."

"I can email them to you if you like?" Ryan knew the answer before he spoke; it was polite to offer nonetheless.

"No, lad, you know I don't like such things. I need to see the real pictures. They never appear quite the same on a screen, do they?"

Ryan shook his head. "How's that ancient typewriter of yours holding up with all the writing?"

"Splendidly. She's as loyal as ever to the cause."

"Tell you what. I'll bring back what I've got so far and print it up for you on Monday. Then I'll have to come back this way and finish off the rest. Would that be all right?"

"Bring me the receipts you've accumulated so far, and I'll get working on settling your expenses. You can tell me all the old stories you've been hearing. A few of them would be an interesting addition to the book. People love a good legend."

Years ago, it had been those same old stories that had begun Trevivian's fascination with the stone circles near his home on Bodmin Moor. To this very day, the Hurlers, the first site he remembered visiting, was still his personal favourite.

"I can tell you many old tales, they're essentially variations on a theme," Ryan laughed. "They've been giving me the weirdest dreams. I may have to charge for psychological damage at this rate. I've got to ask you about the significance of the many Maiden sites when I see you."

The phone line crackled as the washing machine downstairs hurtled through the final rinse. "Come for dinner, Monday night, I could do with the company," the professor said. "We'll order in, I hate cooking. Then we can go through the pictures and tell tales late into the night."

An idea popped into Ryan's head. "If it's good food you're after, maybe you should come back to Pembrokeshire with me. I'm staying in a great pub that does the most wonderful food, all home cooked and very generous portions." He stared down at his own stomach; he could swear it was expanding.

Trevivian laughed; the laughing then turned to coughing. "Don't try and distract me, Ryan." The professor sucked in breath; it rattled in his throat. "I'm having enough trouble ploughing on with this book as it is. I would much rather be out in the field than stuck in this stuffy study. Where exactly are you then?"

"Maenddu, close to the Ring of Maidens."

"Ah yes." The professor sounded dreamy, distracted. "A very fine example of a western style circle. A true enigma, that one."

Ryan continued, "I've also bumped into one of your old students. She's been showing me around and being my personal tour guide."

"Oh, who?" Trevivian pried.

"Siân Derwyn."

"Indeed? I did wonder whatever happened to her. A very dedicated student, a serious soul. There was talk of her staying on for her Masters, then she simply fell off the radar. Had to go back home for some family crisis, I think. Such a shame. My, my, how is she?" He paused for more coughing.

Ryan squirmed and fidgeted; he puffed up the pillow and shifted on to his elbow. "She's fine."

Trevivian had sensed the pause. "I'm glad you've had some company. I'd best leave you to your day of rest. Don't do anything I wouldn't do."

"Take care of yourself, Trev."

"…And there's not a lot I wouldn't do at my age. If only I'd figured that out all those years ago. Bye, Ryan, see you on Monday."

"Bye, Trev." Ryan buried his head in the pillow. He did not want to go back to Cardiff yet; he wanted to stay here. At least he would be able to come back in a few days, once he and the professor had got the first round of pictures organised. He would have to tell Siân today about the change in plans. He hoped she would not mind; after all, this way he was coming back. Would she believe him? It could hardly look encouraging from her perspective, him rushing off like that.

They met outside the front of the pub. His mind raced with options; should he tell her now, so they could savour this day together, or should he tell her later? Ryan pursed his lips and gathered his courage; he might as well get it over and done with now. "Siân, I have to go back to Cardiff for a few days. The professor wants to go through the photographs."

Siân turned to him and smiled, though her eyes were sad. "Oh…"

He took her hands in his. "I promise you I'm coming back, I've booked it already with Ffi."

She nodded, uncertainly.

"How about I try and get Trev to let me have a copy of some of his notes so far about the Preseli monuments?"

This time the smile reached her eyes. "Good luck; he always was a secretive old buzzard!"

"Would you like to come up and see the pictures?" He led the way to the side door and pulled the key from his pocket.

"Would you like to live until the end of the day?" she gibed.

"Huh?"

"Ffi would have your guts for garters; they don't like guests to have visitors in their rooms. Anyhow, I live here, remember; I'd never live down the gossip."

"Good point. What about your place then?"

Siân snorted with laughter. "How is that any better? The gossips will have a field day. Maybe when you come back…" She left the suggestion hanging in the air provocatively. "For now, let's set up in the conservatory, I'm sure Ffi would like to see the photos as well."

Ryan opened the door and waved Siân in before him. She called out to Ffi. "Helloooo, may we borrow the conservatory for a bit?"

Ffi was in a fluster, clearing away the breakfast things; her face was worried, flushed, and her concentration elsewhere. "Come in, my dears; make yourselves comfy, I'll be out of your hair in a minute."

"Ryan's going to show me some of his pictures; would you like to see them?" said Siân as Ryan dashed off upstairs to fetch the laptop.

"Normally I'd love to, dear, but I'm a bit busy right now. Maybe later?"

Siân piled the sauces and mugs into her hands and took them through to help out. "What's the matter, Ffi?"

"Nothing that I want to worry you about, dear." Ffi's heart sank; she wanted to tell Siân to warn her. But what good would it do? Only worry the poor dear girl. She had already had so much to deal with in her short life; it did not seem fair. "I'm getting rather behind with the work for the exhibition, that's all." That at least was true; she despised lying to such a close friend.

"If I can help in any way…" Siân knew that Ffi was not telling her the complete truth, she saw it blazoned across her face; Ffi was such a bad liar.

Ryan came hurtling down the stairs, sleek silver laptop in hand. "Is it all right if I plug it in down here, it's running low on power?"

"Help yourself, dear. Can I make you a cup of tea?" Ffi attempted to avoid Siân, for fear that she would realise something was horribly wrong.

"Please," they said in unison. Ffi bustled off into the kitchen and splashed some cold water on her face as she filled the kettle.

Ryan uncurled the lead and plugged the computer in. It sprang to life, with a stunning silhouette of the long, thin stones of Callanish against a glorious sunset for its wallpaper. "Did you take that?" Siân asked in admiration.

"Yep, it will be the cover of Trev's book on the 'Megaliths of Scotland', due to be published next month. This 'Megaliths of Wales and Cornwall' is the next in a series he's planning to do."

"It's so enigmatic, is it Callanish?"

"Yup, it's an astonishing place, completely timeless. Here we go, I've set it up as a slideshow."

Siân sat back patiently to watch. Each shot was well constructed, deliberate and atmospheric. She smiled inwardly. Ryan was a very skilled photographer, a skilled artist in his own right, borrowing his colours from Mother Nature rather than the paint pot as Ffi did. Each were wonderfully artistic in their own unique way, each showing you another way to see the world around you. Shot after shot ran before her eyes, of various different sites. Some she knew, others were new to her. Several took her breath away.

Ffi watched through the hatch from the kitchen, waiting for what felt like an eternity for the kettle to boil. Not bad for such a young lad. She herself had only discovered her talents much later in life; it was something she regretted not exploring earlier. Leaning back against the kitchen top, with it squarely in the small of her back, she took in both the sights of the pictures and of the young couple. Feelings of apprehension and anxiety knotted in her stomach. She rubbed it, trying to ease the sense that it was going to eat her up. Another slide appeared, rolling on to the screen like a leaf of paper. It was one of the shots of the Ring of Maidens. He was there; the spirit of the circle, as a dim grey shadow. She could see his long white hair blowing out behind him; his hand reached out towards the person behind the camera, reaching to Ryan. Again, another picture poured on to the screen; there he was again, closer.

"Stop!" screamed Ffi. Ryan and Siân turned around in alarm as Ffi came rushing into the conservatory. Their faces were a picture of confusion.

"Ffi, whatever's the matter?" asked Siân. "Come and sit down."

Ffi stood there in front of the computer, clenching and unclenching her fists. The colour drained from her face. "Don't you see him?"

"Who, Ffi? Who can you see?"

"That man, standing there in the circle. He's reaching out to you, Ryan."

Ryan's jaw dropped. "When I took these, I saw a shadow in the circle. I thought it must have been a dog walker off in the distance. When I checked the pictures they were clear, to me they still are. I can't see him; Siân, can you?"

"I'm sorry; all I can see is the stone circle and lots of gorse and the mountains."

"He's right there. Tall, old, with long white hair, with a cloak around his shoulders."

Ryan still had not taken his eyes off Ffi. "Ffi, no one here is saying we don't believe you, only that we can't see him. Where do you see him?"

Ffi stepped forward, watching Ryan closely. Was he humouring her? She pointed to the screen, to the very centre of the circle. She traced the figure as she spoke. "This is his head, his tunic, and see here, the cloak and his hair here."

Ryan nodded. "That is exactly where I saw the shadow."

Siân looked from one of them to the other, utterly bewildered; it was as though they were talking a whole other language.

Ffi put her hand on Siân's shoulder. "You of all people know the tales about the circle. The shadow is the spirit of the guardian of the circle, the old Druid who was buried there thousands of years ago. He is a hawk spirit and he watches even now." Ffi sat down opposite Siân. "Siân, dear, something strange is going on at that circle; someone is trying to do something sinister." Siân opened her voice to speak, but Ffi continued. "I didn't want to tell you this, but someone is making dark spells against you." Ffi plucked up the courage to ask something that had been bugging her since her animal reading. "Ryan, what is your full name, my dear?"

"Ryan David Ackley. Why, does that have some relevance to all this?"

"David, as in Dave. As in Damh, DAMH to the Celts, Damh means Stag. Yes, you're the Stag. That's why you couldn't tear yourself from that picture."

The younger woman was extremely puzzled. Over the years she had heard all sorts of things from Ffi; some were interesting, others more 'out there'; nothing before had been quite as crazy as all this was. She laughed nervously, as she patted her friend's hand. "Ffi, the pressure's finally got to you."

"No!" Ffi snapped. "Please listen to me! Ryan, tell her. Ryan is here to protect you. He is the stag to your deer. Damh and Elain, the Stag and the Deer. The Druid brought him to you, to ward and protect you. That's why you have been brought together. Ryan, you must not go back to Cardiff, you must stay here with Siân, please."

Ryan had no idea what to say; the old woman was crazed, hysterical. Her words made no sense. So there was some similarity in their names, so what? Yet it nagged at him and she had seen the shadow; he saw that very same shadow. She could not have known; he had not said anything to anyone about it.

"I don't know about any of that, but I did see something at the circle. Only a vague shadow though. A streak of grey, not anything more than that."

"Please don't go back to Cardiff," she repeated, more firmly.

"I have to; I'll be back in a few days."

Ffi knew she was not getting through to them, so she changed tack. "Siân, have you ever known me to lie to you?"

"No."

"Then trust me, dear, I am not lying to you now. You must be very careful, both of you. Someone has been casting black spells against you. This morning, I went up to the Maidens to try and destroy them, but I couldn't find them. I could feel them though; they are truly evil. You must both be very careful and take good care of each other."

Ryan could see that this conversation was going nowhere; Siân was becoming increasingly freaked, and Ffi was losing it. He grabbed the laptop and unplugged the cable. "Siân, shall we head out? You said you'd take me somewhere today."

"OK. We'll be fine, Ffi, honestly. Will you be OK?"

"I'll be fine, if you're both together, dears."

They walked away in silence, leaving Ffi to her own troubled thoughts. Neither spoke until they reached Ryan's vehicle. Siân knew this vehicle; she had seen it often enough around Cardiff. "Hey, this isn't yours."

"Nope, it's the professor's. He calls it the monster. He lets me borrow it while I'm on the road for him. Personally, I'd never want such an environmentally unfriendly vehicle, but I need it on these roads. Don't worry, he's using my smart car, and holding it to ransom until I get this back to him."

"That seems fair. What was that all about in there?" Siân knew that Ryan knew more than he was sharing.

Ryan opened the boot and put the laptop safely in it. "When I was up at the circle, I did see a shadow, possibly a ghost. I thought I must have been imagining it. Kind of easy to do when you've been wandering around ancient monuments and hearing ghostly tales non-stop for weeks. I didn't tell anyone; I mean, it's a bit embarrassing to admit to seeing things."

"Was it at the exact time you took those pictures?" Siân stood by the passenger door as Ryan came to open it for her.

"Yes. That's what makes it so odd. Does Ffi normally go a bit bonkers like that?"

"I've never seen her like that before, to be honest. Do you think there's anything to it?"

"I don't know. These circles have so many stories of weird goings-on; ghosts, stones that get up and wander about at night, even UFOs. It sounds like nonsense to me. Quartz and other minerals have been known to have some very crazy properties; it could be some abnormal reflection off a stone. So where am I heading to?" he asked as they both climbed into the vehicle and stretched their seatbelts across their young bodies.

"To my favourite hot chocolate in Cymru, perhaps even the world. Head for the main road. I'll direct you from there." She winked at him as he turned the key and the engine sprung into life.

CHAPTER SIXTEEN

As she watched them go, through the window, Ffi let out a huge sigh. In her desperation to get the message across, she had messed up. She felt alone, painfully isolated. Ffi had to admit to herself that she had never really fit in with other people. Others tended not to understand her, or think she was nothing but an air-headed hippie, a relic from the Sixties who had wandered aimlessly into the Twenty-First Century. She saw things others did not; she felt things that others refused to believe were possible. Perhaps it gave them comfort not to have to worry, or believe in the things she did. It would have given Ffi comfort right now not to be so aware of the feeling of foreboding that was sticking to her like glue.

She stretched, catlike, to shift the sensation, her fingers and toes reaching out, spreading and sensing the web of life around her. The web felt close, smothering her, holding her down. The normally brilliant white rays of light were grey, torn, limp and lifeless. Ffi gasped in astonishment. Leaping up from her chair, she ran towards the phone. Gripping the receiver so tightly that her knuckles went white, she began to dial, her fingers tripping over each other in her haste.

Half an hour later, Ffi sat curled up in a ball by the phone. She held wads of her mousy hair tight in her hands. She looked up with red, bloodshot eyes as the door opened and Bryn and Alun ambled in. "Whatever's the matter?" Alun's voice was filled with concern.

"Everything, everything's the matter. It's too much for me on my own, and no one wants to help."

Alun knelt down slowly to be on his wife's level. His knees cracked arthritically as he manoeuvred himself next to her and placed his arms around her. "What happened this morning?"

"I went up to the circle and it's awful, Alun." Bryn joined them on the floor in the hall, snuggling up to his master and mistress to comfort them. "I thought it was only a local fool messing about with something they didn't understand; turns out, I'm the fool."

Alun hugged her tighter. "You're not a fool, love."

"I did everything I could think of, I clapped the energy away, cleansed it by the elements and even rosemary and sage; nothing helped. The smudging even made it worse; the spell started to feed off it, like it's feeding off the whole life force of the mountains. I don't know how to sever that. Whoever it is has buried something nasty under one of the musician stones; I tried to dig it up."

"Would I be able to get at it?" He tensed his arm muscles, still strong.

Ffi forced a weak smile. "No, it's far too deep now. The marsh has taken the offering."

Alun picked up the black plastic receiver, still hanging down by Ffi on its coiled lead, and awkwardly placed it back in its rightful place with a reassuring click. "Who have you been calling?"

Ffi nestled down into her husband's strong arms. "Everyone I could think of. The rector's not interested; he's too busy with his three parishes and Easter coming up. So much for 'call me anytime'. He said he'd get someone from the Diocese to call me back in a couple of weeks. I don't think we have anything like that long. Rob and Co were also not interested, too busy with the Grove's Ostara celebrations, self-centred buggers. Honestly, when you think what I give to that lot in terms of time and energy. Even MoonRaven's coven were too busy, all apart from Tasha, but I don't think I want her involved in this, it's too much for someone so young and so new to the old ways."

"I see." Alun's lips were thin slits. "Perhaps it's best this way. Perhaps this is what the old Gods want."

"What do you mean, dear?" The words were faint.

"Perhaps this is something that we have to sort out ourselves. You've always said you felt like the guardian of that circle, passing your knowledge on to Lowri and Siân, as your uncle passed it to you. 'The Merry Maidens' has always been more to you than just this pub. I knew that when I married you."

He kissed the end of her nose lightly. "Maybe this is an internal matter, not meant for outsiders. You're always telling me that everything works out as it has to in the end. What do we know?"

"There is someone trying to help; I saw a magnificent hawk at the circle. He could be the old Druid in the story, the one who was buried there. He was trying to talk to me, trying to help, but for all my research, for all my meditations, I didn't understand him. The magic is old, so old. The things were buried to re-awaken it all, like some weird unfinished business." Ffi stared into the warm brown eyes of her husband, the eyes she knew so well and she knew never lied to her. "The spell is to harm Siân and Ryan. I can feel it. I tried to tell them but they didn't understand. They're both involved in all this, I know it." She squeezed her husband's hand tenderly.

"Did they start all this?" Alun idly scratched behind Bryn's ears with his other hand.

"No. Siân wouldn't do something as stupid as that. It's someone else, someone local. Ryan's got mixed up in it somehow; it's like he's a major player in a game that I can see being played out before me, only I don't know the rules or the moves." Ffi was exasperated.

"Then you have two choices, my dear." Alun's logical mind was the perfect foil to his wife's way of thinking. "Either learn the game, and fast, or start playing your own."

CHAPTER SEVENTEEN

S unday lunch at 'The Merry Maidens' was always popular. Ffi's Sunday roasts were traditional, wholesome and meant no messy washing up at home, always an appealing combination. Ffi welcomed the distraction from the morning's events at the Ring of Maidens. The kitchen was hot, and the windows streamed with condensation even though they were open. Ffi's face was bright red, flushed with the heat. Her hair was dishevelled, fluffed around her face, annoying her as she worked. The whole building was scented richly by the cooking meat and simmering gravy.

Alun was serving drinks behind the bar, chatting to his customers and catching up on local events. The clock in the hallway struck one with a loud chime as the twins hobbled in. The twins were real characters – old, stubborn, rude and argumentative. They were elderly gentlemen, their skin leathery and crinkled from their exposure to the elements, year on year. Their legs bowed outwards and they walked with the aid of matching sticks. They were identical twins and, for the most part, functioned as one. They still lived together in the old, rickety farmhouse in which they were born, and were proud of the fact that their house had no electricity and no running water. They put their very great age, of which no one was sure, down to the fact that their water came fresh from their own private spring, that they had at least one pint of beer a day, and long constitutionals every morning and evening. To be truthful, though, their long constitutionals, like everything else they did, were beset by bickering. Each had waited years for the other to move out and bugger off, yet neither had. They were stuck with each other, and this day was no exception. As they came through the door, they poked each other out of their own way with their stick and grumbled at each other.

"Afternoon, Jim, afternoon, John. What can I get you?"

"A pint of your best ale," they chimed together.

Alun poured out their pints, with careful deliberation, half-listening to the two men grumbling still at each other. "I tell you, I saw him, as clear as day." Jim was poking his brother with each word with his tanned, creased forefinger.

"You're lying; you always were one for the silly stories, making stuff up to get all the attention. It didn't work on our mother and it won't work now." John turned his back on his brother and counted the money out on the bar mat.

"I tell you…"

"Will I never get a meal in peace?" John said as a prayer, his eyes closed.

"Everything alright, gents?" Alun felt obliged to ask. He knew he would regret it but it was par for the course of being barman.

"Oh, Gawd, don't get him started. He's been on at me all bloody morning and half the bloody night already. The old sod is seeing things; too much beer last night I reckon. Didn't even share it with me."

Jim cleared his throat; it took some time. Then he paused for effect. "Last night I saw the Gwyllgi, the Dog of Darkness, clear as day," he announced to the whole pub. A soft half hush descended on the gathered patrons. People continued to talk, in hushed tones, still listening out for Jim's latest tale. Alun and many others raised an eyebrow at this tall tale. Jim was famous for telling these sorts of stories; he loved to scare the kiddies, to tell tales in exchange for a pint; oh, how he loved an audience.

John shook his head and his ragged grey hair furiously. "You didn't see anything except through your beer goggles."

"Where was that then?" Alun asked conversationally. He knew he was going to hear all about it anyway, so there was no harm in appearing interested, and something inside told him that after Ffi's recent experiences he had better listen.

Jim settled himself down comfortably on a barstool, his stick next to him. "On my evening constitutional, I went out to stretch my old legs. This lazy old sod was too busy to join me, so I went off on my own. It was nice to have some peace and quiet, I tell you. I was just making my way over the lower fields, as dusk was coming down, and there he was. He was as clear to me then as you are to me now. He strolled out of the hawthorn as bold as brass and stared me right in the face with those horrible red eyes of his. His fur was as black as the night. He was a big bugger, at least as big as a Great Dane, if not bigger." Jim emphasised the dog's dimensions with his hands. "He was built like a brick shit house. Scared me half to death, I tell you."

"So, you'll be dead by the end of the week, will you?" remarked John bitterly. "Once you've stared into the beady, red eyes of the Gwyllgi, stories say you'll be dead within the week."

"I bloody hope not. With my luck, you'd go and die too, to spite me, so's I could never get any bloody peace and quiet, even in Heaven." Jim waggled his twisted finger only inches from his brother's nose.

"You're not going to bloody Heaven, you liar," John roared, his face turning puce.

"I'm not lyin'. Not this time, this is God's own truth. I saw the Gwyllgi." Jim's finger was getting closer and closer to his brother's wide, bulbous nose.

"Oh, shut up, you stupid old sod. I'm fed up with your tall tales, always making stuff up. I'm ashamed to be related to you." John clenched his fists and stuck his neck out, trying to gain height on his brother.

"That makes two of us then," Jim said into his beer as he drank the froth from it.

Alun had never seen them this angry with each other before. "Hey, guys. Calm down a bit, eh? What can I get you for lunch?"

"I'm not eating with him. Not 'til he admits I'm telling the truth. I tell you, I saw him, he's as real as you are. Big black dog with fiery eyes, like the coals of Hell itself."

"You liar!" John launched at his brother with his fist, punching him hard, full in the face. Jim went halfway down, managing to hold on to the side of the bar. His beer glass tilted over and fell to the ground, smashing on contact.

"You bastard," Jim retaliated with his fist, knocking it hard into his brother's nose. Blood spouted forth.

John lurched backward as the patrons began to rise from their seats; he grabbed a glass from a nearby table and cracked it on the table. He aimed forward with the broken glass as a weapon. Jim grabbed the barstool by the legs and brought it high above his head with the intention of bringing it down with all his strength on to his brother, and he would have done so if it were not for Alun. The landlord rushed around the bar as fast as his legs would carry him. He grabbed the stool, tugged it forcefully away from Jim, and chucked it unceremoniously out of range. Various other patrons had grabbed John and were pulling him back. "Stop it," Alun ordered gruffly. "What the hell has got into you two?"

Alun glanced from one brother to the other; their steely, distant expressions each matched the other's. They did not appear as they usually did; there were deep, dark shadows in the irises of their eyes.

"I asked, what the hell is going on in my pub? I will not tolerate a bar-room brawl!"

Ffi came rushing through from the kitchen, tea towel in hand. The glass she had put down to an accident, it happened all the time in a pub, but the thud had brought her running. She surveyed the scene before her in consternation. "What the…"

Alun spoke softly to his wife, without taking his attention from the twins. "These two were just about to explain."

"I saw the Gwyllgi and this stupid sod won't believe me. Then he attacked me. You all saw it," Jim growled at the whole room. Ffi's eyes widened and her breath caught in her throat. A sighting of the Dog of Darkness, even by someone like Jim, was not a good sign. Her legs began to tremble; she reached out to the bar for support as the ground beneath her feet swayed. The evil was spreading.

"He's lying, he's always lying. I've finally had enough. Eighty years I've had to put up with him! Eighty bloody years. I should have kicked you out years ago." John was trying to shake off the people holding him back.

Alun was a smouldering volcano, the calm exterior hiding a mountain of rage beneath. "Sort this out now. Get out and stay out until you sort your little differences out. I will not allow fighting in this public house. This is 'The *Merry* Maidens'. Do you understand me?"

The brothers answered in unison. "Yes."

Alun pointed at John. "You started it, so you can apologise first."

"Sorry," he mumbled. Someone passed him a napkin and he held it to his nose to staunch the nosebleed.

"Now you, Jim."

"I've got nothing to be bloody sorry for." Jim was indignant.

"Now, Jim," commanded the landlord.

"All right, sorry."

"Now, bugger off, both of you." Alun's tone said, 'Do not argue with me, don't you dare argue with me.' The twins shuffled off in shame, still moaning at each other under their breath. Alun and everybody else watched them go, not believing what they had just witnessed; two frail eighty-something's trying to take each other out in a public place. For the rest of the day the tone in the pub remained hushed, lulled into a sense of insecurity and nervousness.

CHAPTER EIGHTEEN

The roads were dark, narrow and winding. There was barely enough room for one vehicle, let alone two to pass each other. Ryan was taking them slowly and carefully. He had no desire to damage the professor's four by four, himself, or his passenger. Siân was issuing instructions as needed and Ryan was relieved; clearly, directional signs were not something much worried about around here. Half the roads he was taking were more like private gravel tracks rather than roads.

"We're nearly there," Siân said reassuringly.

"Great." Ryan was concentrating on the road ahead.

Suddenly, something dark bounded across the road in a giant leap. Ryan slammed his foot down hard on the brakes to avoid hitting whatever it was. The vehicle jolted to a sudden stop and the engine stalled. Ryan and Siân were flung forward and then backwards sharply. Their heads thudded into the headrests. Ryan's hands remained holding tightly on to the steering wheel, his nails digging into the old rubber. "Did you see that?"

Siân was as white as snow, even paler than usual. Her voice came out as meek as a whisper. "Must have been a deer or a dog."

"Gigantic dog, if it was. We missed it anyway. I hope it's all right."

"Probably as freaked as we are. We should just make sure we've not glanced it." Siân was already fumbling for the door handle.

Ryan turned the engine on again; squinting into the dusk. He could not see anything immediately ahead. "I'll go. Stay here, it might not be too happy. There's a torch in the glove compartment; pass it to me, please."

Siân obliged, passing across the huge powerful torch. She rolled down the window and wrapped herself tighter in her long black cardigan. Ryan got out and began to search around the ditches and hedgerows. The spiky shadows cast by the hawthorn and blackthorn gave him the creeps. A hundred thousand tiny black daggers looming out at him, clawing closer like the fingers of death. The flowering blackthorn was like a hundred thousand white phantoms floating on the wind. He shivered. "I can't see anything. I'm sure we didn't hit it, anyway. We'd have felt it, something that big. Bloody hell, it's dark."

"There's very little light pollution out this way. This is what dark is supposed to be like, black and blue, rather than tinted orange."

He came across a gap in the hedgerow, a recent one. The branches had been snapped away as though something big had gone through it. "Take a look at this. It must have been huge, a big stag or something." He shone his torch through the gap, peering after it; still he could not see anything except the fathomless dark.

"Get back in the car." Siân was feeling very uneasy, her palms were damp, and she just wanted to curl up in the warm and well lit indoors.

Ryan flicked the plastic switch on the over-sized torch. He was still squinting through the gap in the hawthorn. His mind willed him back to the car, but his feet were transfixed to the spot. His eyes caught a glint of light in the darkness. A pale light at a very great distance. He blinked, not quite believing what he saw. There it was again; a pale white-green light dancing in the distance; iridescent, shimmering like the aurora borealis. The colours shifted through the spectrum and back to pale green. A noise assailed his eardrums, like a harp being played, like the sounds of dancing starlight. The sound called to him, his feet began to move him towards it. Siân watched him carefully. "Hey, Ryan, have you found something?" He did not respond. "Ryan?" She climbed down out of the vehicle and made her way towards him. "Ryan, where are you going?"

He had gone through the gap now into the field. He had barely noticed the thorns scraping at him as he passed them by. Siân dashed after him, the thorns pulling at her clothes and hair. She grabbed him around the waist with her arms and hugged him close. Ryan continued to take slow paces forward. Hugging him tighter and leaning slightly back, Siân used her own body weight to hold him still. "Ryan, stop, you don't know where you're going. This is marshland."

"Huh?" Ryan was miles away, off in the distance with the dancing light.

"Whatever is the matter with you? We have to get back to the car, this place is dangerous."

"Follow me," called a voice, a soft feminine voice in his head.

"Follow me," Ryan echoed.

"No, you follow me." Siân was pulling at him now, trying to drag him with her back to the light and safety of the vehicle. It was like trying to drag a lamppost; he would not or could not budge.

"Can you see it? Can you hear it?" Ryan raised his arm, his finger pointing off into the distance.

Siân followed his line of sight. A small pale green flame was dancing on the marsh, twirling, swirling hypnotically. The flame was reflecting in a still pool of water. The beauty and grace of the flame was otherworldly. Siân gazed in awe; this was the stuff of fairy tales, literally. The sight of it both thrilled and repulsed her. How many people had been so ensnared by the beauty and magic of the marsh lights over the years? Many, then driven mad or led to their deaths.

"I see it, and, believe me, it may appear beautiful, but it is deadly."

"How can something so beautiful be deadly?" Ryan's voice sounded far away. His eyes were cold and unblinking. Siân put her hands over his eyes and held on tight as he attempted to prise them away. His nails dug into her flesh, hurting her.

"Listen to me, Ryan. It's a marsh light. Possibly some ignited marsh gas, or it's a Pwca, a phantom or spirit trying to lead you over the marsh to your death. Either way, if you go following it you will lose your way in a marsh in the dark and you can't get any more stupid than that."

"It'd make for a wonderful photo." He was wistful, abstract.

"I have no doubt that it would, but it would be your last. Take me back to the car, please." The strain was telling as Siân pleaded with him. "Ryan, please…"

Ryan put his fingers in his ears and turned around. "I can't get it out of my head; can you hear it singing, calling to me?"

"No, I can't. All I can hear is us and the sound of the engine. Follow me; we have to get back now." She took his arm and began to lead him back.

Ryan began to take small unsteady steps back towards the car. His head felt as though it were being cracked in two. The beautiful music had become a loud cat-like screeching, a combination of a wild creature and nails on a blackboard. It clawed at his nerves and every sense. Siân held on tight, determined not to let go; his life depended on it. She pushed them both through the barbed hedge to the comforting light of the vehicle. She opened the passenger door and pushed Ryan into the seat. The more he tried to resist, the firmer she became. Siân made her way to the driver's side and drove them back to Maenddu as fast as she dared. Ryan was drifting in and out of consciousness. Siân hardly dared to glance at her passenger, slumped in the seat. She could still see the mysterious light reflected in his half-open opaque green eyes.

Siân pulled the four by four up roughly in front of the pub. Fumbling in Ryan's pockets, she found his room and door key. She tried to drag Ryan out of the vehicle, and half-carried, half-walked him into the pub via the side door. She did not want anyone else to see, or start interfering, as they were wont to do in this village, and she did not want to hear any more of Ffi's bizarre conversation from this morning. This whole evening was weird enough as it was. She got him into the corridor and up the stairs before Ffi appeared on the scene, and called up the stairs. "Ryan, dear, I need a word before you go…"

Siân cursed under her breath. "Speak to him in the morning then."

"Siân, what are you doing up there?" Ffi came running up the stairs; her expression shifted from angry mother to worried mother. "What happened?"

Siân tried to unlock Ryan's room and hold him generally upright at the same time; it was tricky. "Ffi, please, he's just not very well. Help me get him in for the night."

Ffi was not buying any of it; she took the keys from Siân and unlocked the door. She could see for herself that Ryan was far more than simply not very well. His skin was grey and pale; there were dark circles under his glazed eyes. "Whatever is the matter with him?"

Siân laid Ryan down on the bed; he lay there very still. She placed her hand to his cheek; it was cold and damp. She affectionately pulled the duvet up over him and turned the radiator up.

Ffi was not letting it go. "Siân?"

Siân glared at her old friend. Her irritation and frustration came out all at once. "OK, you really want to hear it? I'll tell you exactly what happened; a Pwca, a flaming will-o'-the-wisp. Out on the marsh, calling to him; him and only him, I might add. How do I know? I saw the damned thing with my own eyes. What the hell have you started?"

The more rotund woman stepped back. "I didn't start anything, I promise you, Siân. Someone has been doing something bad out on the moors, casting evil spells. No doubt it was he who asked the Pwca to lead Ryan away tonight."

"You really expect me to believe all this?"

"Yes, because it's true. All of it, all that I said this morning." Ffi stepped forward, trying to angle in to give Siân a hug. Siân pushed her arms away and stormed out of the room. Ffi followed her out.

"No. Leave me alone. Leave us alone." Siân fumbled with the lock, locking Ryan in. "Keep this locked until morning; do not let him out, whatever happens, until dawn comes." She handed the key to Ffi, who opened her mouth to speak. "Please just stop it, I'm not in the mood," said Siân as she stormed off out of the pub.

* * *

The music was even more enchanting than it had been earlier. The notes soared and danced in perfect harmony; soft, sad and sickly sweet. Each note echoed through his entire being, stirring his soul. Ryan's heart ached with sadness and longing as he heard it. In the same silken voice, she called to him, across the miles and across the years. "Owein," she called as she sang. "Owein, or is it Ryan now? Come dance with me." The other words he could not discern, they were sounds of some ancient language, melodious and rounded. "Siân?" he called out to her, but she only laughed. "Ryan."

She danced closer to him, as light as a feather and dancing on air. Her skin, hair and clothes were all white with a hint of pale mint; they were translucent and ghostly. She shimmered as though she were in full moonlight and starlight. She repulsed him as much as she drew him to her. She was beautiful, the most beautiful woman he had ever seen, with her long pale hair and eyes like saucers. Her intense beauty was eerily unnatural; it felt wrong, it looked wrong. She reminded him of Morwyna, no, Siân, she was now, but this was not her. This woman resembled Siân, if all her wonderful imperfections had been ironed out. Deep within he longed for Siân, for all her human imperfections, her slightly droopy eyes, her mismatched soft lips, all those things that made her truly beautiful.

The figure continued to dance, raising her arms high, twirling and turning, teasing and tormenting him. He could see now that her clothes were ragged and torn. She beckoned to him with her slender, white elongated finger. He followed, he had no choice. Yet with each step he took she seemed always to remain the same distance away. He picked up his pace; still she was out of his reach. She laughed her delicate laugh.

"You must come out to the marsh to dance with me; I have to dance out in the open, under the night sky. Dance with me and I will take all your worries away." Ryan felt dizzy, drunk and disorientated. He tried to put one foot in front of the other but found he could not. Something was holding him back, trapping him. He fought it, determined to follow the woman before him, to join her out on the marsh. Still it would not give; he was caged like an animal while the spirit before him was free. He longed for the freedom, for one touch of her perfect lips. The spirit began to move further and further away, fading away into the distance. He screamed after her to wait for him. She beckoned him again, blowing him a kiss. Then she began to laugh and laugh; at first it was musical, then slowly its pitch and volume increased until it became a high-pitched bloodcurdling shriek. Ryan found himself trembling in its wake; he clamped his hands to his ears to protect himself from the cry. As he watched, her beautiful face faded and lines appeared around her dark eyes, which sank back into the sockets. Her once pouting, kissable lips curled and twisted, her teeth no longer pearly white but dark and rotten. Her pale flesh began to peel from the bone, revealing the even whiter skull beneath. Her clothes became more ragged, barely covering her misshapen form. Ryan closed his eyes so hard that his eyelids squashed into his eyeballs, and prayed hard to whatever deity would listen. He could feel her cold, damp rancid breath on his neck and face.

"Ryan, come with me, I can make you happy. I can take you away from all this. I can give you peace."

"No!" The icy, bony fingers around his throat strangled his scream.

Out in the corridor, Bryn howled, his inner wolf finding his voice once more. He raised his head proudly and closed his brown eyes. The howl was long, soulful and fluctuating. He paused for breath and howled once more. The call was echoed by the well-built Alsatian three doors down; his voice was deeper and carried further. A small terrier nearby also joined in, with a funny, awkward little yowl. Within minutes every dog in the village and the locale was in full pelt, lamenting to the night. Windows trembled with the vibrations, and a sense of unease crept over the village.

CHAPTER NINETEEN

The chorus of the night woke Ryan. He was enveloped by complete darkness. He moved slowly and carefully; somehow he had wedged himself up against the door to his room. His muscles and bones ached. The door handle dug into his forehead, right up against his skull. He rubbed it, feeling the indentations of the ridged metal, which would leave a mark for a while yet. He gently moved himself to a more comfortable position, waiting periodically for the pins and needles to ease. Rubbing his eyes, he yawned. He must have slept, yet he did not feel like it; he felt far beyond tired, into pure exhaustion. Come to think of it, he did not remember coming in last night and going to sleep. His eyebrows crossed as he tried to think of what he did remember of the previous night. The dull aching in his head was annoying. He was driving home, then there was something in front of the car, and then a light. Yes, the light was the last thing he remembered. He closed his eyes, in the hope that he had not done or said anything bad or stupid in front of Siân. Damn, he had meant to make last night special, to properly bid her farewell before he went back to Cardiff. No doubt he had messed that up. He coughed, his throat dry and sore, and climbed back into bed.

Ffi awoke with the dawn, what little there was of it. The morning was grey and overcast. She tiptoed barefoot cautiously along to Ryan's room. Bryn was outside it, lying right across the doorway. He raised his head as his mistress approached. Ffi leant down and scratched him behind the ears. "Good lad. Have you been guarding him or guarding us?" She unlocked Ryan's door as silently as possible; it would not do to get a reputation for locking guests in their rooms. Her hand rested on the door handle; she wanted to go in, to make sure everything was fine, yet she also did not want to go in for fear that things were not all right at all. She flexed her fingers nervously and chewed her cheek as she weighed up her options; in the end she went back to bed and hid under the cotton bed covers. She would deal with things at breakfast. Everything was better with a good breakfast and a morning coffee. She rolled over closer to Alun to get warm, and listened to the sounds of the early morning, or rather she found herself listening to an unnerving silence. The birds had been so active in recent days, welcoming in the dawn each day, and singing more or less until nightfall. The song of the blackbird had been especially wonderful to hear this year. Even the chirruping of the little baby birds in the eaves was absent this morning. "Alun?"

"Waaaa?" he responded, not amused at being woken.

"Can you hear that?"

"Hear what?" He put his head under the covers to drown out his wife's voice.

"Exactly." Ffi sat up in bed. "I've never known it as silent as this, not even in the depths of winter."

"Very nice." The automatic husband answering machine was definitely on this morning.

* * *

"I hate Mondays," grumbled Mandy into her hot, steaming mug of tea.

"Don't we all," Siân answered with meaning as she checked the contents of the shelf before her. Monday was always her day for checking all the best-before dates.

"They are sooo depressing. Have you noticed how all our delightful customers can be such gits on Monday mornings?"

Siân agreed wholeheartedly. "They don't want to be up and about any more than we do."

"They don't have to be quite so grumpy about it. Gryff was being a complete shit to you this morning. It's not our fault that he forgot to tell us that he wanted that stupid car magazine. We're not psychic. God, can you imagine that; wouldn't it be fab to be psychic?" She took a slurp of tea, warming her insides against the chilly drizzle outside.

"The poopy weather doesn't help; people are naturally more miserable when it's like this." She tilted her head to watch the rain falling down the windows, like tears. "When the sky cries, we want to cry with it. Besides, I reckon we're all fed up with winter. Last week was so nice, I really thought spring was coming, and now look; it's all yucky and cold again."

"You mean like that seasonal thing?"

"Yeah, winter always makes me feel miserable. I long for the spring to kick winter's butt. Come on, daffodils and tulips! When they turn up, you know the warmer weather is on its way."

"Hey, I forgot to ask you about your date." Mandy's eyes opened wide in disbelief. "Oh my, it must be a crap morning if I'm forgetting the hot gossip."

"What date would that be?" Siân feigned innocence; she was surprised it had taken until now for Mandy to start the questioning.

Mandy shifted on the spot with annoyance. "With Ryan, your lover..."

"Very funny. It was nice," Siân said, non-commitally.

"Oh my God! It was nice?" Mandy laughed so hard she had to make a real effort to keep tea from bubbling out of her nose and mouth. "Nice is not a word to be used. Come on, was it steamy, passionate, and sexy? Spill the beans, I'll find out anyway."

Siân had to admit she probably would. "OK, it was great; I had a really great time. He's perfect, you know, almost too perfect. He's like a list I made years ago for the perfect man. He ticks all the boxes. We spent almost the whole weekend together. But… he's going home today." Siân decided to leave out the small detail that he was supposed to be coming back soon; she could not bear the pity she would get if he did not return. Also, part of her was worried that he may not actually come back at all.

"So, how was he in bed?"

Siân was horrified. Mandy's gossip and usual reading matter was full of colourful events and references, most of which were not only unlikely, but probably downright silly. "You gutter brain. I wouldn't know," she said, smiling sweetly.

"Prude."

* * *

Bryn barked as Ryan came into the conservatory. "Hey there boy." Bryn had wagged his tail warmly once Ryan started fussing him. The conversation was sparse at breakfast, the bare minimum required for politeness. Alun had not been too chuffed with his wake-up call, and Ryan was having trouble not falling face-first into his cooked breakfast. Ffi kept looking at him funnily; every time he caught her eye, she glanced away, then he glanced away and she was staring again. Ryan was worried. Had he done something bad last night? Had he upset anyone? It was not like him to do that kind of thing, so why did he have this sinking feeling in his stomach about something this morning? He knew he should ask, but felt he did not know these people well enough.

The silence was going on too long; Ryan felt he had to say something, anything to get things going again. "I'm really going to miss these hot breakfasts."

"Ah, but your arteries will be grateful," Alun smiled weakly.

Ffi was burning to find out more of what had happened the previous night. Siân had said so little, but what she had said had confirmed Ffi's own theories. She was worried that Ryan would leave and never return; she had noticed the tenderness between Siân and Ryan. Poor Siân should not have to cope with all this on her own, and Ffi feared that she would not bear the heartbreak very well. "So, did you have a good evening last night?"

Ryan dropped his knife; it crashed on to his plate. The noise was deafening. "Er." Ryan had no idea what to say. "Siân took me out to a few places."

"You didn't look very well when you got back." Ffi was pushing for answers.

Ryan picked up his knife again and cut up a sausage. He kept his eyes lowered. What was she trying to get at? Ryan desperately thought back; all he remembered was feeling a bit groggy, and having the father of all headaches. "Bit of a headache, I think." Something flashed neon in Ryan's hazy memory. "I hit my head on the steering wheel."

"Siân said you saw something out on the marsh." Ffi's tone was level.

"Maybe. I think something leapt out in front of the car; a big stag, must be plenty of them around here." Ryan was squirming in his seat by now, and Alun was puzzling over what was going on in front of him.

"What colour was it, this stag?" The conversation was being replaced by interrogation.

"Dark, black I think. Why?"

Ffi raised her eyebrows at Alun. "Don't get many black stags around here. Get black dogs sometimes. Big black dogs out on the moors. Could it have been a dog?"

Ryan shrugged; he was eating the remainder of his breakfast as fast as he could now so he could gracefully get away. "I don't really remember."

"Did you see anything else; lights maybe?"

Alun decided to put an end to this. "Ffi, go and make some more toast, now please."

Ffi grumbled as she bustled off into the kitchen.

"I'm sorry about her; I don't know what's with her lately," Alun apologised. "I don't think she wants you to go. Women, eh?"

Ryan nodded; he did not know what else to do. He and Alun fell back into silence. He finished off the last of his meal and packed the last of his belongings into the four by four. As he was packing the last bag, his overnight backpack, Ffi came running out to him. "Before you go, here; this is for you." She passed him a jute bag. Peeking inside, Ryan saw the painting of the stag he had seen a few days before. "I can't take this; this is yours."

"No, dear, it's yours." Ffi placed her hand on his arm. "It always was and always will be. Now, you make sure you come back to us; you're needed here, Ryan. You come back to us safe and sound."

Ryan did not wish to seem discourteous. "Thanks very much, Ffi." He placed the picture on the back seat, so it would not run the risk of being squashed by his luggage. By the time he turned around, Ffi was gone.

Running his hand through his short hair, it was now or never to say goodbye to Siân. He wanted this not to be 'goodbye' but a 'see you later'. Leisurely, he strolled up to the village shop and pushed open the door.

Mandy got all excited when she saw who the visitor was. "Oh my, it's lover boy." Both Ryan and Siân blushed hotly.

"Let's nip outside for a minute. Please." Siân bustled him out of the door again. "Sorry, her hearing is amazing. What's the matter with your head?" She ran her fingers over the mark on his forehead. He tingled at her touch.

"I think I must have hit my head on the steering wheel last night. That and I woke up with a door handle there this morning. Look, did I do anything wrong last night?"

Siân leapt up and hugged him warmly. "No, what on earth makes you think that?" she said into his warm, comforting chest.

"I don't remember very much about last night and I was worried that I'd done or said…"

"You were fine, it was just an accident."

He let his hands fall to her waist. "I had the weirdest dreams though last night."

She kissed his forehead. "Probably just that knock on your noggin."

Ryan returned the kiss. "I remember the weirdest light, like a burning butterfly."

So he did remember after all. Should she say anything, and risk scaring him off for good, or keep quiet, hoping that the Pwca would leave him alone now that he had not gone to her? Would she try again? Was that what he had dreamt? "Marsh lights," she said, trying to be dismissive.

"I'll be back as soon as I can. I'd like to try and come back tomorrow if I can."

"That soon?" The words popped out of Siân's mouth before her brain shut her up. That had not come out very well at all. "Sorry, what I mean is, that would be great, if you can, that is." They squeezed each other tight in a big bear hug. Ryan leant down and kissed her full on the lips. The perfect, even lips of the Pwca echoed in his vision; he put the thought away. The imperfect version was what he wanted; he wanted Siân and only Siân. They melted into each other in a combination of drizzle and bodily warmth. Mandy knocked on the door, her face pressed up so close to it that her nose was distorted. "Go on, girl!"

"Ignore her." She pulled him down for another kiss. His breath tasted of toothpaste while his lips were sweet, laced still with a delicate taste of something tangy and orangey. He must have had some marmalade on toast, realised Siân.

Ryan gave in, but the audience was putting him off. "I have to go. The quicker I go, the quicker I get back."

"I like that idea. Drive safe." She waved to him as he headed off. She could still taste him on her lips and as the distance between them increased the tang of him faded; her heart reached out towards him and sank ever further into despondency.

Badden watched his rival leave, his grey clothes camouflaging him against the grey stone of the chapel. No one ever paid any attention to this body anyway; it was too insipid, too insignificant. He could walk down the street as bold as brass and no one would give him a second glance. He rubbed his cold fingers together in glee. They seemed unable to retain any heat after he had pressed them to the ancient stones. This body was always so cold to inhabit; beggars cannot be choosers, he thought. He had to make the most of what had come to him, pathetically begging him for his powers and magic. The Pwca had done her job well, though not as well as she was meant to; his rival was still alive. She would be dealt with accordingly, if he could manage to work his magic against her, once Morwyna was his. He had a feeling, though, that the Pwca would not be subject to even his darkest, most ancient spells; she was older still and more powerful than he was. Ryan had resisted the Pwca's call; that was no mean feat, but at least she had scared him off. He watched Siân turn and go back into the shop. "You're mine now, Morwyna."

He watched as Ryan drove away, chugging off down the road, running back to the city, no doubt. Well, he was well out of it, good riddance. At last, things were going right. Badden began to laugh, a cold hollow laugh. He stuffed his fist into his mouth to silence himself.

CHAPTER TWENTY

Ffi was painting in her art zone, a poky corner room with a disproportionately large window that took up almost a whole wall. The tiny room was crammed full of paints, brushes, silk and canvasses. The walls were splattered with excess paint in so many colours. This was to be a feature piece for the gallery's inner core, and was much larger than her usual paintings. Ffi was revelling in the challenge, but exasperated by the pressure. This image could make or break, not only the exhibition, but her own future in the art world. This was the first time she would be shown in a professional gallery, and the initial excitement had worn into worry and panic.

New Age music was blaring out; today's choice was an unusual combination of drum styles from around the world. The beat lulled her into a deep trance. Her painting was wild, fluid, impulsive and energetic. In large, sweeping strokes the brush formed an image. She channelled her intuition and the power of the Awen, the flowing spirit and energy of inspiration. She was so absorbed in the process that she paid no attention to what was manifesting at the end of her brush; for now there was no need. Then, from within the sounds of the drumbeat, another sound, another thumping began, more rapid and more focused. The banging on the old wooden door went on and on, reverberating along the narrow corridor. It brought Ffi back down to earth with an unpleasant jolt. Her enthusiasm and inspiration faded in one brief moment. Ffi wiped her brush on the cloth and rested it across the paint pot, swearing to herself. Then she wiped her paint-ridden hands on the cloth.

Making her way down the stairs, she wiped the back of her hand across her cheek and jawline to stifle an itch. A damp sensation followed the wake of her hand; she had just painted herself. The knocking continued frantically. "I'm coming!" she shouted down the corridor. "Hang on!" She peered through the frosted glass in the door. "Who's there?"

Agitated fingers scratched on the pane of glass. "Ffi, let me in. It's Rosie."

Ffi fumbled with the door and wiped black paint on the handle as she opened it. A blast of cold wet weather hit her full on. Standing before her was Rosie, her shoulder-length red curly hair darkened and plastered to her head by the rain, wearing only a cardigan against the elements. Her face was red from crying and an angry red welt was swelling up across her cheek and eye. Her two little girls were also standing there; they at least had proper coats on. The girls were miniature versions of their mother, with their dark eyes and auburn hair, and they too had been crying.

"Come out of that weather. Whatever's happened?" The three stepped forward into the warm, Rosie casting a glance behind her.

"Let's get you some hot drinks," Ffi knelt down to the girls. "Would you like some cocoa?" Ffi herded them into the kitchen, where she popped the kettle on. Then she led them through to the conservatory, where she turned up the heating. "Make yourselves comfortable. Take those wet coats off, you can put them on here to dry." The two girls took off their little coats and shoved them on the warming radiator as they were told. They ran over to the dining table and popped themselves up on to the chairs, their little legs swinging in mid air, still sniffing from the cold and the tears. Rosie stayed close to Ffi.

"Who hit you, Rosie, dear?" she whispered.

"Who do you think?" Rosie whispered back. "It's so not like him, though, he's always been such a softie."

"Did the girls see it?"

"No, thank the Goddess. They were upstairs."

"Tell me what happened." Ffi led her friend into the kitchen and made ready mugs for two teas and two cocoas as the kettle bubbled into life.

"I was getting breakfast ready, pouring out the girls' cereal. We were all running a bit late, you know what it gets like. Anyway, I spilt some of the milk and Neil just went for me. He went crazy; I've never seen him like it before. He made no sense, yelling and screaming. I was so frightened. As I went to mop it up, he pulled me across the table with one hand and punched me right in the face with the other. I grabbed the girls and came straight over; I didn't know what else to do. I mean, I know he's been worried about work lately; do you remember I said that they were making layoffs at the last Grove meeting? I didn't think it was going to affect his department yet though. You should have seen him; it was like it wasn't really him."

Ffi raised an eyebrow. "You're making excuses for him? Rosie, he crossed the line."

"I know; he didn't mean it. He's not a violent man. He's never even smacked the girls before to discipline them, let alone anything else." She absent-mindedly alternately pulled and coiled her corkscrew hair with her fingers as she spoke.

Ffi put her hand to her friend's face, and tilted her jaw. "He got you good, dear, your eye is starting to swell. You'll have to go to Doc MacKenzie. Whether or not you take this to the police, though, is your business."

"I know," Rosie moaned as the kettle boiled. "I don't know what to do; he was so apologetic after, fawning all over me. He genuinely seemed to feel so guilty about what he'd done. But it doesn't change the fact that he hit me."

Ffi made the drinks, the steam rising high from the mugs. "There's some colouring stuff in that drawer; your girls must be getting a bit bored by now." Rosie opened the drawer; it was overflowing with crayons, coloured pencils and blocks of paper. Pulling some of the items out, she took them through to her girls, who by now were teasingly kicking each other under the table and giggling. "Why don't you draw something for Mummy?"

"I dunno what to draw," wailed the bigger of the two girls, while the other immediately picked up a coloured pencil and began to draw on some coloured paper, her pink tongue firmly stuck out of the corner of her mouth with concentration.

"I don't know either, sweetie." Rosie examined the room, which had yet more of Ffi's animal pictures. "Why don't you draw an animal, like one of these?"

"OK, Mum." The girl picked up a pencil and began to tap it against the one front tooth that she still had as she thought about which animal to draw.

Ffi had brought through the four mugs on an old-fashioned tea tray. She laid them out on the table. "I popped some cold water in the girls' drinks so they can't scald themselves."

Rosie smiled, a dry sad smile that only twisted her lips up a small fraction of the way; it never reached her eyes. "I'm so sorry to put you out like this, I didn't know who else to go to."

"You're welcome to stay; you know you are, my dears. However, at the moment, maybe getting away from Maenddu for a bit might be a good idea."

Rosie set her jaw firmly and looked over her daughters' shoulders to their drawings. Ffi, for fear of making a mess out of all this again as she had done the previous day with Ryan and Siân, went on carefully, "You are welcome to stay here, of course you are. There are just some decidedly odd things going on around here at the moment. As I said on the phone yesterday, someone has been up at the Maidens, messing about, only whatever they've done is having a major effect on things. Perhaps it's best to get away for a few days, put a bit of distance between you and Neil," she said quietly, so as not to upset the girls.

"The dogs this morning? That was weird."

"Oh, more than that. Believe me. Jim claims he saw the Gwyllgi the other night, up by the boundaries of Fferm Hafan. Then, last night, one of our guests encountered a Pwca."

Rosie almost dropped her mug as her mouth dropped open; she gaped at Ffi. "Did he follow it?"

"No. His heart is already spoken for; he was fine."

"Could that be what set Neil off?" Her heart hoped it was.

"It could well be. D'ya know, Jim and John got into a nasty fight yesterday. Really swung for each other, right in the middle of our bar. We all know they grumble constantly at each other, but I've never known them to lay a finger on each other in all the time I've known them. It could be this negativity is getting to people, but whether it's making people do things they would not otherwise have done I don't know." She picked up her mug of tea and took a long gulp. "This horrible energy is getting under everyone's skin."

The redhead idly played with her curls with one hand, sipping from her mug in the other. "Oh, Ffi, what can we do?"

"Nothing that I know of. Not now, anyway. I tried to undo the magic, but that didn't work; I spoke to Rob and begged for some help with this, but he was rather rude as usual. I fear it's my fault that things have got so much worse."

Rosie exhaled sharply. "How on earth can you have made the situation worse? What did you do?"

"I tried to spread some love and light. I cleansed the place with light, air, water and earth. For a whole minute, I thought it had worked as well. Then the damned thing negated it, whoosh, like I'd not done a thing. Maybe I shouldn't have meddled. You know, Alun thinks this is some local thing that has to be resolved by those involved in it, like a story that has to be played through. I'm not sure the people involved know that they are, though."

A soft, rustling noise disturbed them, as the youngest girl began to colour in her picture with sweeping sideways strokes of her pencil. "Who's involved?" Rosie whispered.

"I'm not sure I should say, in case words can fuel this. You know how our ancestors viewed the power of words." She flexed her fingers nervously.

Rosie looked over at her daughter, rubbing her pencil wildly across the paper. "What are you drawing, sweetie?"

"A doggie, the doggie I dreamed of last night." Her little voice was high pitched and unclear as children's voices often are to the uninitiated.

"Neil's been promising to get them a puppy for ages," Rosie said. "And, of course, both of you do like to keep reminding him, don't you?" The two girls nodded, their auburn hair bobbing. "I want a big doggie like this one." The girl held up her picture proudly for the two women to see. The dog was roughly drawn, but there was talent there under the rough edges and childish form. He was as big as the tree drawn next to him and jet-black in colour, with one red eye that had been drawn with flames, or rather streaks of red and yellow erupting out of it.

The two women gasped, while the other girl carried on regardless. "I want a little dog, I want to be able to cuddle him. He's too big to cuddle."

"Uh huh," said their mother, her eyes on her youngest daughter. "Was it a bad dream, Melanie?"

"It was OK." She shrugged.

"Are you sure, sweetie?" Her mother stroked her hair.

"Yes, he was a really big doggie. He came into our house when we were all asleep. He was nosing around, he was after somebody. He came into my room and he was being so noisy that he woke me up. I thought it was like Christmas. Daddy said he would get us a doggie for Christmas, but he didn't."

Ffi fussed over them in full motherly mode. "Where's Neil now?"

The other woman shrugged. "At work, I guess. We just left him there."

"Give me your keys; stay here while I go and pack you some things."

Rosie pulled her bundle of keys from her dark blue jeans and passed them across. "I'll come."

"No, stay here with the girls. I'll go and see if he's there still before you come. Don't answer the door or the phone. I'll let myself back in, then we can go together if it's safe. Is there anyone else you can stay with, someone not around here?"

"My sister's in Caldicott," she said uncertainly.

"Good, call her now and arrange to stay a few days. Call the doc as well, and get an appointment to get that eye checked over, this morning; don't let that stupid assistant of his put you off. I'll drive you down to the station when we're done." Ffi knelt down by the girls. "You'd like to go and see your auntie, wouldn't you?"

The elder girl held up her picture for the adults to admire. They smiled and made all the right noises as adults do. Her drawing was of a much smaller, spaniel-type dog. Though a neater picture, it lacked the power and talent of her sister's work. "Yes, I like Auntie Tizzie. She has a really big tree house in her garden."

"Well, there you go then!"

CHAPTER TWENTY-ONE

A distant tinny thudding accompanied the chime of the shop door opening. Only one person in the village made that noise. "Oh poop, I'm going out the back," hissed Siân, sneaking into the back room.

"Huh?" Mandy looked from her fleeing friend to Huw. "Ah. P'nawn da, Huw. What can I get for you today?"

Huw pulled one earphone out to hear and grabbed a plastic basket from near the door. He then pulled out a tattered shopping list. "Mam wants some baking powder, where would that be?"

"Come on, I'll show you." Mandy led him to the back of the shop, to the cake section, and showed him the little tubs.

"Cheers. Um, is Siân in?" His eyes were questioning, shining with the dark lustre of black diamonds.

Mandy's seventh sense, her gossip detector, was clanging like an alarm. What had been going on here then, between Siân and Huw? Was she seeing two men at the same time? Mandy had to know. Mandy had to collect gossip, as the bee has to collect pollen. "She's busy doing something at the moment. I'll see if I can get her." She turned and yelled, "Siân!" There was no response; Mandy headed back to the counter area. Huw kept his head down; he picked up a pot of baking powder and put it in his basket. He checked his list and worked his way around the shop.

Mandy peered into the dark stockroom. "Somebody wants to speak to you," she cooed.

"I don't want to speak to him."

"Oh, go on, he's harmless enough. You've not been leading two men on, have you?"

"He's not harmless; he went for me the other night. Tried to scare me off Ryan. Right outside my house. Scared the poop out of me, if you must know." Siân remained in the shadows of the stockroom.

Mandy spoke through a fake smile, barely moving her lips. "Oh my God, really? You'd never think it of him. He always seems so drippy. Are you sure it wasn't just lustful jealousy?" The sarcasm was thick.

"Ha ha, was that the title of your latest piece of reading?" Siân responded, with an equal dose of sarcasm.

"Touché, he's coming to pay for stuff in a minute. You're going to have to deal with him sooner or later; that's the curse of living in a small village. If I have to drag you out of there by your hair, you know I will."

Siân was not happy; she had no intention of speaking to Huw after his brutish behaviour. He had done wrong and both upset and angered her. Inside, her heart raced and her breathing shallowed as she thought back to that other night, to the fear when he had tried to grab her. She knew that Mandy would bully her into it. What a mystifying friendship they had, she and Mandy. She both liked and disliked her, often at the same time. Siân answered with one swear word. "Sguthan."

Mandy said simply, "Language!"

"Welsh or English? I can swear just as effectively in each, you know."

Mandy reached around the sturdy grey doorframe of the stockroom. She was not meant to leave the shop floor while there was anyone in, and she was going to be good. Her fingers connected with the material of Siân's sleeve. She pulled hard and fast.

"All right, I get the hint." As she appeared in the doorway, Siân's face was set, expressionless and emotionless. She wanted to be cold to Huw, to make it clear that she was not interested and never had been, then when he was gone she planned to have some serious words with Mandy about her always encouraging and harping on about Huw.

Huw approached deferentially, his face cast down, his actions slow and shy. He placed the basket on the counter and Mandy pushed Siân physically forward to attend to it while she started some conversation. "So, how's your Mam these days, Huw? I've not seen her for a while."

"She's OK."

"I know what I meant to say to you. Mr Collins is after someone to walk Bessie for him, since he's been having a bit of bother getting around. He can manage little walks, but he's after someone to take her out for a proper long walk, two or three times a week. He's happy to pay you a bit, minimum wage rate. Pop up and see him if you're interested, he could do with the company."

"Oh, yeah."

The till beeped in the background as Siân ran the goods through, the electronic, artificial sound grating on her already delicate nerves. Huw turned to her, shuffling. "I'm so sorry about what happened the other night." Mandy watched with baited breath as she packed the goods into paper bags.

"Yes, you should be," Siân said icily.

Huw fiddled with the loose, hanging earphone. "It's only cos I care about you. You deserve better than that bloke."

Rage boiled inside Siân; it stemmed from her anger at Huw's interference. How could he know what was best for her, it was none of his business! It also stemmed from her deepening love for Ryan. She raged at the thought that one idiot could try and destroy her feelings for him. The rage was boiling over, her face was heating up, and she could feel something rising in her throat. She calmed it with great effort. She would not be rude to a customer at work. Outside work; well, she would have to wait and see, but not in here and not now.

"I thank you for your concerns; however, you have no right to interfere in my life, Huw."

"I know." He shook his head sadly; in trying to protect someone he considered a friend, he had ruined their friendship. He had known her so long; twenty odd years now, and he had loved her since he could remember, even at school. He had dreamed of marrying her since he was about seven. Everyone had commented how well they would go together, yet she had only seen him as a friend and not a particularly close one. He did not know how he had borne her three years away at university. He had missed her so much that he had not been able to function. For three years he had no one to talk to, no one to share things with, no one to understand him. He spoke desperately, "I'm so very sorry; I was wrong to say what I said, how I said it, but I do worry for you. I don't want to see you get hurt." He placed his mother's debit card in the slot and pressed the four keys for her pin number.

"That's very gallant." Her tone was softening. "I need to make my own mistakes, get it? And I'm sorry, but I don't fancy you. You're a good friend, Huw, so don't cock that up, OK?"

He smiled. Hope was his again. Maybe he had not completely screwed their friendship up then. Maybe there was still hope for him yet. Hope that one day she would see him for all his love, and fall head over heels in love with him. He prayed for that constantly. Huw took the bags from Mandy and walked away a happy man.

Siân turned to Mandy. She told her all the details of the encounter between her and Huw that night, how he had attacked her and cursed at her. The rage rose again, screaming to be let free. Her blood felt as though it were boiling, her brain running red. Siân fought to keep it in check but some slipped out in a turbulent, tactless torrent. "How could you do that to him and to me, Mandy? I'm supposed to be your friend. Friends don't manipulate and hurt each other and then bitch about it! You should not have led him on. You know I've never fancied the poor sod, so why did you do it? Do you revel in his misery? Or mine? He's wasted time hanging on for me when he would have been so much better to look for love somewhere else. You can't begrudge him some happiness, can you? The poor guy has it tough with that mother of his."

Mandy appeared to be duly ashamed of herself; it was a first. Siân thought she was going to cry; well, so what? She had caused so much upset she deserved to feel some of it herself. Her endless interfering, her social and romantic engineering, it was playing with people's lives and emotions for her own entertainment. It was about time she realised that people got hurt in her silly games.

She whispered in her own defence, "I thought you'd be good together, you're both so lonely. I was only trying to help."

"No! You weren't, you just wanted to fit things into your neat little boxes. Pairing up for the sake of it. Is it some weird compulsion with you?"

Her head hung in shame, Mandy checked her watch. Where was Lloyd? He should have been here ages ago. She would have to leave now to collect Alice or ring Pete to go and get her and bring her to the shop. She wanted to go anyway, to get away from Siân's yelling, to go herself to collect her daughter. Lloyd would go mad if she left Siân alone, health and safety or something.

"I'm sorry, Siân, but I'm going to have to ring Lloyd." She reached for the old grubby phone on the counter.

"Whatever," Siân replied, going back to checking dates. "You weren't even listening."

Mandy tapped the receiver with her fingernail as it rung on and on. Lloyd was not answering, perhaps he had already left, but it was not soon enough, he was not here to relieve her in time. She replaced the handset and then picked it up again; she would have to ring Pete now. She dialled the number carefully. It rung three times before a happy, sickly sweet voice answered. "Newport Accounting services."

Mandy cleared her throat. "Hi, Pete please, it's urgent."

"Thank you."

"Pete speaking." Pete said gruffly.

"Hi love, can you pick up Alice please? Lloyd's not turned up and I daren't leave." She could hear his annoyance in his breathing.

"Can't you do it? I'm at work. I've a meeting at four with a client."

She pleaded with her husband. "No, Lloyd will sack me if I leave Siân alone. I'm sorry, please go. Bring her here to the shop, then you can go back to work."

Pete exploded with consternation. "For Christ's sake, Mandy! What part of 'I am at work' do you not understand? I can't piss about all day like you do."

Tears welled up in her eyes and caused her throat to constrict. "Please, Pete, I don't often ask this of you."

"Fine, but don't moan at me if I end up being one of the people who gets made redundant." He slammed the phone down; the first time it thudded down the line, the second time it cut her off. The tears fell on to the phone.

CHAPTER TWENTY-TWO

A throaty, silver diesel car pulled up outside the shop, its brakes and tyres squealing. A car door opened and then closed in quick succession and the car zoomed off, leaving a cloud of fumes in its wake. Alice came into the shop, her red uniform sweatshirt creased and crumpled from the day at school. "Hi, Siân."

"Wotcha, Alice, how was school?"

The girl plonked herself on a chair behind the counter and began pulling her exercise books out of her little red bag with the school logo on. "Boooooring, as always. Where's Mum?"

"Hiding in the loo. What homework have you got?"

"I've got to write a bit on Florence Nightingale and then I've got some maths to do. I might need some help with that." Alice, her mother in miniature, pulled out a pencil and started to write on squared paper.

"Let me know when you do."

"Who's your friend?" the girl asked.

They heard the bathroom door open into the stockroom and then the stockroom door open. Mandy's face was blotchy and damp. "Hello, Alice, how was school?"

Her daughter did not even glance up. "We've done that, Mum."

"Oh, all right. What are you doing?"

The pencil was being twirled between Alice's fingers. "Maths. Mum, I need to concentrate."

Mandy's eyes glistened with moisture and her mascara was smudged. "I'll be out the back for a minute if you need me."

With her neat, elfin features and sparkly eyes, Alice eyed Siân. "Is Mum all right?"

Siân leaned on the counter, her face resting in her hand. "She'll be OK in a minute."

"Dad was really cross when he came to get me, he was being well rude about Mum."

"I think everyone is having a bad day."

Alice nodded; that seemed as good a reason as any. "Does your friend ever speak?"

Siân's eyebrows lifted; other than her and Alice, the shop floor was empty. "What friend?"

"Her." Alice used her pencil to point directly behind Siân's right shoulder. "That lady."

Siân turned her head to see, and saw no one there. First Ffi creeping her out and now Alice. "There's no one there."

Alice was curious. "Yes, there is, can't you see her then? Is she your sister? She looks like you."

An odd sensation crept over Siân; this was weird. "I'm an only child; I don't have any brothers or sisters."

"Me neither. I can see her, I'm telling the truth." Alice's voice was growing higher and higher in pitch.

Siân leant forward and held the girl's hand. "I'm not saying you're not, only that I can't see her." Her words echoed Ryan's words yesterday, to Ffi. Why was she not seeing what others could see as clear as day? "Can you tell me all about her?"

"She's so much like you. She has long dark hair with an old-fashioned pin thing in it; she has your face and the same funny nose. Only she looks much sadder. Her clothes are torn and dirty. She's got a checked shawl and a bluish tunic; she looks like the Iron Age women at that museum you took me to last summer."

"Can you speak to her?"

"Hello! Can you hear me?" Alice waved her hand in greeting and waited for a moment. "I don't think she can hear me."

Siân shivered uncontrollably. It spread through her limbs like a quake, and she knew now that she would have to speak to Ffi again, properly this time, and listen to what she had to say. "Thanks anyway. So, what's the maths you're having trouble with then?"

"It's this." Alice turned the book around and talked Siân through what her homework was.

Finally, not long before closing, Lloyd arrived. He sauntered into the shop and straight out the back without the courtesy of greeting anyone; he rarely did. Siân and Alice watched him go, though neither dared to look directly at him. His woolly dark hair seemed ever more grey; his age was catching up with him of late. His temples were now far more silver than dark, and he was starting to get an elegantly distinguished air. He had the kind of face that would grow well into grey hair, if only he could lose the permanent expression of disgust that graced his rounded features. The grey had also spread to his skin; usually a delicate tan, it now looked pallid and lifeless. Deep lines were forming around his sunken eyes and his mouth. Siân was struck by the irony; they seemed like laughter lines yet she had never, in two years, seen or heard Lloyd laugh. The creased grey fleeced top and faded black trousers served only to extend the aura of greyness that he radiated. Siân and Alice each pulled a face as he turned his back to them; they then had to stifle the girlish giggles that threatened to erupt as they each saw the other's face.

Within moments Lloyd returned, holding and dragging Mandy by the arm. Her arm and his knuckles were white with the pressure. "What is *that* doing here?" Lloyd pointed dagger-like at Alice.

"*That* has a name, thank you. What did you expect? You were late again, I had to get Pete to go and get Alice." She was indignant, and rightly so, in Siân's opinion.

"She should not be here; what would health and safety say if they came in now? What would the customers think?"

Tears beaded on Mandy's long, dark lashes. "The customers don't mind at all. I couldn't leave her home on her own, could I?"

Lloyd's eyes were cold steel, his pupils and his nostrils dilated as his voice rose in volume. "She should not be here, Mandy. It's unprofessional, and it's not safe."

"You should have got here on time. You didn't even bother to ring and tell me you were going to be late. You're always going on about not having this place single-staffed, but you're never bloody well here to help out, are you?" Her lip quivered with a combination of anger and upset. This was the last straw; it was a crappy day and Lloyd was wrong to berate her like this in front of her own daughter, when he was in the wrong. She turned to try and walk away, but Lloyd tightened his grip. She yelped in pain and watched as her daughter began to cry. "Take your hands off me, or I'll do you for assault," she challenged.

"Let go of her," Siân warned.

Lloyd kept his eyes on Mandy; cool, calculating, and with no regard for anyone except himself. His face blanched and his ears went crimson, the veins filled with purple blood. He loosened his grip reluctantly. "If that's what you want. Mandy, you're fired. You never do any work anyway; all you ever do is sit and gossip. Now, get out and take your brat with you!"

Mandy smiled at her daughter, a cold smile. "Wait in the car for me; I'll be there in just a sec, yeah?"

She passed her the car keys. Alice took them and bundled her belongings into her school bag and glanced at her mother, then at Siân, who nodded. She went outside and climbed into her mother's car. Slowly, Mandy turned around to face Lloyd. She cast him a glare a basilisk would be proud of. He was smiling; he was amused. Mandy shook with anger and frustration, and what little courage she had was failing. She spoke through gritted teeth. "How dare you speak to me like that in front of my daughter? How dare you bully me? You're the one who should be fired, you lazy bastard. You hardly ever bother to come to work, you treat us like dirt and, you know what, I won't have it anymore. I quit anyway. I won't work for a piece of shit like you anymore."

She grabbed her coat, tearing it when it caught upon the hook; she wanted to go in a blaze of glory, and if it cost her a coat, so be it. Inside she was seething. Jobs were hard to come by, especially jobs that had child-friendly hours, and she and Pete did need the wages, pitiful though they were. The relief and guilty pleasure of leaving that dump thrilled her; no more dirty working conditions, no more working for an idiot like Lloyd, no more being bullied. She was an adult for goodness' sake. She stormed out of the shop and slammed the door behind her; the glass panel trembled in her wake.

Siân watched the scene in utter disbelief. She started on Lloyd, "How could you? We have enough trouble staffing this place with only three of us; why did you go and do that?"

"What use was she anyway? You do all the work, don't think I don't know that." He winked at her and it made her want to vomit; Lloyd was odious and obnoxious at the best of times.

"How would you know? You're never bloody well here and when you are you're just twatting about out the back. I'm not working in here all on my own, Lloyd."

Lloyd watched her closely. "You won't be working on your own anymore; I'll be taking over Mandy's hours. It'll be you and me from now on."

"You're never here," she pointed down to the floor, stabbing the air several times. "You're never on the shop floor. I doubt any of our customers even know that you work here, for they've never seen you actually in here, doing any work."

"Then it's time for a change."

"How exactly are you suggesting we cover sickness or holiday, with only two of us?"

Lloyd snarled, "Cancel your holiday leave and we won't be able to be sick."

Siân was shaking. "No. Call Mandy and apologise. We need her."

He enjoyed watching Siân beg. "No, we don't! This is my shop, Siân. Don't fear, I won't sack you, you work very hard." He stroked the stubble on his chin. "Perhaps you need a pay rise, say a pound an hour?"

Siân dismissed his pathetic blackmail with a wave of her hand. Tears were forming in her own eyes. "Bring Mandy back."

"Do you want me to reconsider your job as well?" Lloyd threatened, his voice low and even. Siân was shocked; she needed this job, she needed the money; it was, other than the tours, her only source of income. She realised it was seriously time to start searching for another job. The shop was beginning to spin, strange shapes and lights were forming before her eyes, and she fought a sense of nausea that rose from her stomach, and her head was beginning to ache. She leant heavily on one of the shelves for support. Lloyd was satisfied with her lack of response. "Time to lock up in a minute." He strolled into the back room, leaving her alone on the shop floor yet again.

CHAPTER TWENTY-THREE

Ryan's flat seemed poky, unwelcoming and empty. He longed to be back in Maenddu with Siân. The journey home had been depressingly lonely; once or twice he had caught himself trying to talk to Siân, thinking she was beside him. Each time he had been disappointed to find she was not. They belonged together, she felt like a part of him, a part he needed, a part that he missed wholeheartedly. Ryan tripped over the mail as he opened the door. His nose wrinkled from the dank smell from the lack of airing over the last few weeks.

The darkness of the flat had always worked to his favour, it meant only a curtain was needed and this place was the perfect photographer's dark room, but now it seemed too depressing and dingy. He downloaded his hundreds of pictures on to his main computer and selected two dozen to print up for the professor. He would, as always, take the laptop, in the hope that Trevivian would want to see them that way, but he never did, always preferring the pictures on paper to make them real and tangible.

The pictures of the Ring of Maidens from the first day, the day of the shadow, appeared before his eyes. Ryan plugged in the projector and projected the images on to the expanse of empty wall above his bed. He zoomed in on the areas where the shadows had been, and lay back on the bed to study them closely while the others printed. The Ring of Maidens rolled on before him, empty and devoid of anything out of the ordinary; no peculiar figures or shadows lurking. Was there anything there, he wondered; had Ffi been speaking the truth; had he really seen what he thought he had that day on the moor, or were the shadows simply the product of an overtired, overwrought imagination? The clock in the kitchenette beeped the hour, informing Ryan that it was time to go. He had spent so long staring at the wall that he had forgotten the time, forgotten to shower, or even change his clothes. He grabbed the pictures, laptop and his coat, and was pleased to get out the door.

* * *

Ffi was exhausted by the time she got back home. She had seen Rosie and the girls settled on the train to their aunt's, and well away from here. She longed to go with them, to go anywhere away from here, away from all the sinister strangeness. It was not in her nature to run away from anything, but this; this was different.

Driving back towards the village, the atmosphere had become increasingly depressing; her skin was still crawling with the sense of trepidation that hung in the air and seemed to radiate from every blade of grass, every branch and every stone. On the journey home, she had noticed how the many sheep of the moors were hiding in corners, all clustered together, staring into nothingness. The wild horses seemed restless, moving about, running without any sense of purpose. The atmosphere was not only spreading; it was intensifying, pushing things, whatever they were, towards a head. It felt like a cone of power being raised, as she had felt many times within group ritual work with MoonRaven's coven. Only this cone was eating up the power of the land and of the people and animals living on that land in a most unhealthy way, like a vampire sucking out the very lifeblood.

Alun was right, she realised. Things had to be settled, they had to run their natural course through to the end. Powerful magic was in motion and it was unstoppable. The key was to make sure that the end result was a beneficial one, a positive one; not the negative one that everything seemed geared towards.

She racked her brains, desperately trying to think of ways to help young Siân and Ryan. Who was it? Who was the boar? He had set this all going. Today she could have believed it was Neil, but no; until today he had been a devoted and good husband to Rosie and a good father to the girls. Who was obsessed with Siân? Who had it in for her? Huw? No, he was a bit odd, but was he capable of all this? This was damned powerful magic. Yes, he had followed Siân and Lowri, especially Siân, around since anyone could recall, following her around like a little dog, even at school. Everyone knew he fancied her, except Siân, it seemed. She was oblivious to him, she considered him a friend – a killer for romance if ever there was one. Until now, Huw had always seemed patient; perhaps he was waiting for Siân to see him as something more than her friend.

Sometimes that approach worked, she thought wryly. Alun had certainly waited long enough for her to figure out that he was head over heels in love with her. Though not happy with the situation as it was, for he clearly longed for her to return his love, he had done nothing untoward, nor anything very much to declare and make her aware of his feelings.

Ffi trudged up the stairs, her feet feeling like blocks of lead. She caught her reflection in a mirror; she still had a stripe of black paint accenting her jawline. Normally she would have been annoyed at herself for going out in public like that, but she was so tired she was past caring. Pushing open the door of the art zone where the large canvas still stood, unfinished and unseen, Ffi waited with baited breath to see her latest creation. Would it be any good? Would it be the perfect centre piece?

Something on the floor caught her attention. She must have stepped in a dollop of paint on her way out earlier. She had trampled it for several paces and would have to get the carpet shampoo out to clean it up. If she squinted, it almost appeared like a giant paw print. She raised her head to the canvas and was in awe. The canvas was almost entirely in blues, greys and black. Despite its dark colouring, it was intensely vibrant; the work was a little rough, perhaps, but staggeringly sharper and more realistic compared with her usual style. Deep clouds in varying hues loomed over the scene. They filled the background along with angry, arched, angular mountains. The painted lightning seemed to slice the very air on the horizon. A lonesome megalith stood in the mid ground, leaning threateningly towards the viewer. In the foreground stood a dark, menacing creature, the black Gwyllgi with eyes aflame. His mouth was open, revealing his bone white fangs. Blood, gore and drool dripped from his mouth. He was staring right at her and through her, his piercing gaze eating into her soul. As she stared she heard him snarl, a low rumbling grumble. The fire of his eyes moved, the flames reaching out off the canvas. The heat reached her face and Ffi ran, screaming, from the room.

* * *

Ryan pulled the vehicle into its usual home, the gravel drive of Trevivian's old house. He was reassured by the sight of his own black smart car sitting close to the house; he had missed her, missed her quiet hum. The noisy roar of the diesel engine he was currently driving thrummed through his head, irking him. The professor's house was always a difficult place to find, located on the outskirts of Cardiff, obscured from the road by ancient yew trees. Light was streaming through the latticed window, showing that the professor was definitely home. Ryan knocked on the door; two dull thuds as the sound reverberated through the wood. The large oak door swung open on iron hinges. A broad smile crossed the professor's sharp, narrow features and raced up to his watery, pale blue eyes behind thick glasses, which lit up in joy. "How are you, my boy? You sounded rough on the phone."

"Good thanks. More importantly, how are you?" Ryan noticed how large the professor's clothes now seemed on him. He was lost in his black woollen jumper, like a child wearing an adult's clothes. He had lost a significant amount of weight in the last few weeks, his white hair was long gone and his breathing sounded raspier.

Trevivian appreciated the enquiry, especially made so genuinely. Since his illness had developed, people had at first pitied him and then avoided him like a leper, as if cancer was contagious. He waved Ryan in over the threshold and into the mellow, olive green study. "Can't complain. Chemo's bloody awful, but I'm still here so that's good. Might have to knuckle down and get this book finished soon."

Ryan was surprised at the mess; the professor had never been what you would call a tidy sort, but this, this seemed like he did not care anymore. Someone had been dusting and vacuuming, but only in the few clear spaces that existed. Files, papers and books were strewn over every available space. Ryan could not see anywhere clear to put either his photos, computer or himself down. The famous typewriter lay on the oak dining table.

"I've brought the pictures, as requested, in the good old-fashioned medium."

"Splendid! Sit down, make yourself at home. Shove that lot over there. Now, can I get you a cuppa?"

Ryan was about to say yes, then checked himself. There were mugs under some of the items littered around. Some had things growing in them. "No, thanks. You've been busy then?"

Trevivian removed his glasses and wiped them over with his greying handkerchief. He held them up to the light, only to see that he had made matters worse. "Yes, firing on all cylinders. Everything was going rather well, though I do say so myself. Then, a couple of days ago, I lost the flow somewhere. Haven't been able to find it since. That's why I needed you back with some evidentiary inspiration."

The professor coughed, his face and body screwed up with the agony it wrought.

Ryan dashed through to the kitchen, found the cleanest glass that he could, and ran some water from the cold tap. He brought it back through to Trevivian, who accepted it gracefully. He sipped it slowly. Ryan cleared another seat of books and papers, and the old man sat down, exhausted. "Thanks, my lad."

He glanced up at Ryan's face, a picture of concern. "Don't worry so. I'm hungry, what do you fancy? Chinese, Indian?"

"Chinese, if that's all right with you."

"Sure, the menus and some money are by the phone. I'll have a special fried rice and chicken in lemon sauce. Would you mind calling them? Only…" He rasped.

Ryan did not mind at all. He felt guilty at having been away for so long. To him, Trevivian was not only a client but also a friend, a good friend. They had struck up an extraordinary friendship since they had first met at the exhibition; they felt they had known each other for a long time straightaway, and both shared a similar dry sense of humour. He organised their order, after procrastinating a while over his own choice of dishes, much to the amusement of the professor. "All sorted, thirty minutes."

Trevivian's eyes were still watering from the coughing. He wiped them casually with his handkerchief and put his glasses on. "Good. Now, may I take a peek at your pictures?"

Ryan carefully cleared the dining table, stacking the books on others to make way. He laid out the pictures. So far, he was pleased with them, but as to what the professor thought, that remained to be seen.

"I see," he said guardedly as he assessed the pictures before him. "These are excellent. You know how to show the presence of the place, the power of their history. I'm rather jealous. I would much rather have been out and about exploring them with you, making notes and being there for myself."

Ryan opened his mouth to say something, but the professor silenced him with a glare, the effect amplified by his peering over the top of his glasses. "I know, I'm too ill now to go gallivanting about in this weather, more's the pity. Perhaps some of the old magic of the stones could keep me going a bit longer. A fancy idea, but who knows and I've got nothing to lose. There's plenty of old tales about the stones; that water that comes into contact with them is meant to be magically infused with healing properties. Did you hear that one yet on your travels?"

He nodded. "Yes, I heard it from a friend of yours actually."

"Ah," Trevivian had a knowing glint in his eye. "Yes, you mentioned Siân." His attention rested on the picture of the Ring of Maidens at sunset. "I do rather like this one. Can we warm it up a bit, add in more of a glow here, around this stone, see how it makes a halo? Can we silhouette it a bit more, show the stones rather than the lichen?" The dreaded red pen emerged from Trev's shirt pocket. Ryan grimaced; his beautiful image was desecrated with redification. "There, I think we've found our front cover. This is good." Trevivian pointed to a picture of his favourite, the Hurlers. "You've done well with this, it reminds me so much of the first time I ever saw them. We can leave that one as it is, for the centre piece or inside cover."

Trevivian proceeded to work his way through the images, marking and making notes on all bar that one. Ryan took all his comments on board; after all, this was the professor's book.

The food arrived and they sat down to eat. Now that their business was out of the way, their conversation turned chattier.

"I want to hear all about your adventures, spare me no details," the professor said. Ryan relayed as much of the last few weeks as he could remember, deliberately omitting the more bizarre goings-on of the last week. He described the places, the people and the photography. Trevivian watched him closely as he spoke; there was another story under the one he told, he glimpsed it occasionally in Ryan's eyes before he hid it away again under another part of the account.

"You forget, Ryan, I know you too well. I asked for your adventures, not a sanitised journal entry. Your essay failed to answer the question," Trevivian chuckled kindly. "I've never known you to be so unsettled. Something has got to you, more than the stories."

Ryan ran his hand roughly through his hair, messing it up. "I thought I'd got used to it. All the stories that everyone tells you when you mention you're looking for the stone circles and burial chambers. If I had a penny for each ghost story, haunted site, miracle, time vortex, entity, orb, UFO, or all the rest of it, I'd have a small fortune by now."

"So what changed?"

"I saw something myself, with my own eyes. And it's left its mark on me, or something. It's under my skin. Actually, that's a lie," Ryan corrected himself. "I saw things, multiple things. I consider myself rational, logical, but these sights I cannot explain away. I mean, perhaps they're the delusions of my own imagination. Perhaps I've been conditioned by all the tales I've been told and it finally got to me." Ryan stood up and began to pace the room impatiently. Once he had begun to start expressing his confusion, it came flooding out as a flow of self-doubt, fear of lunacy and rapt inner turmoil.

"Everything was fine, normal, perfectly normal, before I visited the Ring of Maidens. There I was, minding my own business, taking photos, and then there was this shadow, then lights on the marsh. I hit my head and I've had the weirdest dreams ever since. I think I'm going mad, Professor!"

Trevivian appeared concerned. "Has anyone checked you over since you hit your head? Did you get a concussion perhaps?"

Ryan laughed dryly. "They'd lock me up in a heartbeat; seeing things is never a good sign, is it?"

"Good point. Sit down, you're making me nervous." His curiosity got the better of him. "The Preseli Mountains are certainly an unusual place, not quite a part of this world. The Welsh call it the land of magic and enchantment. A part of the Otherworld in this one. Why don't you tell me what you saw?"

This time, Ryan left nothing out; he described his dreams, the mysterious shadows and the lights of the marsh. The professor listened intently and attentively, making mental notes. When Ryan finished, exhausted by the remembrances, the professor spoke up. "I don't think you're going mad at all. What you've described is in the stories from way back, when an intrinsic part of the culture and mythology of the area. As you say, it could be just your imagination overloading, or have you considered that perhaps you really saw what you think you did, and explained it to yourself in the terms you know from the legends? Odd nocturnal lights or marsh gases become the will-o'-the-wisp;

shadows become ghosts and you dream of the woman you love, but torment yourself because you live so far apart and so she becomes a phantom who haunts your dreams."

Ryan blinked. That was a logical conclusion, a comforting one to put his mind at rest. However, there was something more to his experiences; something he could not find the words to express. His soul was singing at him when he was in the Preselis, making him feel alive, but not solely alive; more that he was living out the echoes of another life. Reliving events from the past; real events, not imaginary ones. All he could bring himself to say was, "I do think I love her".

"Thinking doesn't come into it, my lad. Love is something to be felt wholeheartedly. It defies everything you thought you ever knew." Trevivian looked at the sideboard, where he proudly displayed the most beautiful picture of his wife; it was such an ordinary, impromptu picture, yet it showed her radiant beauty. He gulped as a lump formed in his throat. Twelve years had not eased the pain and grief of her passing. Soon enough they would be reunited; he hoped there was an afterlife. Years ago he had thought the afterlife a silly notion but now, now he needed the idea. He sighed longingly. Could it be that Ryan had glimpsed aspects of another world, something beyond this one, as once, just once, he had done?

Trevivian sought to console his friend. "Eight years ago, I was at West Kennet, we were doing some research into the landscape of the area. I saw the spirit of my Inger by the stream there. The stream had just emerged after winter, fresh and pure. Inger looked as beautiful and young as when we were married, she was a stunner. How I got her I will never know. No one else saw her, but I did. She was wispy, white and transparent; it was definitely her. It was a bad time for me then, I always thought I had conjured her up to console myself. Now I am not so sure. Maybe what you saw was real, maybe it was not, only you can know."

They faded into silence for some time.

"I thought it was real, I could see it all clearly. The shadows are not on the pictures though." Ryan passed across the relevant images. "See, nothing there. One of the locals did tell me she saw it there in that picture, but I can't see it. The will-o'-the-wisp; I wasn't the only one to see that. Siân saw it too. If it is some lunacy, it's a contagious one."

The professor stretched in his chair, yawning. "I think I should like to return with you to the Preseli Mountains. I feel so cramped and restricted in this place. The fresh air would do me good, and perhaps I too can see if there is anything of interest there."

"But…" Ryan began; a glare from Trevivian silenced him.

"I may not have much longer, I'll be damned if I have to spend much more of it sandwiched between these four walls. We'll go back tomorrow, no arguments! Pick me up at midday; I have to drop some stuff off at the publishers and we'll go down together. You said they did good food at the local pub and now that my appetite has come back, I feel I owe it some decent home-cooked meals."

Ryan grinned; when the professor got an idea into his head, there was no earthly way to sway him. He felt better that Trev seemed to not only believe him, but understand him and his concerns. He went home a great deal happier that night.

CHAPTER TWENTY-FOUR

The thundering noise inside Siân's head sounded like persistent, even, hoofbeats. The noise was getting to her, scratching on her nerves. She had the urge to flee; to escape, and run away from the driving sound, yet she knew she could not escape the pain that held her firmly in its embrace. The hoofbeats reminded her of something; a terrifying memory lurking at the back of her brain, but, try as she might, she could retrieve only the feeling and not the memory itself. Nothing could block out the sound; she had tried music, the television and just lying on her sofa quietly. Nausea washed over her in waves, the lights dancing before her eyes, whether they were open or closed. Zigzags, bubbles and squares bounced in and out of her view in various hues, all tinged with green. Why green? she wondered; her vision was darkened, but always with green. Every tiny movement made her want to vomit, and each time she fought the sensation with increased urgency.

She had taken two migraine tablets the moment she got home; they had done nothing to ease the sensations that were overloading her body, mind and spirit. Migraines made Siân feel awful; not only ill, but awful about herself. They were belittling, humiliating and debilitating. Nothing functioned correctly when a migraine was upon her; her speech slowed to make her sound like a drunken fool; words came out of her mouth out of order and made no sense to anyone, not even her. She wanted to scream with the agony, the stabbing pains in her head and eyes as real as any sense of pain could be.

She tried to ease the pain; she staggered to the fridge and, by feel, found her cooling eye mask, which she tied over her eyes. It eased the burning sensation and the coolness served to awaken her mind just a little. She had to ring Mandy; she had to, migraine or not; she had to apologise for earlier, for shouting at Mandy and for the way Lloyd had fired her. If she did not, Mandy would only be angry at her, thinking her in league with Lloyd. That was how Mandy thought, seeing patterns and plans even where there were none, and if there were none that she could see, she filled in the blanks or made her own. Groping her way back to the sofa, using the furniture and door jams as a guide, Siân picked up the phone and dialled Mandy's number from memory. It rang only once before it was picked up. "Russell residence."

The words were spoken by a youngster; Siân had to fight to remember who it was who had picked up. She had hoped it would be Mandy right away. "Alice? Can I speak to your mum, please?"

"OK, I think she and Dad have stopped yelling at each other." Alice was saddened.

"Mmh?"

"I'd tell them to shut up and behave if I didn't think it would get me grounded for a month!"

Siân tried to form a comforting sentence. "I'm so sorry, honey; your mum had a really bad day and it can't be easy for your dad either."

"That's no excuse." Alice was adamant; such behaviour would never be tolerated if it was her giving the attitude, so why was it all right when her parents gave it to each other? "I'll pass you over now, Mum's here. See ya soon, Siân."

"Siân?" Mandy's voice was rough; hoarse from shouting at first Lloyd and then Pete, in the raging argument after she had broken the news.

Siân kept her eyes closed; the red, black and green shapes were still performing an opera of confusion. "Hi, Mandy, I'm sorry about what happened today."

"Is this you, or is this that idiot trying to get you to get me back?"

"It's me. He's clear he doesn't want you back. I tried for you, I begged him, but he's stuck too far up his own arse to admit to messing up. He's such a complete pillock."

"Well," Mandy's voice developed a cold, calculating tone. "Would you act as a witness for what happened if you were asked?"

"Of course I would."

"Pete tells me that I could take this to the authorities, a tribunal or whatever. Apparently cacky Cullen had no right to sack me the way he did, and I could push for unfair dismissal."

"Really? That sounds good, for you I mean. Yes, I'll say what I saw, it was bang out of order him treating you like that, treating us like he always does."

"Erm, Siân? Are you all right, only you sound a bit funny?"

"Migraine."

Mandy's face slipped from a hard expression of a woman ready for the fight, to a concerned friend.

"Sorry, was it all this crap that brought it on?"

Siân began to shiver uncontrollably, the motion making the bile rise in her throat. "Dunno."

"What's that noise on the line, like a drum beat or something?"

"Dunno, I can't hear much over my head throbbing. I gotta go, Mandy. I'm sorry, I'll ring you tomorrow or when I feel better, OK?"

"All right, take care of yourself. I know it wasn't your fault lewdy Lloydy sacked me." She chuckled at the nickname; they had a fair few for Lloyd Cullen, he was so easy to take the mick out of.

Siân attempted to replace the handset and failed; she did not notice. She lay back into the comforting sofa and pulled her legs up, curling up to her private tortures. Readjusting the cushion under her head took effort, and she sank back to watch the room spinning wildly out of control and the colours and images that dragged her awareness with them into the dark. Images of a woman running across the marsh, images of a horse, sweating with effort as its rider rode it hard, chasing the woman. Images of other animals; of a deer, a boar, a stag and a hawk spinning, as though on a roulette wheel. Then Siân felt herself within the Ring of Maidens, spinning with arms outstretched as children do, twirling and spinning, until the stones and mountains blended into one; spinning until, in her dizzy spell, her feet could no longer support her and she fell down face-first into the mud. She was sinking into the mud; the more she struggled against it the faster it took her, sucking her lithe body down with it. The dark, damp coldness paralysed her, its weight pushing on her limbs and lungs. She screamed. She became too weak to fight and watched the world above her grow dark as the mud closed over her. Then she was through and under the mud, into a deep, dark cavern within the earth. She could smell the earth and the water, hear it dripping down the walls, feel it dripping down her. She began to shiver violently again.

Mandy stood with the phone still to her ear; the noise on the line was peculiar. Crackling, popping and hissing she was used to, but not this sound, not the sound of something beating. A heart, a drum, footsteps, stomps, more like. The sound echoed down the line.

Alice grabbed at her mother's shirtsleeve. "Mum, come and look at this."

"In a minute, love."

"Now, Mum," whined Alice.

"I said, in a minute, Alice!"

"Mum!"

Down the phone line came another noise, sharp and short. It made the hairs on the back of Mandy's neck rise, and her knees tremble. A woman had screamed, and there was only one woman on the other end of the line. "I have to go," she said to Pete, who was through in the other room, quietly watching some action film, as his way of winding down after their set-to. She heard him get up, the sound of the cushions released from his weight.

"Mum, you have to see this," her daughter grumbled.

Mandy was exasperated, the blood pounded in her ears. She raised her hand to strike at Alice to hush her up, to push her away. She stopped herself just in time, and looked at her hand in horror. Pete stood in the doorway, regarding her with an equal expression of horror. Meanwhile, Alice, so keen to show her mother whatever it was, had turned away to pick up a piece of paper, and had not noticed. Mandy brought her hand down to her side hastily, before Alice turned back to face her. Her mouth and throat were suddenly dry with fear, fear of what she almost did. Dryly she said, "What is it, dear?"

"Take this to Siân for me; it's a picture of her friend, who was with her in the shop today. She asked me what she looked like so I drew her for her. That all right? Mum?"

Mandy reached for the drawing, taking it from Alice without looking at it. "Yes, all right, love. I'll take it over now." She faced Pete. "I have to go, I'll be back soon." She refused to look either of them in the eye; she was too ashamed of herself. How could she nearly have struck her own daughter? She was reviled with herself, what had she become? Today had been a bloody awful day, but that was no excuse. Something bad had leapt up within her, seeking an outlet; it had felt wrong, evil, sinister, like it was not even her at all. That thought scared her the most.

Pete took the picture from her, almost tearing it as Mandy refused to release her grip. "Alice, it's time for bed." Alice was about to protest, but the thunderous look that her father gave her dissuaded her. "Night, then," she responded sulkily. Pete watched as Alice climbed the stairs, pausing only once to view the scene of her mother and father confronting each other. Pete found himself angry at his wife and her behaviour again for the umpteenth time today. "What is the matter with you?"

"I have to go out to Siân's."

"Why? Have you not seen enough of her today?" he scorned.

Mandy was quiet. "No, I heard her scream, on the phone."

Pete was annoyed; his mouth turned up in a sneer. "I'll go, you'll only get hysterical. It's probably nothing. The stupid girl probably bumped into the coffee table, there's so much damn junk in her hovel."

"No!" Mandy exclaimed, grabbing her husband by his upper arms.

Pete shook her off easily. "For God's sake, woman. I'm going. You stay here and sort your head out, or Alice and I will be out of here."

"You can't do that to me, she's my daughter too. I don't deserve that, and you know it."

"If you don't get some help, I'm going and taking her with me. You nearly hit her, for Christ's sake. What is wrong with you?" Pete stormed out of the house, slamming the door behind him. Mandy broke down, sobbing as the echo vibrated around the house.

Pete threw the picture on to the passenger seat and twisted the key in the ignition. He sped around to Siân's house, not far from his own. He pulled in past the chapel and down the muddy track. There were no lights on, so he knocked on the wooden door and waited. He decided to post the picture through the letterbox. It took most of his strength to push the brass plate open, he had to screw the paper up to get it through. He did not care anyway; he could never understand the close friendship that his daughter and wife had with this girl. There was no response; he knocked again and again, but there was no sound from within. Pete was pleased; he detested having to talk to Siân, and only ever did so under duress to keep his wife from having a go at him for his lack of personal skills.

Knowing Mandy would not let it rest unless he had made some effort to check that Siân was all right and still in one piece, Pete made his way past the thorny rose that grew by the door to look into the nearest window. His feet, although he did not know it, found themselves in the footprints of another, larger shoe. He could see nothing in the darkness, even when he cupped his palms around his eyes and pressed his face up to the glass.

As he continued to stare into the void, a faint glow appeared from under an internal door. It was dim, but gave enough light for him to see that Siân was not lying anywhere injured or screaming that he could see, as his wife would have had him believe, drama queen that she was. Pete was about to go when the light moved closer. If Siân was up and about in the kitchen, why had she not bothered to answer? It was late, he realised; a good reason for not answering the door. How odd that the light moved, but maybe she had a candle in there. No, the light was too silvery for a candle. The light appeared to radiate through the wooden door, as though there were almost nothing there; it cast a silvery glow that made Pete feel very uncomfortable all of a sudden. The light moved closer and Pete could see that it was made up of a million tiny iridescent particles shimmering as though under the light of the full moon.

Siân walked through the door; she did not open it, but passed right through it, as though it was not solid. Pete wanted to blink, but, his eyes watering, he could not tear himself away from the sight. Siân was entirely white; her hair, skin and clothes and she were transparent. She did not walk, but glided close to where the sofa was and lay down. Pete crossed himself, his Catholic upbringing coming back with a vengeance. Siân was a phantom. Now Pete understood the power that she had over his wife, and his wife's odd behaviour; Siân was an evil spirit, and had to be dealt with accordingly. Pete was resolved; he would ring the rector first thing in the morning, and would ban his wife and child from ever having anything to do with Siân ever again. He raced back to the car and drove home at maximum speed, gripping the steering wheel tightly with fear and in a vain attempt to anchor himself to reality.

* * *

The pile of post, still not dealt with, blocked the door from opening the whole way. Ryan had not been in the right frame of mind earlier to deal with it, nor was he now. He pushed the door hard with his shoulder to get his laptop and himself through the aperture, and bruised his shoulder in the process as the door argued back, bouncing back from the obstacle. He almost dropped the laptop but managed to hold on to it, while the paperwork he was carrying slipped to the floor. As he bent down and reached towards the pictures, he once again saw the shadow he had seen on his first day in the Mountains of Preseli; the same shadow he had seen at the Ring of Maidens. Unbelievingly, he blinked; the shadow vanished.

Ryan swore aloud. Why was the shadow playing hide and seek with him? What possible reason could it have for doing so? Or was he simply seeing what he wanted to see, to assure himself that he was not going bonkers? He dropped from crouching, to land heavily on his behind. Touching his hand, palm outstretched to his forehead, he exhaled heavily. Exhaustion was creeping over his mind and body; he was beginning to feel that he was swimming in a mere or lake that was so big that he could not see the shore or dry land. The feeling wore him down; it took a great deal of effort for Ryan to get up, to plug in the projector and set up the images on the wall again. He lay back on the bed, sinking gradually into oblivion as the exhaustion won, creeping over his nerves and sinews, stealing his awareness and consciousness.

The darkness was welcoming, warm and comforting; it was easier to let go than fight to stay awake. The images rolled on before his steadily closing eyes, the images appeared on the wall and on the inside of his eyelids. The shadow reappeared, whether on Ryan's lids or the wall he did not know; perhaps it was real, perhaps a dream. The shadow was that of a man, just as Ffi had described. He was tall and thin, gangly even. His bones were slightly twisted with great age and his hair was long, white and flowing out behind him. His cloak was also blowing in some breeze, of another place and time. The figure reached out towards Ryan, reaching out beyond the confines of the picture in which he was caught. As he leaned forward, his features became more defined; his eyes were watery but still as keen as those of a much younger man; his sharp equine features were narrowed with worry. The old man's arm reached towards Ryan, pale with age and dotted with age spots, the fingers twisted with arthritis.

"Owein, you must protect Morwyna. He is back and I cannot stop him. I cannot protect you here; you are too far from me. Badden is back… You must return…"

CHAPTER TWENTY-FIVE

Pete burst through the door, his face contorted with emotions. "Amanda!" he shouted. His wife was asleep on the couch before his grand entrance; she stood up and blearily approached him. "Is she all right?"

"Damn you, damn you all! You bunch of evil witches!"

Mandy was still half asleep; she could not tell if he was joking or serious. "What?"

He was spitting as he shouted, "I see what you're up to, all of you with your prancing around under the moon, casting evil spells and corrupting our poor innocent child. Is Siân your High Priestess, your Chief Witch then? I always thought it was Ffion with her stupid blatherings, but it's Siân, isn't it? What is she, a demon? An evil spirit? A succubus? What?"

Mandy rubbed her eyes. "What on earth are you on about, Pete? It's one thing to have a go at me over what's happened, but I don't understand why you're bringing Siân into this."

Pete laughed, and the noise chilled Mandy to her core. "She's the problem, how could I not have seen it before? It's all down to her, it all began when her Gran died; did she kill her? Oh Christ, did she?" He paused for breath as he ran out. "Pack some things for you and Alice. Now! We're leaving here tonight. You will never see Siân again; you must promise me, or I will have to take Alice away from you; I have to protect her from all this evil."

"Evil? Have you gone mad?" Mandy cried. "The only evil thing here is whatever peculiar idea that has got into your head and wrapped itself around your common sense. What the hell is going on? Please, Pete, talk to me," Mandy pleaded desperately, hanging on to Pete's sleeve as he tried to storm up the stairs.

"I saw her, I saw your so-called friend. She's an evil spirit, you know, all see through and floaty." He waved his arms in mock ghostliness. "How can you not see it; you always were a bit thick. I should've known, this whole place is under her spell. Maenddu, black stone, ha! Black as in evil!"

Mandy shook her head pathetically against the onslaught; this was all far above her comprehension. Siân was solid and real, alive and most definitely not a ghost. Mandy had been to MoonRaven's Sabbats a couple of times to see what they were like, and to satisfy her own curiosity. As far as she could tell, there was nothing evil there, just people praising nature and singing songs. It had been fun, not sinister. She had never taken Alice, and had never seen Siân there.

"You must calm down before you hurt yourself." She studied the enlarged vein pulsating in his forehead. Every argument of the day, more or less every sentence, seemed to have enlarged and angered it, so God only knew what was happening in his chest to his already-stressed heart. She wrung her hands with the stress that she was feeling; the skin was soon turning red. Oh Lord, was this him snapping, was her getting sacked the last straw that broke his sanity? She cleared her throat, dreading the reaction to what she was about to say. "Pete, do you want me to call the doc? The hospital, maybe? Do you need some help?"

Pete held his face close to hers, his eyes wide and crazed. "I don't need help, my dearest wife. You do, you all do. We're leaving now, get Alice and some stuff together! Either you leave with us or we go anyway…"

Mandy chose her family above her friend; she had to, there was no choice really. At least if she went with them she would know where they were, and be able to work on getting Pete to seek the help he so obviously needed. Besides, she was tired of arguing; she felt as though she had been doing that all day. "I'll wake Alice and get packing."

A wan smile crossed Pete's sweating face. He knew he had won.

* * *

Siân woke up at some unearthly hour in the morning, desperate for the loo. The darkness of the night was soft and enveloping like a black duvet. The rustling of bats' wings in the yew trees close by sounded like an oncoming train. Gingerly she eased herself up into a sitting position, taking it as slowly as she dared with her bladder nagging her for every second it took. The room was dark, pitch black, and Siân knew it was. The inner lights from her malfunctioning brain failed to deceive her. She half-walked, half-crawled to the bathroom; in an old cottage such as this the bathroom was located downstairs, behind the kitchen. It was a surprisingly recent addition to the house; her Mamgu had built it on to the house when Siân had come to live with her; before then it had been at the bottom of the garden. Siân, at that moment, was very grateful that it was now so much closer.

As she made her way through the main room and kitchen, Siân could feel something wet and sticky on the floor. She could not yet see it, and dared not turn on the main lights for fear of adding to her blinding agony. Her hands and knees slipped in it more than once, and she held her hand to her nose to sniff it. Was it water leaking from a faucet in the kitchen? Had a mucky cat got in to escape the rain outside? Whatever it was, it smelt terrible; the smell formed images in her mind. There were earthy, rich tones, a peaty aspect, a dank wetness, something organic and something else, something dead. "Ugh," she exclaimed.

Great, now she had to go to the bathroom for two reasons; to pee and to throw up. With great relief, she finally made it to the bathroom and in time. She could hardly breathe between each ejection as her throat and stomach muscles cramped out of control. She gasped for breath, trying to breathe through the qualm and to calm herself from her rising sense of panic. She retched until her throat was raw and she felt she would pass out with the constancy of it. Finally, a break came and she felt much better for it. Slowly, gradually, the thunder and lightning in her head eased back enough to let her think straighter than she had done for hours.

In the cold sink, she washed her hands and then her face in freezing water. She cleaned her teeth thoroughly, the minty flavour and foam negating some of the acidity in her mouth; anything to make her feel human again was most welcome. She clicked on the small, faint yellowish light above the mirror and stared into her own eyes, blinking wildly at first as her eyes adjusted. Her sight was still fuzzy, still clouded by green, though now she could at least make out the shape and contours of her own being and the room around her. Her pupils were tiny black holes, barely visible against the cornflower blue of her irises. Her shadow was cast upon the opposite wall; it moved though she had not. Within the shade of her shadow, silver particles – dust motes, thought Siân

– danced elegantly. Narrowing her eyes, squinting to see more clearly, Siân watched as her shadow moved again. It was moving as though she were taking a step forward and then a step back, once, twice, thrice. The fourth time, the shadow stepped forward two steps and disappeared from view.

Shivers racked Siân's slim body as the cold of the chilly bathroom in the middle of the night caught up with her. She pulled her old, knotted cardigan tighter around her and rubbed her forearms briskly in response. She looked down at the floor, to her bare feet on the cold slate floor, and then out of the room, following the floor into the tiny gangway that housed the washing machine and back door and then into the kitchen. The wet dirt that she had crawled in earlier spread from the back door off into the kitchen. Fear terrorised her heart. Time seemed to freeze; she held her breath. The marks were bare footprints; they were no longer well defined, they were smudged and spread where she had clambered through them.

She stepped cautiously to the back door and tried the handle. Breathing only once, she found it firmly locked and bolted, top and bottom, as it should have been. She twisted on her heel so that her own foot was in line with one of the prints, one that she had not disturbed. They matched her own feet perfectly in size and detail.

Siân ran her hand through her long hair, forgetting she had tied it back; she struggled to release her fingers. She was puzzled; had she gone outside, sleepwalking, earlier? She had never knowingly done so before, and hoped she would not do so again, she had left such a filthy mess everywhere. Lifting her feet, one by one, she checked her soles; they were clean, completely clean. The soreness in her head was ebbing, but her thoughts were still confused. She had no recollection of walking in the dirt of her garden, nor of washing her feet. She followed the prints; they continued right up to the sofa, where they disappeared. Surely the steps would have had to lead to the bathroom, if she had gone to wash her feet? Yet these were in the wrong direction. The confusion was winding her tender nerves in circles, and the ache was using this to stealthily creep back into her brain. Giving up, she flicked off the light and made her way back to the sofa, to sleep the rest of the night through.

* * *

Siân swore as the alarm chimed and rattled against the table. As always, it was set as late as was possible to get her to work on time. Her hand reached out, almost subconsciously, and swiped at the blasted thing. It clattered as it bounced against the wooden beams of the floor and broke into half a dozen pieces. She swore again and raised her head. The alarm clock had broken into its constituent parts, the battery was still rolling across the floor, the battery case had made it to the carpet, and the main frontage was forlornly rocking on the table. She reached down and began to pick up the sections, pushing each back together again as she had done many mornings before. One piece was still missing, the screw that held the front and back sections of black plastic together.

Sliding off the sofa on to her knees, she placed her head to the floor to get a better view. It could not have gone too far. She peered under the sofa, saw the missing screw, and was displeased to also notice a collection of grey dust; she would have to clean under there after work or at the weekend. She extended her arm and reached around to retrieve the screw; feeling its spiralling metal against her fingers, the coldness was intense, as her senses were still heightened after her migraine. There was some other cleaning to do, from the mess made last night. She ran her fingers through her hair, trying to recall what it was she had meant to clean this morning. Looking down at her bare feet against the soft floorboards, she remembered. Last night there had been slimy, muddy footprints and smears throughout downstairs. She tilted her head to the left and to the right, but there was no sign now of any mud, or of any footprints on the warm toned wood. She ran both hands through her hair and smoothed down its morning frizz as her brain went into overdrive.

Last night there had been a real mess; she could recall the sight, the smell and the presence of the mud; it had been real, hadn't it? She walked softly through the kitchen and bathroom, and there was still no sign of the mess. There were two options; either she had been cleaning in her sleep, bizarre but possible, or she had simply dreamt it, the dream given added reality by her messed-up head. She laughed aloud to her reflection in the kettle as she flicked it on; how lovely it would be to clean in her sleep! This place was difficult to keep clean, filled as it was with her Mamgu's numerous knick-knacks and ornaments. If she could clean this place in her sleep that would be perfect, burning off calories and keeping the place clean, without knowingly having to do it. She despised dusting; always having to move all the knick-knacks seemed so unnecessary; so time consuming and polluting.

Putting a tea bag and spoon into her favourite brightly coloured mug, Siân knew now that it was time to tidy away the ornaments and surplus decorations. This place, this lovely cottage with so much potential, was hers now, and although she loved the memories the objects stirred in her, now it was time to make some of her own, preferably with Ryan. The possibilities thrilled her and made her feel more alive than ever before. The steam of the boiling kettle mixed with the blur of her own hazy eyes as she drifted away for a moment to daydream of Ryan. He had said he was coming back in a couple of days, and today was one day closer to his return. She poured the boiling water into the mug and stirred, causing a maelstrom to appear in her mug, matching the maelstrom of emotions swirling in her own heart.

Lost in her emotions and the rhythmic purr of the shower, she failed to notice the time, and it was not until the kitchen clock chimed quarter to eight that she realised she was running late. She rubbed the towel vigorously over her body and hair and dashed naked up the stairs to find some clothes for the day ahead.

CHAPTER TWENTY-SIX

"Have we got room for all this stuff?" Ryan teased Trevivian. "The monster is only so big."

"Nonsense, my dear boy, this is all vital equipment." Trevivian spread his frail arm, indicating the piles of tied-up papers and books, as well as a medium-sized, battered suitcase. "And of course I'm not going anywhere without my most precious possession." He indicated a second similar-sized suitcase, which was in much better condition, lying on its side, next to the other. Within it, well wrapped up, was the typewriter.

Ryan grimaced. "Does all that really have to come with us? I do need some space for all my stuff too. Photographic equipment is very useful for a photographer, especially one working for you."

The professor grinned, the years and fatigue momentarily fading from his face. "And that is why I am only bringing the most essential items; I would have much rather brought far more. This is nothing compared with what Inger used to try and take whenever we went anywhere. Why a woman needs so many clothes I will never know. And as for shoes, they need even more of those to match the clothes."

"Fine," Ryan gave in. "I guess she is your car, after all." He began to pile the equipment into the boot of the monster, repositioning his own luggage and equipment as best he could to accommodate it.

As he picked up the suitcase with the typewriter in, Trevivian weighed in. "No, that's going on the back seat; I like to be able to keep an eye on her."

Ryan shook his head. 'Only a man with a bow tie has these kinds of eccentricities and gets away with them,' he thought to himself. The bow tie had been the first thing he had ever noticed about the professor; it had given him a clear idea of the type of man he was as soon as they had met, and his initial impression had been perfectly accurate. He opened the back door and heaved the typewriter on to the seat; damn, it was heavy. Using the seat belts, Ryan managed to wedge it in place and keep it secured for the journey ahead.

"Are you ready yet?" nagged Trevivian with jollity, having in the meantime planted himself firmly into the passenger seat and belted himself in. "I'm raring to go."

Ryan knew that he was; the professor, many decades his senior, was full of beans, like a child going on holiday. Ryan, however, was still rather tired from a poor night's sleep, and when he did sleep the strange dreams had haunted him still. He had expected the dreams to die away once he was back in the familiar confines of his own flat, but instead the dreams seemed to follow him and beseech him to return to the mountains. He remembered an old man beckoning him back to the mountains, and Siân standing at the Ring of Maidens, calling his name over and over, the word echoing and bouncing around the cauldron of hills at Maenddu until he had dreamed his head would break apart. As Ryan climbed into the driver's seat and belted himself, Trevivian opened a battered old map. "There's a couple of places I'd like to visit on the way…"

* * *

As she dashed towards the door, and slipped on the hallway rug, Siân caught sight of a damp, screwed-up ball of paper resting on the mat. Funny, it was too early for the post, and she had not heard anything come through the door. She popped the slice of marmalade on toast between her teeth to hold it while she retrieved the paper. She had been craving marmalade on toast ever since her marmalade-laden kiss the previous day, the sweetness reminding her of her love. As she bent over, a cloud of dizziness took hold and she was filled with a sense of unease; her spine tingled as though icy water was running down it, but she dismissed it as not having dried herself off well enough after her shower.

Turning the paper over in her hands, she recognised the slightly yellow hue of Alice's drawing pad, which Siân herself had bought Alice for her birthday. Holding the paper against the front door, Siân evened the crinkles out as best she could, first with one hand and then the other. As she smoothed the paper the picture appeared, rough and pale in coloured pencils. The picture was of a girl, the girl that Alice had described to Siân the day before, the shadowy friend whom only Alice had been able to see. As a child's drawing, it was not distinct enough to give Siân a clear impression, but Alice had drawn this other girl in the same manner as she had always drawn Siân, except for the palette of colours she had chosen, which were more muted, more grey. Even the skin and hair colour, so often shown in black and pink, were pencilled in shades of grey. The clothes were as Alice had said, very Celtic Iron Age in appearance, like the costumes worn by re-enactors, the tunic again coloured in with grey pencils. She laid the paper down on the table, by the small money tree, one of the few plants she had been able to keep alive after her Mamgu's death, and headed out the door with the rapidly cooling toast still held firmly in her mouth.

Half-running, half-walking, Siân scampered down the street towards the shop, still munching on her breakfast. A police car was stopped outside the village shop, and a sombre-looking policeman stood by the door, pacing in irritation. He was not the usual community officer for the area, which puzzled her. As Siân approached, her throat and mouth ran dry. The police always made her fearful; they always seemed to be custodians of bad news. She closed her eyes and was back, aged four, watching a young policewoman break the news of her parents' death to her and Mamgu. She remembered the hollow horror that she felt that day and the tears that would not stop. She opened her eyes and moved forward hesitantly. As she drew closer, she could see the problem. The windows were gone; piles of broken security glass lay on the ancient grey carpet in small piles like melted snowmen. The shattered surfaces, catching the early morning light, reflected it back in a thousand directions. The sight was beautiful and creepy. "Bore da, can I help you? I work here."

The officer turned to face Siân. He looked to be in his mid-thirties, lines were starting around his dark eyes, accentuated by his serious demeanour. He was of a solid but not stocky build, bulked up with the paraphernalia of the uniform. His dark hair was cut very precisely and there was something equally neat about his voice, with a decidedly Northern Welsh accent. Neatness and order shone off him. "Oh, hello, seems you've been vandalised. We've been trying to get hold of the owner for ages. Do you know where he is?"

"Probably still at home, he's never in before midday. I'm Siân, if I can help you, let me know."

The policeman's shoulders sank; he smiled wearily, attempting to be polite when he was evidently annoyed. "I'm Constable Tony Nash. I've been assigned to be your liaison for this. Can you tell me if anything is missing? We've got quite a lot to deal with at the moment and I need to get on. I've never known it so busy around here."

Siân unlocked the front door; the act seemed utterly pointless as she could just as easily have walked through the wooden frames that once had housed the windows. She led the way, with the officer following carefully in her footsteps. The till remained where it was, as it was the night before. "No one's been at the till, and nothing seems to have been taken. I'll go and check the safe." Bracing herself with a deep breath, she pushed down the handle and walked into the dark stockroom to the safe. The previous two days' takings were still there, waiting to be banked today. All was present and correct, so why had anyone bothered to smash the glass?

In the next room, Constable Nash's radio beeped into life. He pulled it across him, to hear more clearly. An older male voice, filled with a sense of necessity, crackled through the radio. Siân could not hear the words but it sounded important. The constable pressed the button allowing him to respond. "Will do, Sir."

Siân emerged from the stockroom. "Everything's OK in there, too. Nothing's been taken or moved. How very peculiar!"

"Thank you," responded Constable Nash, who was already making his way back to the door. "There's been an accident on the A478, I have to go. We'll be in contact when we can about this. I'll get you a crime number so you can go ahead and sort out the insurance."

"Erm, thanks!" Siân called after the departing policeman. Alone in the store, Siân took stock of the situation. The glass was at least in fairly neat piles; only odd fragments lay scattered around. Lloyd was not here; that was to be expected. She had not believed that he would make any effort to get in and do any work, despite his empty promises; it was not in his nature. Mandy was not here either; hopefully she was enjoying her time off and away from this dump. Part of Siân was jealous. Loneliness is a swamping emotion that is more than capable of drowning an individual in sorrow and despair, and it was that which Siân now felt. She honestly had no idea what she was supposed to do. Should she clear up the glass, or leave it for the police to come back to? One thing she was sure of was that she did not feel safe or happy to be here. Lloyd chose that moment to arrive; he stomped through the hole where the glass of the main window had once been.

"What the hell happened here?" he demanded, his voice loud and booming. The shards that remained tenuously in place wobbled with the noise.

"I don't know; I only got here a couple of minutes ago. The police were trying to get hold of you, but they had to go." She spoke through gritted teeth; working alongside Lloyd was going to be difficult, everything about him grated on her soul.

"What? That's bloody typical." He ventured past her, entering her personal space with no regard, too close for comfort. He stank of sweat and something more peaty.

"Hey," Siân interrupted him, "What do you know? There was an accident. I, for one, think that's more important than a few busted windows."

Lloyd's voice echoed from the backroom; he had already turned the computer on, the hum and thrum of the darned thing was audible. "You wanna clean this place up or what? You should have cleaned it up when you got in. We don't want to be late opening."

She turned away and took one of the disposable cameras from the stand. She then took a whole film of the scene that lay before her; the piles of broken glass, the empty frames and the untouched shelves. Now if anyone needed a visible record, they would have it. Taking the dustpan and brush off the hook on the wall, she began very carefully to sweep it up, using a box from under the counter to contain the glass; God forbid anyone would hurt themselves on it after it left the shop.

"How nice of you to help," she called sarcastically to her boss; there was no reply except a rallying of mouse clicking, so he was already playing games. It was a relief in some way; at least if he was out the back he was out of her way, but this shop was too much to run on her own. Villagers were flocking by to see what had happened; she exchanged a few courtesies and promised to be as quick as she could so they could soon all come in and get their morning supplies. As she swept the glass sang; as shard connected with shard, notes were sounded bright and lucid in a complete contrast to the low tones of conversation of those gathering outside, queuing to come in. The song was bright, cheerful, yet barren and forlorn. It screeched against her nerves like nails on a blackboard, yet at the very same time it was the most beautiful sound she had ever heard; it was the song that snow and ice would sing – cold, crystalline, crisp and clear.

Her reflection stared back at her a thousand times over and, with some presumably peculiar trick of the light, it reflected back to her a double image. The first was her as she knew herself to be; the colours of her skin, eyes and clothes were true, and the other was an icy image; clear, transparent and devoid of colours, except pale whites and greys. The sight left her cold.

An empty chill gnawed at her stomach and the back of her brain; the hairs were rising on the back of her neck and goosebumps were erupting all over her flesh. This was the woman that Alice had drawn; her picture rather accurate as it turned out. Siân's breath seemed to cloud into mist as soon as it parted from the heat of her body. "Who are you?" she found herself whispering, not wanting to be heard by those outside. The second figure remained in the reflections; Siân recalled that the lady had not responded to Alice either. "Please tell me who you are?" Siân hissed, trying to keep her voice courteous and friendly against her natural sense of terror at seeing this ghostly version of herself. The woman seemed to be staring both at Siân and into some great chasm of space; her expression was distant, disengaged, and disconcerting. Siân tilted her head and the echo of her mimicked the movement.

Slowly the figure raised a hand and pointed to Siân in the reflection, or was it to herself; Siân could not quite work out the angle as they were both so close. She was about to ask if this pale, shadow image of herself was a ghost, or a vision of her own self in death, but realised that in fact she was too frightened to ask that particular question, she was too scared of the answer. Surely to see one's own ghost or doppelgänger was not a good thing; was that not something that was said to be a premonition of death? However, this woman was dressed differently, so did she still constitute a doppelgänger?

Siân could not take her eyes from her double reflection; she had so many questions to ask, most of which seemed rather inane or ridiculous, but then so did talking to herself or the ghost of herself. "Why are you here?" seemed vaguely intelligent and to the point. Siân softly said it aloud to the glass mirrors. The ghost continued to stare vacantly ahead, her eyes full of a cold sadness. Siân was mesmerised by this second image of herself; her skin seemed lifeless, corpselike and dewy. Tiny water drops glistened on her skin, mirrors within mirrors, an infinity of reflections. Siân inched closer to the pile of glass, to get a better viewpoint, moving her knees carefully so as to avoid any loose shards that had escaped the piles. The droplets of water on the ghost's face were frozen into minute crystal balls, and in each Siân could see herself, but her surroundings of the shop were not reflected. Instead, she could see herself standing under starry skies, the twinkling stars yet more mirrors in this universe within the glass. Squinting to the point where her eyes burned, she saw the stones of the Ring of Maidens around her, their polished surfaces of dark stone with white inclusions reflecting the skies above.

A knock on the wooden frame of the front door jerked her sharply back to reality. "Brysio, I want my paper," demanded Jim, coarsely as ever. Siân cried out in pain; she had inadvertently cut her hand on a piece of broken glass when the old man had surprised her. She turned her hand over very carefully and the broken glass moved with her, it was stuck into the flesh of her hand.

"Perfect!" Dark red blood was flowing freely around it, dripping blobs on to the floor below. The glass had not gone all that deep and the sharp stabbing pain was already easing away. Getting to her feet, Siân went through the shop and the stockroom to the small bathroom that was only large enough to accommodate a toilet and basin; even getting in and out around the door was a squeeze.

"Lloyd?" she called. "You're going to have to sort the rest out, if you want to open any time soon; I've had a little accident."

"Are you OK?" he called. Siân was shocked he had actually asked, and did not know what to say to him.

"I'll be OK; I caught myself on some of the glass." Under the blinking neon light she wrapped some toilet roll around the other hand and removed the glass, wincing in pain for only a second.

Lloyd stuck his head around the bathroom door. "Here, the first aid kit." He passed it around the door and saw the blood in the sink. "Oh, Siân. Let me look." The habitual coldness in his voice was mixed with a warm tone that Siân had never heard before; it sounded like concern and that was a little creepy coming from Lloyd, who only ever cared about himself.

She was already unpacking the bandaging. "It's fine, honestly. Only a scratch."

"You'd better write it up in the accident book. Then you can go home if you want. We won't be opening today." His attitude was messing with her head.

"Is this so you can dock my pay for a day?" she queried as she pushed past him to get out of the bathroom; she was not fond of enclosed spaces, and certainly not the bathroom when a creepy man was trying to get into it.

"No, I'll pay you. Perhaps it would be better not to open today, the place isn't safe. I'll stay and get the glaziers in; there's not a lot you can do like that." He indicated her bandaged hand.

"Hello?" called a voice from the main shop.

"Oh, that's the policeman," Siân said to Lloyd. "He wanted to speak to you."

"Hi," Siân greeted the constable as she emerged from the stockroom. Lloyd hung back in the shadows.

"Is everything all right?" Constable Nash asked, looking at the drops of blood on the carpet in front of him and the dressing on Siân's hand.

"It was the glass. Lloyd, he's the owner, is here now if you want to speak to him." Siân stepped aside, the light from the shop now illuminating Lloyd as he stepped forward.

Officer Nash pulled out his black notebook. "I have a crime number for you to give to your insurers."

"Thank you." Lloyd was curt with the policeman; his tone was business-like with added unpleasantness. Siân listened to the conversation that followed as she filled in the incident book, which was kept under the till. Thankfully it had been her left hand that had been cut, so writing was not a problem. The officer was being professional and polite, even in the face of Lloyd's hostility. Siân could not help but wonder why Lloyd was being even more of an arse than normal; had he had some previous run in with the law, or was he just being unpleasant for the sake of it, deriving some perverse pleasure from it?

"Do you have any idea who might have done this?" questioned the policeman. "Any disgruntled employees or customers?"

"Well, yes, now you come to mention it," started Lloyd. Siân's ears pricked up. Oh God, no, he was about to lay this on Mandy. That was why he was being such an idiot; he was waiting to drop her in it.

Lloyd continued, "I had to let a member of staff go very recently; she wasn't very happy about it. You may want to speak to her – Amanda Russell. She lives in Pantyffynon, on the new estate."

Constable Nash made a note of the information. "May I ask why you had to let her go?"

"The usual. She was lazy, inefficient, not a team player."

Siân nearly choked. Mandy was far more of a team player than Lloyd would ever be; at least she knew what the shop floor looked like and had actually cleaned it. Enough was enough.

Siân stepped into the conversation. "I don't think Mandy did this." Both men stared at her. "Sorry, but Mandy's not like that. She was only fired because Lloyd was late and she'd ended up having her little girl in the shop with her."

Lloyd cast her a black glare and spoke to her patronisingly. "That ain't quite true is it, Siân? Mandy was in a foul temper when she left here; she almost broke the glass panel on the door on her way out, she slammed it so hard. I wouldn't be surprised if she came back later for a smashing time, to get back at me. She's always had a problem with me; some authority issue. She has a spiteful, small-minded side to her personality that I never did like. You'd do well to remember that, Siân."

"I'm not going to stay here and listen to this. Mandy did not do this! You need to look elsewhere." She stormed out through the gaping window and past the still growing queue.

CHAPTER TWENTY-SEVEN

Siân took her frustration out in the best way she knew how, in de-cluttering and cleaning the cottage she called home. Donning her unglamorous marigolds, and having bother getting one of the gloves over her bandaged left hand, only fuelled her anger and determination. Her foul mood was ideal for being severe and harsh with all the many trinkets and the quintessential Granny aura of the place. Neatly, she packed away all of the ornaments into cardboard boxes and old shoeboxes. All but one box were piled up by the front door ready to go to charity; the other box, with those very special ornaments of Mamgu's, those which had special memories for Siân, were placed out of sight in the old pine dresser. They could be dug out in the future when Siân wanted to spend some time remembering and reminiscing; that way, Siân could allay the guilt she felt for what she was doing, removing the essence of her Mamgu to make way for her own.

Surveying the room with a cold and moody eye, for the first time Siân could see the room for what it was; dingy, cramped and fussy. The surfaces, now clear, shone brightly where the ornaments had rested; elsewhere the surfaces were dull with grey dust. The furnishings and décor looked old and slightly shabby, the theme was allegedly terracotta but time and use had aged it to a muddy brown. All it needed was a fresh coat of paint, perhaps a paler colour to invite in more light and give the place a fresher, younger vibe. With a bright coloured duster, a complete contrast to her shabby surroundings, Siân began to dust the main living area downstairs. The surfaces gleamed with an enlivened newness as she passed by, and the cottage came back to life. She bypassed the kitchen, which she always kept scrupulously clean; the slate worktop and pale wooden units had been replaced only a few years before, and so, for now at least, this one room did not warrant her attention. She moved through to the bathroom, the worst room of the house, with its ancient green fittings. Getting out the cleaning products from behind the sink, Siân saw her reflection in the dark mirror. Alone she stood, alone she was, there was no sign of her double anywhere within the scope of the mirror. The absence of her shadow was more troubling than her presence.

"Hello? Are you there?" She leaned forward, the sink pushing into her stomach. "I need to talk to you, please? I want to know who you are and why you are here?" The continuing silence frustrated her. "Please… I only want to understand," she begged. "Maybe I can help you?" The words faded into silence. Still she searched for her double, scrutinising the surface before her, looking at herself and then trying to look deeper through herself. The previous days and the migraine had left her tired, her eyes sunken in greyness, her skin sallow and pale, but she was oblivious to her own blanching, too busy searching for her own shadow.

In those few moments in the shop, Siân had got used to her ghost's presence, and now being alone felt wrong in a way she could not put into words; it was a feeling of isolation, abandonment, and a prickling that would not go away. Part of her felt lost, separated from the rest; if only she knew what was going on. Ffi was away for the day, setting up the new exhibition. Mandy would not understand, and Ryan; well, he was not back yet, and a thing like this could terminate their relationship before it truly began. The energy drained from her, the impetus gone, the anger now diffused and fading; cleaning and consigning was exhausting, and so was searching for spirits. She had only one option, to hit the internet; perhaps there she would find some answers, some significance to what she had seen.

The laptop, bulky and black, lay across the brown armchair by the fireside. The wires curled under and around the chair to the phone point. Switching on the power point and then the machine, it bleeped into life. While it awoke from its slumber and loaded whatever it had to that made so much noise and took so long, Siân made herself a piping hot mug of peppermint tea. The computer ran slow; it had not even been a recent edition when she had been gifted it to help her at university, yet it still worked and that was what mattered. When, after a few minutes, the laptop was ready for use, she made herself comfortable on the armchair, fidgeting then falling back into its firmness and familiarity. A few taps on the keyboard brought up a couple of search engines. She typed in the word 'doppelgänger' and the page showed her thousands of results, the majority of which did not appear to be much help with her research. A few mouse clicks led to an encyclopaedia detailing what a doppelgänger was. Scanning through the confusing terminology, Siân saw the words she had known she would see but hoped she would not.

Doppelgängers were an omen of bad luck and/or death. References to astral projection, bilocation, fylgja and vardøgr – whatever they were – only confused her. Outside, the sky darkened quickly; the dusky, yellow light and sudden crispness in the air gave only a fleeting warning before the heavens opened. The rain was hard, the globules large; they smacked against the windows and the roof, making a thunderous din. Glad of the shelter, she reached out to her hot mug and cradled it in her hands, expecting the comforting warmth to warm her skin. Instead it failed to reach her, and her hands remained cold and clammy. Bringing her attention back to the screen, she flicked through several more pages of text, which concurred with what she had formerly read rather than providing her with additional information.

Deciding to change the parameters of her search, she typed in 'ghost' as a search term. As she depressed the enter key, the wires under and around her fizzed and popped. Sparks flew from the power point, blackening the wall. Siân shrieked in surprise and brought her hands up to her head defensively. The laptop's screen went dark as it lost power; the powering-down noise was drowned out by electrical crackling and the rain outside. Siân pushed the laptop away from her with the back of her good hand and, as she made physical contact, the screen flashed back into existence, only for a microsecond, barely enough to be noticed. The Ring of Maidens flashed before her, the picture she had uploaded to be the laptop's wallpaper. It was not a great picture, taken as it had been on a murky summer's day. When next she saw Ryan she was planning to ask him for a digital copy of one of the pictures he had taken of the Ring of Maidens at sunset. Preferably one that did not show her, as she had never liked pictures of herself. The crackling ceased as the electricity supply failed entirely. Pushing the laptop to the floor, she dashed through to the kitchen and checked the fuse box. The trip switch had gone, so she reset it, and switched on the kitchen light to see if that sorted the problem. The light resolutely refused to light up. She rubbed her lips together in consternation; that was her limited electrical know-how exhausted.

Rummaging in the kitchen drawers for some candles, she was thankful that there was at least some light left in the miserable day this was turning out to be. Heading back to the telephone, she picked up the receiver, to hear only the rain and her own breathing; there was no dialling tone. Reaching into the pocket of her mother's checked coat, she pulled out her mobile phone and tried that; it too was defunct.

Throwing on her coat and wellingtons, she paced down to her neighbours, stopping briefly to leap into the puddles, which were begging to be splashed in. Maisy was already looking out of her window as Siân approached and had the door open as she arrived.

"Come in, come in," she said, waving her arm in an overblown gesture of welcome. Her soft blue woollen cardigan swung with her arm. "Has your power gone too? I was watching one of my soaps and the telly popped at me, I think it might be ruined."

"Oh no." Siân knew how much her soaps meant to Maisy; often the characters were a kind of surrogate family to her own, who had long since left the nest. She patted Maisy on the arm.

"I would offer you some tea… Do you think it could be all this weather, all these storms we keep having?"

"Probably. Will you be all right, or can I get you anything?"

Maisy's head shook slightly from side to side. "I'll be fine, dear. Alfred will be back soon; he's taken the car in for a service. Oh, he'll have got caught in all this rain, and I won't be able to get the heating on. Seems so silly when we have all those wind turbines so nearby, doesn't it? I guess it can't be helped."

Siân followed Maisy through to the living room, with its vivid floral wallpaper and furnishings. "I've a gas canister and camping fire if you want to borrow it; that way you can make him a nice hot cup of tea," she offered.

"Thanks, Siân. I should be able to get the fire on the go with a bit of help. Would you mind, only my hips aren't too keen on me crawling on the floor."

"Sure." Siân sank to her knees before the fireplace and piled up some logs from the copper coal scuttle. Using some old papers rolled together for kindling, and the matches Maisy handed to her, she soon had glowing flames roaring in the fireplace. She held her hands, palms out, to the intense heat, longing for the fire to warm her frozen flesh.

CHAPTER TWENTY-EIGHT

On their way to Preseli, the professor and Ryan took multiple detours; a couple of places had converted into a stop / start programme of leaping in and out of the vehicle and in and out of the rain. They visited site after site, cromlech after standing stone, each as drab and damp as the next. Ryan was becoming increasingly wet and miserable. The professor, though equally wet, revelled in the experience and the excitement, his enthusiasm rekindled by his explorations as he soaked up the atmosphere and ambience. Ryan was struggling to keep his camera dry as he listened to Trevivian talk on and on in excited tones about each site. He enjoyed the narration; it gave him something to focus on, other than the damp clothes that stuck to his skin or the trees overhead dripping rain down the back of his neck.

Siân must have learned her art from the professor; they both talked with the same exuberance and candour. He realised how much he had missed being with Siân. It had been less than a day that they had been apart for, still it seemed far too long, an unwanted eternity. Ryan became aware that, for the first time since they had set off that morning, the professor was silent. He was leaning with his left side against one of the rocks of what once would have been a burial chamber. The rock was half hidden under the overgrown hedgerow. He was turned away from Ryan, attempting to hide his distress until it wore off; only it was not going away. Trevivian was breathing hard, his whole body moving with the effort of each breath. His right arm hung heavily by his side, while his left was clutched close to his chest, both hands balled as fists and his eyes bulging with the pain. He held back coughing for as long as he could; once he began, would he ever be able to stop? The tickling in his throat was driving him mad and at last he gave in.

"Trev? Are you OK?" Ryan rushed over to him. The professor nodded but did not speak; it was too much effort for him. Ryan took his arm gently, to help him back to the car. Trevivian winced in further pain and shook Ryan off, making the OK sign with his hand. This close, Ryan could see the veins in Trevivian's neck and forehead pulsing erratically. "I think we'd better get you back to the car, you've been pushing yourself way too hard."

Trevivian nodded in both annoyance and defeat, and allowed Ryan to lead him the short way along the footpath back to the car park. They climbed into the shelter of the four by four and remained there in silence for a few minutes. The professor stared resolutely ahead as he tried to get his breathing back, not wanting Ryan to see him struggling, as he did not want to worry his friend. By now he was getting used to the failings of his own mortal shell, but others' reactions to it he could not get used to. Damn it, he knew he was dying, everyone has to die sometime; it was time people got used to it and allowed him some damn dignity. Ryan also stared ahead through the dappled windscreen, to give the professor some time and space to recuperate. Eventually he said, "I can take you home if you want, we don't have to do this today, we can come back another time."

Trevivian cast Ryan a filthy look and shook his head emphatically. "No," he aspirated. "We go on."

"Are you sure, only…" said Ryan.

"We go on!" he repeated, with even more tenacity.

"Well, you'll be assured of a good meal where we're going; you'll be feeling better in no time," Ryan said to reassure himself, as well as his friend. Trevivian patted Ryan's hand, which was resting on the gear stick, with fatherly affection, then pointed ahead to the road. Ryan got the hint. "Let's go then, shall we?"

* * *

Leaving Maisy warming herself before the fire, waiting for her husband's return, Siân headed back out into the rain. It had eased into a constant, even drizzle, the kind that seeps through your clothes without you noticing until you find yourself thoroughly soaked through. A car pulled into the lane, its wheels grinding on and disturbing the gravel. Siân turned around, not expecting any cars to be coming down here at this time of day; she was surprised to see a police car slowly driving towards her. The occupant opened the window a little way. "Get in; I need to speak to you," called Officer Nash from within. Siân acquiesced, nervously, not sure why he needed to speak to her with such urgency as his voice seemed to suggest. She dreaded what he had to say.

"I've just been to see your friend," he said flatly.

Siân coughed; why did she not like this conversation? "Oh, yes?"

"Yes. There was no one there."

"She was probably out."

"You misunderstand me. There was no one there, and the front door was wide open."

Siân turned to face him directly. "What?"

Constable Nash looked closely at her, watching her reaction. "I don't mean to worry you. How did your friend take losing her job?"

"She was angry, but I don't think she'd go around breaking windows. Her husband was at risk from redundancy; he works at Newport Accounting so the timing sucked, but, even with that, she's not going to be that stupid. In some ways she was glad to be out of there; it's not exactly a fun place to work. Lloyd has a funny way of running things."

"And the relationship with her husband, how was that?"

She wriggled in the uncomfortable car seat. "Where are you going with this? Has something happened to one of them?"

The policeman leaned forward, fixing his hazel eyes on her. "All I know at the moment is that apparently there were a series of serious arguments last night at your friend's house; they disturbed several neighbours with shouting, objects being thrown, and so forth. Then apparently they drove off in one hell of a hurry, burning rubber into their driveway in the middle of the night, and they've not been seen since. One of the neighbour's children said that the daughter had not been at school today. None of the neighbours have any idea where they might have gone. Have you?"

Siân's mouth formed a perfect circle in shock.

"Have you any idea where Amanda is, or where her daughter is right now?"

"Um, no."

"What about family, friends, people they might take off and stay with?" Constable Nash got out his notebook, and his pen hovered over paper hopefully.

"Her parents live in Portugal now; they go over once a year to visit them in the summer. She has a brother in Liverpool. Andrew, Andrew…" She struggled to remember what Mandy's maiden name had been, her face screwed up with concentration; it was right on the tip of her tongue. "Woodley, yes, Woodley. He runs a Driving School, named it after himself, says a lot about him. They've never got on though. To be honest, I don't know anything much about Pete's side of the family; I'm not even sure he's got much of one. As for friends, most of them are local, around here. I'm probably her best friend; she's also good friends with Ffion, who owns the pub, and Mari, who lives up at Fferm Ffynon. She was also good friends with Cerys somebody, but she moved away. Pete's friends tend to be his colleagues; I think his best friend is a guy from work called Mike, or is it Mick? Something like that anyway."

"My concern is for your friend's daughter right now; in light of that I'm going to file a missing person's report when I get back to the station. If you hear anything from any of them, you must let me know. Let's hope that they've just decided to go off on an impromptu holiday."

"Do you think they're all right?"

He tried to reassure her. "Probably, most people turn up after a few days after letting off steam. Sorry, I have to get back to the station; the radio and phone have gone completely dead. Take care of yourself, yes? And let me know the moment you hear anything from any one of them."

Siân nodded dumbly and got out of the car. She watched as the police car turned around in her drive before heading back to the main street. The drizzle coated her hair, her skin and her clothes in a delicate mist of water droplets, like a thousand tiny crystal balls. Each showed the Ring of Maidens and starry skies above.

* * *

The mists hung heavily over the mountains; Trevivian and Ryan were into the mountains before they even saw them coming. Sheep bleated miserably from nearby fields, their woolly cream coats obscuring them in the mist. The road ahead appeared to be leading to nowhere, or perhaps the land of Fairy. Thorn trees hung on a ridge, bowing over the road menacingly, while black and red pillars on the other side lay at peculiar angles, no doubt from where vehicles had left the road behind. Dusk was swiftly approaching; the mist was darkening before their eyes. They thought they knew where they were, but the signs and local landmarks they recognised from previous trips seemed somehow different in the misty half-light.

Trevivian recognised the gates to the cemetery; they were close to the Ring of Maidens. "What a spooky atmosphere; what do you say to getting a few pictures of the Maidens? If ever there was a time to see shadows and ghosts, this is it. You might even be able to catch some on camera this time. That would be an interesting aside for the book."

Ryan's brow furrowed. "Professor, you're crazy! The weather is awful, you're clearly not feeling too good, and it's getting dark. I don't fancy getting lost on the moors tonight…"

"Ah, but this is the perfect time. Don't you remember all those ghost stories and children's tales of the veil between the worlds? At dusk and dawn, and certain times of the year, we find ourselves in in-between times, when the barriers between this world and the Otherworld are said to be as thin as can be; so thin that beings can cross from one to the other. The dead and the Fairy can come into our world and the very brave or very stupid can journey to theirs. Mortals may think only a day has passed in Fairyland, but hundreds of years have passed away in our world, and all their friends and family are long dead. Did you never hear the tale of Tam Lin?"

"Not that I know of." There was now pavement by the side of the widening road. "We're almost at the pub, and I for one want a hot drink and a hot meal. We can do the Ring of Maidens first thing tomorrow."

Knowing when not to argue, Trevivian responded as they pulled into the pub car park. "Sure, first thing tomorrow. What do you recommend for our dinner?"

"Steak and ale pie," said Ryan, with his hand on the door release. "You go straight in; I'll bring the stuff in."

Trevivian headed straight for the door, and as he opened it a welcome blast of warm air and scent of cooking hit him. He removed his glasses, wiped the raindrops from them and popped them back on. He surveyed the room. At the bar, a young woman was eating what looked like melted ice cream from a tub, while talking to a young man with messed up black hair. Their heads were so close they were almost touching, in their secret, intense conspiracy. They were the only souls in the place. Presumably even the regulars had been kept in their homes by the weather.

Trevivian coughed politely as he neared the bar to attract attention. The young woman looked up, a vision of pale skin, dyed red and black hair, heavy kohl lined eyes and a black and red velvet vampire-inspired dress. "Hiya, what can I get you?" she said cheerfully, spoon still in hand.

"Erm, two steak and ale pies, two mugs of tea and two rooms please," Trevivian replied.

"Tad!" she shouted at the top of her voice. Trevivian was shocked that someone so petite could be so loud. She had almost blown him backwards with the noise. Ryan came through the door, groaning with the weight of all the luggage he had brought in. Seeing the girl behind the bar, he greeted her. There was no doubt who she was from the description Alun had given; the bold hair and jewellery and the strong resemblance to Alun. "Hi, you must be Lowri."

"Yup. You must excuse us; we've no power so we're winging it right now. I've been back, like, five minutes and already Tad's got me behind the bar."

"Oh, I see." Trevivian looked around the room. He had wondered at the darkness in the room, and now he saw the reason; the room was lit only by the fire and a candle on each table.

Alun appeared from the corridor, beaming as he saw Ryan. "Welcome back! Couldn't stay away, eh? At least you've stayed out of the mud this time around. How long will you be wanting to stay this time?"

The professor butted in. "Two rooms, three nights."

"OK, we've plenty of space. Sorry, I should have introduced myself. I'm Alun, and you are?"

"Gavan Trevivian; everyone calls me Trev." They shook hands.

"A Cornishman? You're most welcome. What can I get you? You must have some dinner. What doesn't get eaten will only get chucked, power's gone. Thank God we've got a gas oven and a good fireplace."

The Gothic beauty piped up, "They want steak and ale pie and two teas; can we do tea?"

Alun scratched his stubble. "Yeah, we've got a whistler, I can bung it on the hob."

"Can I have one as well then, puh-lease?" asked his daughter. She did not wait for an answer, but instead resumed her hushed conversation with the lad at the bar who sat nursing a beer. He cast daggers at Ryan.

"Shall I show you to your rooms? Ryan, are you OK with the green room again?"

Ryan nodded as he picked up the luggage. Alun led them through and up the stairs. Ryan made his way to his room, while Alun showed the professor the adjacent room, with a bright turquoise door.

CHAPTER TWENTY-NINE

After freshening up and changing into dry clothes, the two men regrouped in the bar room, where two steaming hot mugs of dark tea awaited them, on the table closest to the roaring fire. Logs crackled noisily as they burned.

"How're you feeling, Trev?" asked Ryan, searching his companion's pallid face for an answer.

"Much better, now that I'm warmed up. The damned damp is the problem, makes me cough so much and yes, I know it's getting worse." The warm air of the pub and the vague scent of pine from some of the logs were enabling him to breathe more easily than he had done for quite some time.

Sensing that Trevivian did not want to discuss the matter any further, Ryan turned their conversation to the job in hand. He smoothed out the map on the table. "Where else did you want to go tomorrow?"

"So many places. You can't wander around for more than five minutes round here without falling over a standing stone or cairn. Where do you still need to photograph?"

"Don't worry about that, where do you want to go?" Ryan picked up his mug and began to sip the hot tea.

Trevivian grinned mischievously. "Everywhere. Would your friend like to come? She would be more than welcome. I'd like to see how she's getting on. "

Colour flushed to Ryan's face as he spoke awkwardly, "She's probably working".

"You haven't asked her yet?"

He leaned in. "I don't know where she lives, only where she works."

The professor caught the approaching Alun out of the corner of his eye. "Why don't we ask our host?"

153

"Professor!"

Alun overheard the last section of the conversation. "Two pies, tuck in. What did you want to ask me, gentlemen?"

"Where does Siân Derwyn live?"

"I'm not sure I should be telling you that, even you, Ryan. That's for her to tell you when she's ready, she's a private one. I'll give you her phone number though. I'm sure she'd be keen to hear from you when the phones are working again. From the latest gossip it sounds like she's had a rough couple of days." Alun noted the number on the corner of the map. "Dyna ni."

"Is she all right?" Ryan leapt to his feet, almost knocking the chair over.

"She's OK; the shop's been having a few, how should I say, problems lately. Didn't you see it on your way in? Someone's smashed all the windows."

Ryan sat down again. "We came the other way in. What was that about the phones; are they not working either?"

"No, it's like the good old days. Lowri's livid she can't call anyone or check her emails. How did we all cope before technology, eh?"

Trevivian pushed his glasses up his nose. "This is why my typewriter is so marvellous; unlike your laptop, she works!"

Ryan gave the professor a look, that of a child being berated for something silly. "Alun, have you any idea how long it'll all be down for?"

"No, but I reckon it'll be a while yet. Sorry, I must get some cleaning done before I go and get Ffi. Today was the start of her big showing at the Green Gallery in Swansea and she'll murder me if she comes back home and thinks I've left it for her to do."

"I hope it went well for her."

"So do I," prayed Alun under his breath. "So do I."

"Are these your wife's pictures?" Trevivian nodded towards the nearest wall, adorned like the others with artwork.

"Yup, there's not a wall in the place without one of her pictures on. Enjoy your dinner, gentlemen."

The young man at the bar watched Alun returning to the kitchen. He scowled across at the two other guests, muttering to himself under his breath. He downed the last of his beer, said something to Lowri which left her with an expression of puzzlement, and then stood up and went over to Ryan to vent his frustration.

"So you think you can come back here whenever you feel like it?" he growled. "What, did your other girlfriend kick you out? Siân deserves better than you, city boy. She deserves someone who'll be there for her, forever, not just when he wants a shag."

Ryan stared straight ahead, not wanting to give anything to this young idiot. He was not going to get drawn into an argument or a fight. He continued to eat his meal. Trevivian glanced from one young man to the other, and kept his head down too.

Lowri called over from the bar, "Huw, go home mate." It was an order, not a request. Huw shrugged and left.

"I'm so sorry about him, he can be such a grumpy sod," she complained. "Without that, he might just make good boyfriend material," she added quietly.

Trevivian found it all highly amusing. "I see you have yourself a rival for the maiden's affections."

Ryan shrugged and drank the last of his tea; he did not know what to say. Having a rival for a girl's affections was not a situation he was familiar or comfortable with.

To break the overlong silence, Trevivian tried to assure his young travelling companion. "Don't worry lad, I think he's jealous because she fancies you. He'll get over it."

Ryan raised an eyebrow and turned his attention to the pictures on the walls. Trevivian followed his line of sight. "I rather like that one, the grey cat. Reminds me of a student. Right little pain he was, brilliant mind, but far too arrogant and lazy. He used to sit there preening during lectures, always trying to catch the eye of some girl or other. That one there has to be my favourite."

Ryan turned around and looked to where the professor was indicating.

"The hawk?"

"Yes, he's magnificent. His eyes are so full of power and intelligence. It's almost as though he were looking right through me; no, make that at me. Well, Gavan means white hawk, he must recognise a kindred spirit." The professor laughed.

Trevivian set down his knife and fork neatly on his plate. "I'm full. That was delicious." He sighed contentedly and pushed his chair back to give his stomach space. "Are any of these for sale, do you know?"

Ryan was still eating; he gulped down his mouthful. "Most seem to have little price tags on."

"Splendid. Back in a second." The professor stood up and walked across to the hawk picture, checking the price, which, to him, seemed very reasonable for such a quality piece. The hawk's yellow eyes followed him. He stood there, studying the picture intently. The hawk was perched atop a yew tree; those prickly spikes were unmistakable. The bird of prey was painted beautifully; the beak, the feathers, the talons, all so three-dimensional. Trevivian peered closer, half-expecting the bird to launch off the canvas into flight. In the background, possibly by the base of the yew, stood a trilithon, two upright stones capped by a third horizontal stone. The trilithon loomed, a gateway to the beyond; it gaped wide open, menacing yet inviting. Above it stood a planet or possibly the moon, grey and blue in appearance with a misty halo of pale light. The planet had been painted in a sparkly paint, which helped it to glow and radiate off the image. The professor sighed as the painting absorbed him, his breath momentarily clouding the canvas with condensation.

Alun emerged from the kitchen, wrapped up in a robust dark coloured coat and dangling his car keys from his hand. "Right, I'm off out for a while, gentlemen. If you need anything, ask Lowri here and I'm sure she'll do her best to help." He turned to his daughter. "Won't you, please?"

Lowri nodded and smiled, the ice cream spoon still in her mouth.

Alun saw Trevivian standing close to the painting of the hawk and he saw the resemblance. Trevivian had very hawklike features; the sharp nose, angular chin, fingers that tapered like talons, penetrating eyes and the same quick intelligence. He had heard Ryan address him as Professor; that fitted. He knew how his wife liked to introduce people to their totem or guardian animal through her art and through her work, empowering them to make that connection to learn and live more fully, or some such thing. Here before him was a case in point; Trevivian was connecting as he watched with his own animal spirit, the wise and spiritual hawk. Alun smiled wryly to himself, wondering how many other people had done the very same thing today through the exhibition.

He checked his watch; the weather was terrible, so he hoped he was leaving himself enough time to get to the station before Ffi's train arrived at Fishguard.

He headed for the main door. "Well, gents, I'll see you in the morning for breakfast."

"Bye," said Ryan. There was no response from Trevivian; Alun was gone before his words roused him from his deep concentration. Lowri popped out to collect their plates. "Will you be wanting any dessert; there's some apple pie and some chocolate cake that should still be all right."

"I'll have some apple pie, please. Trev, would you like any?"

Trevivian's voice was distant, dreamy. "Any...?" he echoed.

"Any dessert?"

"No, no. Couldn't possibly manage another morsel. Wouldn't mind another cup of tea though. And I'd like to buy this painting if I can."

* * *

From deep in the shadows, Badden watched the pub landlord drive away into the night; at least he had the sense to keep well out of it, unlike his silly, interfering wife. He sat outside the pub in the car that belonged to his body, glaring at the four by four which belonged to the lad still inside. How dare he come back? How dare he show his face around here again? More to the point, how had he come back? How had he got through the stormy and misty miasma, the enchanted boundary that he had set up? He had poured so much energy and power into it; how on this mortal earth had he breached it? Badden was furious; his blood boiled, and rushed wildly in his ears. A primal scream raged inside him, the scream of the wild animal within. Every muscle tensed in pure, unadulterated hatred of his rival.

Was this the pathetic boy child, Owein, come back to exact his revenge? No matter, he had killed him once; doing so again would double the pleasure. Had Gwalchwen found a way to interfere; had the hawk called the boy back? Or had Morwyna called to him? No! Morwyna would love him this time. He would make sure of that this time around; this time she would welcome him with open arms and they would be together for the rest of time. Badden glowered hatefully at the four by four, hoping that with his fiery hateful gaze he could set it alight, even on this dank evening. Then he could push Owein into the flames and watch as he burned to death, screaming in terror and pain. His eyes narrowed with intent focus; if looks could kill he would be long rid of

Owein, or whatever he called himself in this life. Ah but even he was not that powerful… yet. Instead, subjected to his piercing glare, bubbles and blisters began to appear in the black paintwork as the metal underneath became hotter and hotter. Steam poured from the vehicle into the cold of the night and Badden felt a sense of satisfaction.

* * *

"You'll never believe who bought the Gwyllgi picture," Ffi said to her husband as they drove back from the station.

"Who?" asked Alun obediently, in automatic husband mode. His concentration was firmly locked on the road ahead. The rain was so heavy now that the windscreen wipers could not keep up. The windscreen was a wall of running water. The limited visibility and the nature of the roads made Alun hyper aware. Accidents were common in these conditions, he knew that, but he was determined that it would not happen to them.

"Arabella Sinclair-Pierce. She loved it, claimed it was perfect for her new Gothic pad in Oxfordshire. I was so thrilled. She was quite nice, actually; I thought she'd be a right snob, but she was ever so charming. She even came to my talk."

"Who is she?"

"The actress, well, socialite, really. She's in all those trendy gossip magazines that Lowri reads."

"Eh?"

Ffi continued, the excitement of the day still coursing through her veins. "I also sold two to Taimi Kivela, the Finnish art expert. I'm not expecting you to know who she is," Ffi laughed. "She's expressed an interest in selling some of my pictures as prints. Can you believe it? She has galleries in London and every major Scandinavian city! At this rate I'll have sold them all before the week's gone."

Her husband still looked resolutely ahead. He was driving by instinct; he knew these roads well and was following the markers of the twists, turns and bumps. "That's great news. Lowri's back, by the way."

"Oh, lovely, I can't wait to see her." Ffi's heart rose with joy at the prospect of seeing her daughter again.

Alun nodded. "Now the bad news. We've had a major power cut, been off all afternoon."

"Oh no," Ffi interjected.

"We also have two guests with us for a while. Ryan's back already, and he's brought his boss, Trev. Nice old bloke, bit frail. Definitely a hawk; as I left he was standing stock-still, staring at your hawk picture, the one in the bar."

"A hawk… Oh, Alun! Do you remember what I said about the goshawk at the Ring of Maidens? Is it him, come to help us, come to help Siân and Ryan? I must speak to him as soon as possible."

The car stalled and the engine died. Alun turned the key over and over to try and get the engine going again. "Damn, sorry, love. I don't know what happened there." He paused. "I'll get her going again in a minute." The mist outside thickened and the rain eased off. Their hearing became clearer as the constant splatter of the rain faded; small sounds from the moorland around them suddenly became audible. Ffi watched as the mist thickened, becoming a dense wall of white all around them. The high beams of the foglights could not penetrate the wall at all. Closer and closer came the wall of mist; a cocoon of white that ensnared them as it wrapped tighter and tighter. Alun and Ffi found their breathing becoming shallower and more frequent as the mist moved in. Through the vents and the old window seals it seeped, coming ever closer. The temperature in the car dipped, the white form freezing the air within it. The couple gasped for air, feeling stifled and suffocated.

"Why don't you go and check the engine or the battery or whatever it is?" Ffi asked.

"I'm not getting out of the car," Alun said in a low monotone. "Check the mirror."

Ffi raised herself up from her seat and looked into the mirror. Two red lights and a dark shadow in the mist looked right back at her. She raised her hand to her mouth to stifle a gasp. "The Gwyllgi?"

"What do you know? Jim was telling the truth after all."

Ffi spoke through her fingers, still clasped to her face. "What can we do?"

"You tell me, love. Do you know of any way to get rid of him? Any spells, prayers or the Druidic equivalent of a big stick for him to run after?"

"I've not heard of anything that'll see off a demon dog."

"What about silver bullets or crucifixes, eh?" He put his hand over his wife's to give her courage and to show her affection.

"I don't know. Black Shuck went into two Norfolk churches and killed people in the midst of services, so I don't think a crucifix will work."

Alun looked on as the Gwyllgi came closer. The shadow became more defined in form; he was a huge creature; he could take a man out in no time. The Gwyllgi's red eyes and black shape lowered to the ground in one silent move. "He's lying down now. Waiting, watching us. What can we do?"

"Try the engine again. Let's see if we can get out of here."

Alun turned the key repeatedly. He put more effort into it, almost breaking the key in half. "Where is 'here'? I know these roads like the back of my hand and I have no idea. By my reckoning we went down the dip with the ford, then we should have come to the turn down towards Brynberian, but there was no turn."

"Let's not worry about that right now, let's get out of here. Keep trying." Ffi closed her eyes and called with her heart to the God and the Goddess. She smiled broadly as her mind turned to the most appropriate Goddess to ask for assistance. Quickly, she composed a short mantra or spell to call on Elen, the Goddess of the roads, of the paths and the way ahead.

"Elen of the old trackways, Ancestors of blood and bone, protect us from this strange haze; please get us both safely home."

Over and over, Ffi repeated her plea, until, at last, Alun persuaded the engine back to life. The guttural chugging of the engine startled the Gwyllgi, who slunk away into the mist, the red light of his eyes growing more indistinct and fainter until they were gone.

CHAPTER THIRTY

Trevivian was exhausted, but sleep would not come. He sat in bed, leafing through his notes and books by the gentle light of several candles. Lowri had been kind enough to dig out a multitude of blankets and more candles than anyone could possibly have needed; they made the room cosy and warm. The thrill of being here, in the heart of the Preseli Mountains, surrounded by so much history, kept him awake. How he wished he had spent more time studying the pictures by candlelight, the soft light enhancing the black and white photographs, giving them life. He looked from his notes to the map that lay across his legs, which had many of the sites marked upon it. Why were there so many ancient monuments clustered together in this relatively small area of South West Wales? What was so special about this area way back when? He longed to truly understand them, to understand why they were built and by whom. All the generations, all the people who had built the magnificent monuments, worshipped or communed, or buried at them, all those since who had stood in awe as they looked at them, the weight of all of their souls hung heavily on him. How he longed to be able to talk to them, to ask so many questions; but that was impossible.

The monuments themselves were beautifully and lovingly crafted; moving and carving them must have been an enormous task, yet still they did it and with such passion and honour. To Trevivian, they were the most esoteric enigma in the whole world, and a mystery that maddeningly could never be truly solved. This was their charm and also their curse. Theories came and went, then came back again as though stuck on a loop, only the voices changed. After a lifetime of study and theorising, he was little closer now to understanding their great mysteries than he had been as a young boy looking at the Hurlers in awe.

After writing up his notes for the day, the first time in three years that he had written in his field notebook, he pulled the map closer. Intently he searched the sheet, looking for patterns or signs marked out by the monuments, praying for an epiphany before he succumbed to the mortality of his feeble shell. As the night went on, the candles burned lower and the professor's glasses moved gently further down his nose until they almost fell off. Trevivian pinched the end of his nose and pushed his glasses back up. Sighing, he checked the time on his old and trusted watch, a wedding present from his dear wife. It was still in the wee hours, people would not be stirring yet for an hour or so, and dawn was still a long way off at this time of year.

The stones called to him through the earth, their deep voices responding to his yearning to understand them. Trevivian resolved to go and pay his respects to the Ring of Maidens, to wait and watch as dawn came over the mountains, and while he was waiting he could survey the stones and map out their strange egg shape. He got dressed, collected together his field kit and dug out his set of car keys from the bottom of his satchel. He rapped his knuckles softly on Ryan's door, wanting to wake only Ryan and not the rest of the house. A series of loud snores was the reply. 'Let him sleep,' thought Trevivian, 'He has been working hard and travelling for weeks, he needs some rest.'

Holding one of the candles before him like a lantern, he made his way down the stairs, feeling his way with his other hand. The pub's dog welcomed him as he reached the bottom of the stairs. His tail wagged violently against the professor's legs, nearly knocking him off his feet. "Aren't you a friendly lad?" he said as he stroked the dog's ears, with their short soft fur. Bryn circled the professor, blocking each step he tried to make towards the door. Trevivian tried repeatedly to step over the golden retriever but the dog was too high and he was too frail. "You're a good guard dog. They've trained you well," he said as he shuffled to the door. Bryn barked, a short sharp bark, and looked up at the coat rack to his lead.

"Shhh, they're all asleep. Sorry, lad. Your master will take you out later." Trevivian reached out to the door handle, and opened the door a little way. Bryn whined and shifted on his front paws, blocking the door from fully opening with his backside. Trevivian looked into his big brown eyes and soppy face. "You're good. I'm not usually one to respond to emotional blackmail. I'd love to take you out, but your family would be very worried if they woke up and you weren't here." Bryn moved aside and nuzzled his nose against the man's legs. Trevivian squeezed past and out of the door, closing it quietly behind him. Bryn licked his lips and whined pitifully, louder this time.

Trevivian walked soundlessly over the tarmac to the four by four. The cold air invigorated and awakened his soul. He expected it to be coated in a thick layer of ice on a night this brisk, but the car was warm to the touch and the paintwork was blistered. Trevivian frowned; that was most peculiar; well, there was nothing he could do about it now and he did not want to. The past was calling him. He climbed in and drove the short way along winding roads to the lay-by that served as the parking spot for visitors to the Ring of Maidens. Trevivian got out of the car, shut the driver's door, and opened the boot, where he packed a few things together; his large torch, tape measure and his current field notebook, which he hung from his neck. These were old friends, too long ignored.

Apart from the scuffling noises that he made in the boot of the four by four, there was utter silence in the valley. Not a bird or animal stirred; all were still and silent. As Trevivian passed through the gate, from which the battered metal sign for the Maidens hung, a strange noise surrounded him. He looked down, turning the torch downward to illuminate his boots. Beneath him, the ground was covered with the thickest, crispest white hoarfrost he had encountered in his seven decades. With each step he took, the ground crunched beneath his feet, and the noise then bounced back from the hills that surrounded him. In awe, he considered the landscape around him, the hills cradling the circle as though in a womb or cauldron. Was this the cauldron of the ancient Goddess Ceridwen? The mythical cauldron that was the source of inspiration, known as Awen. Or was this one of many that existed? Was that the effect that the ancient peoples were trying to achieve here? He felt privileged to be here; he always felt that way at these places; they had the holy aura of quiet that could also be found in cathedrals and majestic forests.

Another noise, a soft crumbling behind him, caught his attention. Trevivian turned and shone the torch behind him; his footsteps were marked where he had flattened the frost on the grass and mud, but there was no sign of anything else. He shrugged his shoulders and shook his head; he had only gone and spooked himself. It was probably a solitary badger making his way back to the sett. He ploughed on; grass gave way to gorse and shrubs, which attacked the hems of his trousers, pulling at the threads and his bootlaces. Rocks protruded awkwardly from the bushes; the hoarfrost had made intricate, chaotic patterns in the ice. Curls, swirls and spikes reflected back in the torchlight.

The professor regretted not waking Ryan to come with him; he could have captured the delicate designs digitally for posterity, and the company would have been good. He was starting to regret coming out here on his own; the ice underfoot was treacherous; if he went over, would he get back up again? Curiosity drove him onwards towards the Ring; he wanted to see what patterns the ice had formed on them. Would they be like those on the debris rocks, or would they be something more intricate? He had heard a lecture not long ago about strange patterns forming in water where unusual electro-magnetic forces were present, forces which many claimed could be found at ancient stone circles and monuments.

The quiet of the night was unsettling. Trevivian was becoming more and more convinced that he was being followed, stalked by someone or something that he could not see or hear. He told himself it was nonsense; he was alone here, and began to hum to keep himself company. At last he could see the circle ahead; several stones in an arc reflected the torchlight back to him, temporarily blinding him. They were covered in ice as the other stones had been, but this was out of this world. As he neared the stubby stones, he saw that the ice had formed a coating of diamond-shaped ice crystals all over the surface of the stone. He knelt down and broke one off, holding it tenderly between gloved thumb and forefinger. The heat from his body and his breath melted the crystal as he looked on, enchanted by its beauty, and water dripped away to the cold ground.

A prickling sensation on the back of his neck stirred Trevivian from his reverie. There it was, that sound again, like the soft swishing of clothes and a crumpling of ice. He started, startled; whatever it was that he could sense was close. His heart raced, thumping painfully against his ribcage. He shone his torch in the direction of the noise. "Who is it? Who's there?"

A shadow moved from behind one of the outlying stones to behind a dense gorse bush. Trevivian asked again as he straightened up, "Who is it? I can see you. Show yourself." The fight or flight response in his body was taking over. Adrenaline rushed through his veins, pushing his heart to work harder and his breathing to become shallow; his palms became clammy as the cold night air crept through his clothes and made him shiver and cough. The torch beam shook with his hacking coughs. "Who is it?"

"Fancy that. I wasn't expecting you, old man. But now that you're here, you won't be leaving. Don't you recognise me?" Badden stepped forward proudly, into the beam of the torch. He forced himself to stare down his opponent, despite the bright light which made his eyes water. "Your most talented student, not that you ever bothered to acknowledge that."

Trevivian stepped back, jarring his heel on one of the stones of the circle. "I don't know you… You're not one of my students…"

"Yes, I was. But I'm not a student any longer; I'm the Master now. My powers exceeded yours a long time ago." He held out his hand, held tight as an open fist, grabbing towards the old man's heart and squeezed.

"I think you have me confused with someone else." The professor held grimly on to his torch, still shone at the man's face as he backed away. The coughing was becoming more painful, his lungs burning with the gasps of cold air that he managed to take between coughs. His ribcage felt as though someone were squeezing it, crushing him or weighing him down.

"Oh no, I know who you are, even if you don't, Gwalchwen." Badden listened to the other man gasping for breath; he could hear and feel the old man's heart beating irregularly now; it would not be much longer. His face contorted as he squeezed his fist harder.

The pain in Trevivian's chest was worsening; his eyes were watering as they bulged from their sockets. Stabbing pains struck at his heart and all down his left arm and back, then crept up towards his neck and jaw. He recognised the symptoms of a heart attack and he realised that the stranger was not going to be of any help. He stumbled back towards the four by four, but it was a long way. Each step tired him and made the pain worse. Nausea overwhelmed his senses. He clutched at his heart with his hands, dropping the torch, which spiralled away into a patch of shrubs. Onwards he pushed himself, step by step, until his foot caught on a rock and over he went, face-first into the frost. The fall knocked the last of the air from his lungs; he gasped in agony but no breath could he get into his old body. Trevivian was damned if he was going to spend his last moment on earth face-down in the crud; he pushed himself over to lie on his back. The stars shone brightly above, their twinkling light bright tonight.

The cold of the ground worked its way under his clothes and under his skin, through to the bone. Numbness spread through his body, granting him some peace from the pain, which blackened the edges of his vision and clouded his mind. The figure stood over him, blocking out some of the radiant stars.

"Do you remember now, old man? Do you know who I am? Twice you have interfered, and twice you have paid for it. You are so weak! I will have Morwyna and there is nothing you can do." The stranger ranted on and on as life faded from his victim.

Trevivian's heartbeat slowed, and the throbbing pain diminished, leaving him feeling light-headed. Thinking was becoming difficult; thoughts were unclear, muddled, no longer making any sense. He blinked and no longer were the stars above him, but a thatched roof with smoke curling upwards. Here, as before, the stranger stood over him, ranting about a woman named Morwyna. He, for he knew it to be himself, but not himself, lay dying at the stranger's hands. Badden had his hands clasped firmly over his mouth and nose and was using his weight to hold him down on the floor, strewn with rushes. He felt no fear, no hatred, only a deep sadness and sense of pity for the man killing him. Then, as now, his heart failed him. He blinked again and the smoke from the fire became the faint light of the Milky Way high above him. The starlight faded from Trevivian's perception; star by star they blinked out until all was dark, then he felt the weight of his own body fall away into the earth and his soul soar into the sky on wings of light.

Badden looked on as his adversary's soul departed. He grabbed at the bird-shaped spirit with both hands, attempting to contain it. Badden did not want his enemy getting away that easily; he wanted to trap him forever within the outlying stone where he had been for so long. He wanted Gwalchwen to feel the pressure and pain of the rock and the passing of time. Once trapped, Gwalchwen's spell of protection laid around the stone circle would diminish and die, then Badden could use the power of the circle for whatever he wanted. The spirit slipped through Badden's chunky fingers, still sparkling and spiralling towards the Heavens on outstretched wings. Badden reached up to grab it again but the spirit danced out of reach, screeching as it flew higher and higher. A second hawk flew in from the mountains, hovering in mid-air to await its companion. Badden threw his head back and screeched an array of indistinct sounds at the hawks, his spell to prevent the two combining against him. The hawks screeched louder, their call shriller. As one flew upwards and the other across, the spirit hawk and the hawk merged into one; it circled the moor once before flying off.

Badden stood alone on the moor as the body of his enemy cooled. It gave him pleasure and pain in an intoxicating combination. To extinguish the life of another always made him feel more alive and more powerful; he felt invincible, a living God of destruction. Once, as a young child, all those centuries ago, Badden had dearly loved the old man who became his teacher. That was until the old man refused to teach him the dark magic that he longed to learn; that of power and control. From that moment onwards their relationship had spiralled to distrust, suspicion, and then open conflict. What use was herblore, treelore or starlore if you could not use it to benefit yourself, to poison and destroy your enemies and fulfil your desires? What use were the stories when he wanted to be their subject, to hear the tales of himself as the greatest and most powerful magician that ever lived? Forget Arthur, forget Myrddin, who were they anyway? He, Badden, had cheated death, as a spirit in stone through the centuries. Where were his stories to glorify and deify him?

He understood now how Owein had returned; the old man had helped, but Owein was on his own now. If only Owein had left the old man out of this. If only it had been Owein sneaking out alone tonight. Badden thought it had been Owein, he had been so certain. The four by four was Owein's vehicle, surely; that was what he had been driving around in for the last visit. No matter now, one adversary was gone; the other would be dispatched soon enough. A delay now was nothing after all these centuries of waiting, was it? Badden roared into the silent night a cry of frustration; the noise languished away into the still air. He was fed up with waiting, he had done enough waiting and watching from the shadows, now it was his turn. Today he would make his move.

CHAPTER THIRTY-ONE

"Professor?" Ryan tapped on the turquoise door of the professor's room. "Breakfast's being served." The door stayed shut. Ryan tried the door, but it was locked. Putting his ear to the door he listened for any noise from within. Perhaps he was already down there? Ryan made his way down the stairs towards the conservatory and was greeted not by the rich aromas of cooking but the carbon whiff of burning. The smoke alarm screamed into life and was greeted by a chorus of swear words from two voices.

"Good grief, is everything OK in there?" he asked, peeking into the kitchen and waving the smoke away from his face. Alun was waving a tea towel madly at the smoke alarm, trying to make it shut up, while Lowri removed blackened toast from the oven.

"Sorry! Sorry, I'm trying to make some toast with the grill and it's not bloody working. Oh God, this is like living in the Dark Ages!" She lost her temper and dropped the tray on the surface where it clanged loudly.

"Hush now; you'll wake your mother."

Lowri put her hands on her hips. "Oh yeah, like the fire alarm won't have done that already?"

Aware that their actions were being watched, and by a guest, Alun spoke to Ryan carefully. "Don't mind her, she's always a bit of a grump first thing in the morning, not that she sees many of them in."

"All I want is a cup of tea and some toast, is that really so much to ask for?" she whined. "And I can't have either cos of this stupid power cut."

"What? No tea?" Tea was what got Ryan going in the morning; without it he would be groggy for a while yet.

"Milk's gone off, well off. It's, like, lumpy."

"I can still do most of a cooked breakfast," Alun reassured him.

Bryn whined and paced in the conservatory. "I'll take you out after breakfast, boy. Ryan; would you mind letting him out into the garden for a bit, it should be open."

"Sure." Ryan slid the glass door open enough for Bryn to get through. Bryn sat down and groaned sulkily. "Don't you want to go out then?" The dog barked. "Doesn't seem like he wants to go out."

"Each to their own, I guess. He'll change his mind when he gets his lead on, then he'll want to be off like a shot."

Ryan took a deep breath. "Have you seen Trev yet this morning?"

Alun shook his head "He's probably still asleep. I don't mind doing his breakfast a bit later. Lowri, can you take Bryn out after breakfast?"

"Yep." She was raiding the cupboards in her search for breakfast.

Ryan tapped his fingers on the table. "I don't think so; I couldn't hear anything in his room."

"Maybe he went for a walk?" Lowri settled on just pouring some cereal on to a plate and eating it dry with her fingers. Without lashings of milk to soften it up it was pretty foul.

"He's not that well; he's been fighting cancer."

Seeing the worry blazoned across Ryan's face, Alun pulled a set of keys from his belt, and, selecting one with a blue dot on, he handed it through the hatch to Ryan. "That's the key to his room. If he is still asleep it's best if he's disturbed by someone he knows well."

"Thanks, Alun." He sped up the stairs and tapped again on the door. "Trev? Professor? Are you OK?" He paused with his heart in his mouth, hoping for a reply or at least a snore, some sound of life. "I'm going to unlock the door now." Fumbling with the key, he opened the door. There was no sign of Trevivian; although his bed had been slept in, books were spread everywhere and his luggage was here. Ryan moved through to the bathroom door; he knocked. "Professor? Hello?" The door was already open so he peered around it. The professor was not in there either.

Ryan was wide awake now; he raced out and almost bumped into Alun, who said, "Everything all right?"

"He's not there."

"Probably gone out for a morning walk, or to get a paper from the local shop. Don't worry so much." He was relieved to see Trevivian's belongings were still here; the last time a guest had gone astray he had gone with everything, without paying. "Where's his coat? If that's gone, you know he's popped out for a bit."

Ryan hunted around for the professor's coat. "It's not here; I guess he did go out then." He was about to give in, when he remembered the four by four. He looked out of the window, down to the car park below. "Trev's taken the car with him, he's gone off exploring on his own. Silly old sod!"

"Come and have some breakfast; if he's still not back after that, we'll go looking."

Ryan found eating his haphazard breakfast difficult; he was ravenously hungry but a feeling of unease made his stomach tighten. He rubbed his fingers together as a cold, tingling sensation crept over them. He made polite conversation with his hosts, but the thought of Trevivian rambling alone out in the cold morning made him feel uneasy. Inwardly he prayed the professor was OK. He did not mind that he had gone off exploring; Ryan knew that was on the cards the minute Trevivian suggested he come too. What worried him was how ill the professor was, and how easily the cold got to him.

Alun piled up the plates and took them through. "Where do you think Trev's gone then, eh?"

"Definitely one of the old monuments. One near a road. He can't walk too far anymore. I think it would be the Ring of Maidens first; he's been very keen to visit it again."

"Right, get your coat. We'll go in my car. Lowri, could you take Bryn out for a walk, but only go local in case Trev comes back while we're gone? Put your phone on in case they get the networks going again." Alun wrote a short note on the pad stuck to the fridge. He tore the paper off and passed it to Ryan with a piece of sticky tape. "Stick this on his door in case he comes back while we're out, then he knows to stay put. I don't want us all to be looking for each other all day."

"That's his!" Ryan almost shouted as he pointed to the four by four sitting in the lay-by. "That's his car."

Alun beamed at Ryan. "See, he's fine and there was you worrying. You worry far too much for such a young man."

Ryan was relieved at the sight of the professor's vehicle, but would not be totally at ease until he saw Trevivian safe and well. "I'd like to go and make sure..."

"I'll come with you. Bryn is going to know I've been here without him anyway; he's a clever bugger for a dog. Ffi reckons he's some reincarnated enlightened soul; I reckon he just knows things." Alan tapped the side of his nose.

A spider's web strung from the gate to its post, coated in a delicate layer of ice crystals. Alun frowned to himself. No one had been through here recently then. He faked his usual jollity as he noticed Ryan looking in his direction. The ground was soggy underfoot where the overnight ice had melted. A few areas still thick with ice remained in the shadows of stones and bushes where the sun had not yet reached. Alun unintentionally took the lead, as Ryan hung back, less sure of his footing.

Alun looked around, keeping his head high, searching for any sign of the professor as they walked. Up ahead he noticed something grey sticking out from behind one of the larger stones, which itself was half hidden by some bushes. One look told him all he needed to know; it was a hand and it was bluish-grey. A hand like that belonged to no living person. As they drew closer, Alun turned, and Ryan walked into him. "Ryan..." Alun began; he did not know what to say. He put his hands on Ryan's upper arms to comfort him and to hold him back.

"What?" Ryan already knew the answer; he stared over Alun's broad shoulder. "He's dead?" He shook off the other man and rushed towards Trevivian's body. He lay in a sheltered spot; ice hung on his clothes and had formed over the bare skin of his face. The eyes were glassy and pale; the skin was blue and sagged from the skull. The echo of a smile remained on his frozen face. Ryan fell to his knees by his old friend. His heart; it must have been his heart. His fingers searched for a pulse in Trevivian's neck and when he found none, he placed one hand over the other, over Trevivian's heart, to begin CPR.

Alun stopped him forcefully, pulling him upright by the scruff of his jacket. "No, Ryan, he's been gone a long time."

"I have to try..."

"Leave him be. Don't touch anything. There's nothing you can do, except say goodbye." Alun patted the boy's shoulder as he backed off. Ryan nodded dumbly.

"Take a moment. I'll wait over there. Then we'll have to report his death."

Ryan looked down on his friend, the first time he had seen a dead body. Empty sadness washed over him as the tears began to flow. He turned his eyes upwards and sniffed to stop the tears, and caught sight of a blurry bird flying in the distance. Ryan blamed himself; this was all his fault; he had brought the professor down to the mountains, he should have insisted he stay back in Cardiff. He knew deep down he could not have won that argument; once Trevivian had made up his mind, that was it. He sighed as tears rolled down his cheeks. Trevivian should not have died alone, but at least he was somewhere he loved. "Thanks for everything, my friend," he uttered quietly.

Alun put his arm around Ryan and led him back to the car. "We'll take a drive over to the police station. When someone dies there are certain things we have to do."

CHAPTER THIRTY-TWO

"Lloyd?" shouted Siân as she opened the shop door. "Are you in? Poop, it's so dark in here, ew, and something reeks!"

The empty window frames had been blocked with boards. There was only a little natural light in the shop from the open door and a few cracks between the boards. She flicked the light switch in the hope that power was back; clearly it was not yet. She left the door open behind her so she could see her way around as she opened up. The smell was acrid and made her nose wrinkle in protest. Whatever it was, it hung heavily in the air, pervading and permeating everywhere. There had been no power to the chiller cabinet since yesterday and the whole lot had gone off. Siân took a roll of black bin bags off the shelf, putting the label in the till for sorting out later. She donned rubber gloves and unfurled a black bag, the smell of its plastic much more pleasant than the smell of rancid dairy products. How had the smell got this bad overnight? Surely milk and cheese would survive a little while in the shop, especially as Lloyd was always too tight to pay for any heating. Last night had been so cold; surely this place had been its own fridge?

She reached out and took a bottle of milk off the top shelf; the milk inside was practically solid. Rotating the bottle moved the sludge slowly, and nasty-coloured lumps came to rest by the semi-transparent plastic. "Yuck!" She piled the milk bottles in one bag, reeled off another and started on the butter and cheese. As her slight fingers touched the cheese, she felt something grossly uneven under the plastic. She angled the block of cheese to the light and dropped it in revulsion. It was rancid and rotten, coated in a deep layer of multi-coloured mould. She checked the label in case it was some fancy, deliberately mouldy cheese, but no, it was normal cheese. The smell and the sights combined to make Siân feel queasy; she forced herself to breathe through her mouth.

The man with the papers came through the door and dumped the stack of papers down. "Morning, love."

"Thanks." She wandered over and unpacked the papers; the locals were not going to be very happy this morning. Getting the paper and milk was a regular morning ritual for many people in the village. If the phone had been working she could have rung the dairy and asked for more milk to keep everyone happy, but it had no tone. She tried her mobile; it flashed 'no network' in bold black letters. A figure in the doorway distracted her. "Sorry, we're not open quite yet, I'll be only a minute or two."

"Don't you dare turf me out."

"Lowri?"

"Yep, the one and only." She stepped into the shop. "Puh-lease tell me you have milk."

"Not any that you'd want to drink, it's rancid. That's what that stench is; it's not me, I promise," Siân giggled.

"Noooooooo!" shrieked Lowri, in mock seriousness. "Crap, I wish I'd stayed in Aberystwyth for Easter; they have power there, y'know."

"It's great to see you. I like the red; your hair was green last time, which I have to tell you is not your colour. I want to hear all about what you've been up to. It feels like ages since I saw you last."

"Likewise. Erm, Siân, I've been back a whole day and I've not actually seen me Mam yet. Is she ignoring me? I mean, I know Tad was OK with me moving out, but Mam, she wasn't too happy with it. I thought she would be; you know, some nice time for her and Tad to be alone again, get their lives back. I thought that was meant to be every parent's dream, to see their kids move out."

"She's not said anything like that to me; she has missed you though, that I do know."

Lowri smiled, relieved. "This place never changes, does it? All the faces are always the same, only a little older. Oh, have you got any gossip magazines there?"

"I can order you some in if you want, when the phones wake up. You're not still reading that rubbish, are you?"

"I am," Lowri announced proudly. "Only these days it's called research. How can I be a trendy, cutting-edge jewellery designer without knowing what jewellery celebs are wearing?"

"If you're going to be cutting-edge, shouldn't you know before that? So you can make the trendy jewellery for the celebs?"

"Gawd, you always were a smarty-pants." Lowri changed the subject. "I hear you have a boyfriend?"

Siân laid the papers out. "Maybe... sort of. It's early days."

"I'm happy for you. He's not to my taste, but he seems kind of sweet. Old-fashioned, like a gentleman..."

Siân interrupted her. "Hang on, you've met him?"

"Yep, last night. He's staying with us, him and a nice old bloke."

Siân's face lit up as she smiled widely. "So, he did come back. Please, Lowri, when you see him next, give him my address and tell him I'll meet him in the pub tonight."

Lowri nodded, pleased to see her surrogate sister so happy. "They've all gone off on a wild goose chase at the moment. The old bloke, a professor or something, has gone missing."

"Not another one, it's like a black hole around here. First that tourist, then yesterday I hear the Russells have gone missing, and now another?" Siân stopped dead. "Do you mean Professor Trevivian?"

"Sounds about right. Wears a bow tie of all things, quite funky really."

"Let me know when he turns up. I knew him at Cardiff and it would be nice to see him."

"What a small world we do live in," pondered Lowri. "Anyway, I can't stand here gossiping all day; Bryn's outside and I'm s'posed to get back in case the old guy shows up there. See ya later!"

* * *

The police were kind and understanding. A petite, blonde policewoman showed Ryan into one of the small interview rooms. The room was a cold shade of mint and the faint light visible through the tiny box window only added to the crisp paleness of the décor. The room smelt faintly of disinfectant, and the linoleum floor was still slightly sticky with cleaner. The woman offered a drink and it took three attempts to get an answer from Ryan, whose entire body and mind felt cold, numb and lost. When at last he did speak, Ryan found himself stuttering as though the room were freezing cold. "W-w-water, please."

With a soft, reassuring smile, the young woman left him alone for a few minutes. Outside the door, Alun was busy talking to another officer and then the local doctor.

Ryan was no longer operating in the world around him; he stared at his left shoe, the bright mud was still damp and he had trodden a trail of mud around the police station. His mind was racing, yet also not operating; it seemed as though his thoughts were out of focus, yet bombarding his cold mind; he could not get that Trevivian was dead. Question after question ran through his mind. Why had Trevivian gone out so early? Why had Ryan not realised just how ill Trev was? His ego was well away with the blame game, and Ryan felt utterly wretched with himself. His cheeks coloured with guilt.

The blonde policewoman came back into the room with two little white plastic cups of water. She placed them gently on the old desk and sat down, her chair screeching against the floor. She began to speak, but still Ryan could not hear anything but his own dark thoughts, surfacing in his mind.

"You killed him," they said. "You murdered him. It is all your fault he's dead. If it wasn't for you, he would still be in Cardiff and still be alive. You did this." The voice was twisted; its words seemed gnarled and distorted, as though someone were speaking from underwater. Over and over the voice berated him and blamed him – becoming increasingly venomous and sharp.

The policewoman shook Ryan's arm firmly but politely.

"Wha?" he said faintly as he reached for the cup.

"I'm Constable Davies; I need to ask you some questions about your friend. I'm very sorry; I realise this is a very difficult time for you, but I'm sure you can understand…"

"Whatever I can do to help."

Davies visibly relaxed. Ever since these two men had walked in and bluntly told her they needed to report a death, she had not quite been able to work them out. The death; well, that sounded a little odd to her, what with all the strange stories coming out of Maenddu in the last few days. Normally the area was quiet; last year's small spate of burglaries in Maenddu and its neighbouring villages had been big news. Yet in the last couple of days, the station had been run off its feet with weird calls about demonic creatures prowling the moors, domestic abuse reports, missing person reports, two traffic accidents and even a hit and run. All the incidents had centred in on that one very small village – and now a death? Davies had a sneaking feeling there was more to this than anyone was going to let on, yet these two people appeared to be completely genuine, and the younger man; he was either plainly devastated or he was the best actor she had come across so far. The way he was nursing the little cup of water was something she had seen often enough with beers as men drowned their sorrows. She flicked on the tape recorder and spoke the date, time and her name clearly. "If you could please state your name."

"Ryan Ackley."

"OK, now I'm just going to ask you a few questions..."

The questions seemed endless, but he knew they were important. The female officer asked him all about Trevivian; who he was, where he lived, what his health problems had been, who his doctor was. With his eyes closed he began to relay everything in as much detail as he could remember. As he spoke, tears rolled down his cheeks.

Then they turned to how Ryan and Alun had found him, and what he was doing there. She let him dictate the pace, prompting him only every so often for more information. Talking about Trevivian, knowing that he was dead, drove the fact home. *Is* became *was*, the present tense the past tense, as Ryan talked.

* * *

"Mam," called Lowri, as she opened the back door of the pub. "Are you up yet?" The smell of warm toast told her that she was. Her stomach rumbled hopefully.

"Lowri!" Ffi rushed forward and embraced her daughter warmly. "I'm so pleased to see you. How are you, my dear?"

"Fine, I've got so much to tell you. First, though, I'd really love some toast."

Ffi laughed; she was secretly a little jealous of how her daughter could eat without having to worry about her weight. Her wild energy seemed to burn off the calories as soon as she consumed them. Ffi busied herself making the toast, listening as her daughter relayed her goings-on in the weeks since they had last spoken. Ffi served the first couple of slices up on to a plate and popped another two under the grill. She opened the cupboard door and reached for the strawberry jam, always Lowri's favourite. She raised herself on to tiptoes and groped in the cupboard for the jam, which she knew ought to be there. The tips of her fingers connected to the cool glass and she began to try and tilt and tip it towards her, only she ended up pushing it further back out of reach.

"Do you need some help, Mam?"

"The jam's not playing fair. Go on, your arms are longer than mine." Ffi stepped back and watched as her daughter reached up into the cupboard. Like her mother she reached up high on tiptoe, her arm reaching far out of its socket. "Got you!" she exclaimed triumphantly. Lowri pulled her arm back, bringing with her the jam. The flesh of her hand caught against some sharp metal on the door hinge, and she cried out in pain and dropped the jam. The jar bounced on the worktop then hit the floor, where it smashed in a small, neat pile. The jam leached out on to the tiles, a glistening globule of red and black. A darker, more velvety globule, dropped on to the jam. "Dear girl, you've cut yourself." Ffi went into full motherly mode, grabbing the first aid kit from the drawer and bustling Lowri to the sink, forcing her forearm under the flowing, silvery water. Lowri protested, "It's fine, Mam, just a scratch. I'm not five anymore."

"It may be only a scratch but you need to make sure it's clean." Ffi opened the plaster packet and turned away to throw the wrappings into the bin. Her eye caught the jam jar, still oozing on to the floor. She halted in mid-movement. Her voice was a monotone when she spoke. "Where's your father?"

"Out, with the guest bloke. The other guest, the professor, has gone missing. They went off before you were awake… why, Mam?"

"He's dead."

Surprise and fear crossed Lowri's face. "What? Tad?"

"No, the professor, see."

Lowri turned the tap off and followed where her mother was looking. "It's jam; it's a jammy, sticky mess. I'll clean it up in a minute." Her tone belied her annoyance; her mother was always coming out with weird stuff; some of it was accurate, most of it was annoying. Lowri reached for the tea towel and threw it on the floor. She was about to bend down and begin picking up the glass, when her mother blocked her with one arm. "Mam, there's nothing to see."

"See the letter; T for Trevivian." Ffi drew out with her forefinger the way the jam had oozed into the letter T on the floor.

"C'mon, it's just a coincidence. You don't know that anyone's dead."

"Yes, yes, I do. I can feel it, Lowri. He's gone." She put her hand to her mouth in horror as the jam continued to pool outwards; the image of the T became a flying eagle, gooey against the tiles. A dark thought crossed her mind and blew all other thoughts clean out of her head. "He was murdered. Oh no!" she wailed. "He was coming to help. He knew how to sort this out. He was Gwalchwen!"

Lowri did not say anything; she honestly did not know what to say that would not either set her mother off on one of her mad mystic moments, or deeply upset her. Instead, she decided to make herself useful; she pulled the toast out from the grill as it was just starting to burn, and hoped her mother's attention would soon depart from fairyland and come back down to earth.

CHAPTER THIRTY-THREE

A lun drove back towards the stone circle, leading a small convoy; behind him followed Doctor MacKenzie, and behind him, two officers in a squad car. As they passed through Maenddu, all eyes turned upon them, narrowed with suspicion. Jim watched the entourage pass by and shook his head. He wondered what had actually gone on to need the police and the doctor; it was not going to be anything good. He had known this, whatever it was, was coming. He had expected his own death after seeing the Gwyllgi; the damned thing had nearly scared him to death anyway with its eyes like the devil himself, and he was pleasantly surprised to still be waking up day after day. More was the pity, John was also still waking up day after day, getting in his way. And, day after day, he had seen people growing more agitated, nastier and more violent to each other. He had tried to tell the others, to warn everyone that something was very wrong, but they had all laughed in his face. Now perhaps someone might listen.

Jim looked at his brother and sighed. John was also watching the show. "What's that then?" he asked aloud.

"It's what I've been on about all week." Jim tapped his walking stick hard on the pavement and then used it to bash his brother's identical stick. The crack echoed down the narrow street. "I told you, didn't I say there were some funny goings-on? I tell you. It's him, the Gwyllgi. He's got the 'fluence."

"The only 'fluence round here is your rancid home brew and your damned imagination!"

"It's the devil's own dog."

"Oh, shut up, you boozy old sod."

Jim muttered at his brother, "Then why did you ask me?"

"You and your bloody stories," moaned John. "Get out of my way."

The light of day had hardly got itself into gear before its time was up and the day began fading away. Night seized its opportunity before its rightful time, settling the afternoon into a deepening grey. Clouds raced across the skies at varying rates, each tone of grey from the palest to the darkest represented in the thick, puffy clouds. The atmosphere grew oppressive with tension and pressure. Rain threatened, but never quite came. The atmosphere sapped at the energy of everyone. A van driver fell deeply and suddenly asleep at the wheel as his van coasted down the road into the town; the crash as he took out the post box woke him with a jolt. He checked himself over, thrilled to find himself intact despite the rearrangement of the front of his van and the displacement of the post box. He had not even felt tired before he got to the valley.

The afternoon yoga class at the community hall gave up and went home early, too sticky and tired to do their full time. Several members gave up totally and stopped by the local shop on their way home to buy chocolate, crisps and other things they knew they should not. Their excuse was that they needed it; they needed the comfort and barrier to the depressing, draining cloud that hung heavy over the village. People scurried around the village, for once not exchanging pleasantries or the latest news but only going from A to B in the quickest and quietest possible way. They did not even look up from the pavement to catch each other's eyes.

* * *

Alun and Ryan's entire day had been a carousel of repeating the same information to various people; the doctor, the coroner, and a sea of faces in police uniforms and fluorescent jackets. Everyone had been efficient, matter-of-fact and courteous. Alun had looked on as the doctor examined the body, watched as the officers checked out the area, and witnessed Trevivian's mortal remains being bagged up and taken away by the Coroner's team. How quickly a person became an object once the animation and spirit had departed. Alun had then gone back to the station to answer a few more questions. As the investigation had progressed, the police acknowledged the death was due to natural causes, a heart attack. Trevivian's heart had given out and given up. The doctor assured them that he had not suffered, his death had been quick. Alun had hung around to wait until Ryan was done. The lad was in need of a lift and a friend. The journey back to the pub had been silent; Ryan was too lost in his own thoughts and Alun could not think of anything helpful to say. He knew all too well how hollow the stock phrases rolled out at times of loss sounded. Instead he let his presence, his company, do the talking.

The gentle hum of the engine and the exhaustion of the day lulled Ryan quickly to sleep. Clouds of light and dark raced through his dream vision until he found himself standing on the top of Carn Siân. Mist still surrounded him; this time a foggy sea mist; the tang of salt was palpable. Thunder rang out in the distance and made the ground tremble underfoot. Owein put his hand to his stomach to staunch the flow of ruby flood, which was trickling from the open gash. Badden launched forward with an even harder, fiercer attack. He sensed the weakness now and made the most of it, lunging with sword and dagger. As their blades clashed, metal sparked. Owein blocked each stroke, fighting defensively now. Badden showered blow after blow down on him; there was no chance for Owein to launch his own attack. Sweat poured down his back, stinging sharply, and the blood from his stomach was beginning to trickle further and further down. He needed his other hand on the sword to use his strength to block his opponent's blows, and the blood was now flowing freely. Using the flesh of his arm, Owein attempted to wipe the sweat from his brow as he staggered back. The sweat was pouring into his eyes, stinging and blurring his vision. His blood felt too hot as it raced through his veins, burning him up from the inside.

"Ha, can you feel that now?" cried Badden with glee.

Owein ignored his opponent, preferring to concentrate on their battle. He seized the moment as Badden gloated and struck out hard with his bronze sword, putting all his weight and power into it. Badden seemed surprised and stepped back to avoid the blow. Momentum carried Owein still forward, and he staggered closer to the cairn. He struggled to regain his footing on the smaller rocks that lay around the base of the cairn and landed heavily, one hand against a sharp rock, the other using his sword to lean on.

"Is that the best you can do?" Badden sneered, his mouth turning up in disdain. "Mind you, it's not bad for a *dying* man." He rested the tip of his sword in the soft ground and leaned elegantly against it, the dagger in his other hand, being gently swung to and fro, watching as Owein tried unsuccessfully to get back to his feet.

"You're not leaving this hilltop, Owein." There was the faintest hint of pity in his voice. "If only you had stayed away from my wife. You could have been the leader of our clan, I could have helped you."

Owein pushed himself off the ground with his sword. "Then you would have stabbed me in the back and taken the power for yourself." Raising his weapon high, he lurched forwards. Badden side-stepped and Owein fell face forward to the ground. The sword fell by his side.

Badden picked up the sword as Owein tried to get up and thrust it into the ground several feet from his enemy. "It's an interesting poison." He waved his own dripping sword over Owein. "See the staining on this sword? I knew I could never beat you fairly, so I had no intention of fighting fair. The harder you fight, the quicker your death will be, and the sooner I will have Morwyna. Tell me, does that give you comfort?"

Owein roared. His blood was boiling, he tried to speak, but no words came. Continually he tried to lift himself up on his arms, but each time they gave way and his face hit the ground again. His sword was only feet away, yet now forever out of his reach. The torc he had always worn with pride now held him down.

"It's your own fault, Owein. Morwyna has always been mine. Gwalchwen knew it, you knew it, and you're both dead now. No one gets in my way." Crouching down on his haunches, Badden whispered to the warrior. "I killed him, you know. I would have thought a great magician like him could have easily stopped me with one word! For supposedly such a great man, he was so easy to kill. The great Gwalchwen was a great coward in the end." He issued a deep cackling laugh into his fallen rival's crimson ear.

Owein was enraged, his anger only adding to the unbearable heat that racked through every limb. He raged that Badden had won, that he had not been able to protect Morwyna; he raged that Badden had fought dishonourably and murdered his mentor. Most of all he raged against himself for not being able to stop Badden. His hands curled to fists, the darkening veins throbbing erratically as every muscle in his body tensed.

Badden recognised the final stage of the poison's work and moved away as the convulsions began to tear at Owein's body. Taking a deep breath of sweet victory and salty air, he mounted his skittish horse and rode off to collect his prize.

Vibrations shook the car as Alun and Ryan passed over the cattle grid, waking Ryan with a jolt. He lifted his head and stretched his neck, his dream forgotten in a moment. Seeing they were now coming to the main area of the village, he asked, "Can you drop me off by the circle?"

Alun paused before he spoke. "If that's what you want. Are you sure you want to go back there now, eh?"

Ryan shrugged. "Not really, but that's where the car is."

"The car?" Alun was confused.

"I need to get back to Cardiff, sort a few things out. Arrangements to make…"

Alun interrupted him. "Not today, lad. That can wait a day or two."

"No, I don't think it can." Ryan was desperate to get away from this place, with its spooky goings-on and now his friend's death. He mentally berated himself again for bringing Trevivian so far from home when he was so ill and to such a creepy place. Over and over, the voice in his head told him that he did it, he killed Trevivian.

"At least come back for some food and a good night's rest. You can go back in the morning if you're still keen."

Ryan pleaded, "No, please. I have to go tonight."

Alun was exasperated; the kid was losing it with grief. "Ryan," he said plainly. "You can't go back now. Besides, you'll be wanting to take the professor's belongings with you, and they're back at the pub. Listen, you're tired, you're upset and you're in no fit state to drive." He studied the face of his passenger, looking for a sign that the young man had got the message, but found none. Ryan opened his mouth to speak and Alun spoke again. "Not tonight, do you understand? Here we are," he said as he pulled his car into the pub car park. "Get some sleep; things'll be a whole lot clearer in the morning."

Ryan put both hands to his head and tugged at his dark hair. The voice was still shouting inside his head, screaming at him now. "I have to get away from this place. Don't you see, all this is my fault? I did this. I killed him."

"No, you didn't. The doc made it very clear that this was a heart attack. He died of natural causes, Ryan." Alun knew what he had to do when someone was like this; the lad was in no fit state to be going anywhere. He unbuckled his seatbelt and put his hand out to Ryan. "Give me your keys."

"No!" Ryan shouted, pushing Alun's hand out of the way. He struggled to get out of his seatbelt.

Alun sighed and opened his door. The car moved visibly as he climbed out, and he purposefully stepped over towards Ryan's door. Ryan was already away, out of the car, stumbling and running towards the road. Alun picked up the pace, his knees groaning and creaking. "Ryan, get back here!" He made a grab for the lad's jacket and grunted when he managed to get a handful. Ryan pulled sharply away and the jacket tore. Alun swore and reached out again, only obtaining a handful of air. The lad was fast, with the wiry swiftness of the young. Alun struggled to keep going, as each pace sent pain shooting up his legs and through his knees, to reach Ryan before he got to the road. Ryan was well ahead, getting into his stride. With one more pace, Alun's left knee gave way; pain seared through every nerve in his body as he fell to the ground with a thud. The pain took his breath away and he screamed out hoarsely.

Ryan did not even look back. In his desperation to get away, he ran as fast as his legs would carry him towards the car, his way out. On the road, with its even surface, he found his rhythm, the pace and thudding of his feet drumming out the voice in his head. The cold wind blew against him and he pushed forward, leaning into the wind. Around him, debris and fallen leaves spun in small circles, swishing like whispers on the tarmac. It only took a matter of minutes before he reached the lay-by and, in it, the familiar monster. Within his pocket, Ryan beeped the locks as he approached, and wrenched open the car door fully back on its hinges before leaping into the driver's seat. He wanted to catch his breath and settle his heart which was in his throat, but the moment his legs had stopped running the voice had returned. Without thinking, he re-arranged the car seat to his frame; taller than the professor, he needed to push the seat further back. The seat clicked into its new position as the key in the ignition clicked the engine to roar. Ryan pulled out without checking the road around him and sped off into the distance.

CHAPTER THIRTY-FOUR

Siân was topping up the dents made to the sweet section by the Yoga class, when the time came to close up. A shadow crossed her view as Lloyd came between her and one of the several battery-powered lamps that they had set up to light the shop. "Before you go, I want a word with you."

She continued to lay out more goods. "Why don't you say it now?"

"Now is not the right time."

"I'm here, you're here. What's the problem?" she asked. Lloyd moved back towards the stockroom. "When you're done."

Siân shook her head. With all these odd shadows and goings-on, Lloyd seemed even more creepy than usual. She wanted to go home but her coat was out the back. She did not want to speak to Lloyd at the moment; she only wanted to tell him angrily to get Mandy back, to get off his backside and do some work and to leave her alone. He had been hovering all day, hovering in the doorway, watching her serve the customers. She had felt his eyes on her back, but when she had looked around he was gone again. 'Maybe he's planning to sack me too?' she wondered, secretly edging towards hoping that he would. Then she would not have to stay here any longer. Oh, but where else could she get a job around here? Maybe she would not have to worry; maybe she could go to Cardiff with Ryan. She smiled warmly at the idea.

"Siân, when you're done," barked Lloyd, impatiently.

"What?" she replied as she walked to the back of the stockroom to the coat rack.

Stepping between Siân and the exit, Lloyd smiled. His sharp teeth looked odd when he smiled; besides, smiling was not normal for the man. The hackles on the back of Siân's neck rose and the room grew very cold.

"Before you go home tonight, I wanted a little word with you…" He moved closer and Siân moved back, until the brass hooks of the coat rack pushed against her shoulder blades. Lloyd did not look well; his skin beaded with clamminess and he was pale and grey. The deep shadows under his eyes suggested the man had not slept in days, and with the dark his grey irises seemed obscured by his widened black pupils. She did not like her personal space invaded at the best of times, and certainly not by creepy old Lloyd. She tried to step sideways to clear some space between Lloyd and her, but he counteracted her move. "Morwyna." His smile broadened and the word formed as mist in the cold air.

"I have to go," muttered Siân, pushing past him. Morwyna, that name again, the girl who had died in the marsh, whose name she had heard called by the circle that evening with Ryan. Her heart skipped a beat; was that the woman she had seen? Was that the ghost? Morwyna had been running away from someone in her daydream, someone she feared terribly.

Lloyd grabbed her hair; tied back in a ponytail, it was an easy target. Siân moved forward, trying to pull away, but Lloyd pulled her back.

Siân's heart raced as she went through her options. She had no desire to hurt the man; she did, however, feel the need to get as far away from him as possible. She took one step backwards, towards Lloyd, to give her some leeway, then spun on her heel as fast as she could, slapping his hand away from her hair. His other hand reached around to her neck and got a grip; using his body weight, he slammed Siân bodily into the side wall, winding her. He held her up by the neck so that her feet did not touch the ground. Siân gasped for air, digging her nails into the flesh of his huge, hairy hands. She saw for the first time deep red welts on his hands and arms; they appeared old but she had not seen them before. She gouged into them with her nails to cause maximum pain. Her face flushed as blood remained in her head, unable to flow past his tight grip. Her heart thundered in her ears and the room began to swim. "Let. Go. Of. Me!"

"Why would I want to do that when I've spent so long trying to make you mine? Don't you recognise me, your true love, Badden, who has waited millennia for you?"

"Where's Lloyd?" she gasped.

"Dead." His breath reeked of something unpleasant and Siân found herself turning her nose up in distaste of not only his breath but also the whole of who this man was, by whatever name. She was damned if her last breaths on this earth were going to smell that bad. Consolidating her strength and appealing mentally to Morwyna to help her, she lashed out towards his face with her fists, and his testicles with her knee. All her blows connected with her desired targets, forcing him to let go of her. Gasping for breath, she bolted towards the open door. Badden grunted, an animal sound, as he righted himself, using the aluminium shelving frame. He pulled the frame towards him and tugged even harder, bringing the frame and all its contents down. The battery-powered lantern slipped off the shelf and smashed, immersing the room in complete darkness. The shelving unit knocked against the next row of frames, which also fell, right on to Siân.

CHAPTER THIRTY-FIVE

Alun carefully swung his left leg around under him; it had twisted awkwardly as he fell. When he had got it as far as it would go, he reached down and pulled it the rest of the way. Using his hands and a nearby bush, he edged himself upright. He looked up, along the road, but Ryan was long gone. There was no more he could do to stop him, he was most likely already at the car. Stepping forward, he stumbled again with the pain. Alun's face deepened to magenta as he shuffled home, one small pace at a time.

Lowri intercepted her father as he came through the door. "Where have you been? Mam's been going on about some really crazy stuff and now she's locked herself in the zone."

"Lowri…" Alun puffed, leaning against the wall. "Please. Give me a minute to get my breath back."

Lowri took her father's arm and pulled him towards the stairs. "Talk to her, Tad. I can't get her to make any sense. She was raving about that bloke being murdered, about animals and going on and on about the circle. I think she's totally lost it this time."

Hanging heavily on to the hall cabinet, Alun resisted his daughter's tugs. "Get me some painkillers and some water, eh." He leaned back on the wall and closed his eyes. He heard Lowri rustling in the drawer and the splash of water in the glass, before she returned. "There y'are, Tad."

He gulped them down gratefully.

Lowri was on edge. "What the hell happened to you anyway? You've been gone all day."

"Long story. The professor's dead…"

"Mam said he was murdered!"

"What? No. He had a heart attack up at the circle. How did your mother know, anyway?"

"It's so stupid. I dropped the jam, then Mam started on about murder and eagles. Puh-lease, Tad, I really think she's lost it this time."

"No, dear," he muttered. "Your Mam gets it; she gets more of it than the rest of us." Alun pulled himself heavily and awkwardly up the stairs while Lowri hovered behind him and chivvied him on. He tried the door handle of the zone, only to find the door locked. "Ffi?"

Paper was shuffled within the room. "Ffi, let me in."

"He's dead, isn't he?" Ffi's voice was muffled by the door.

"Yes, he's dead. It was a heart attack."

The door opened and Ffi stepped forward. Her mascara streaked down her cheeks where she had been crying. Ffi threw her arms around Alun. "No, he was murdered. It's all here." She pulled back from the embrace and indicated the piles of papers and books opened on the floor. "He was the one who was to come to help us, and now whoever it is who's been making dark magic against Ryan and Siân has killed him."

"Dear Ffi, it was a heart attack. The doc's confirmed it."

"There's ways to bring about a heart attack; I know of several herbs that'd do the job and be hard to trace; or who's to say the Gwyllgi didn't scare the poor man to death? Or the Pwca? It was murder! I should tell the police."

Alun reasoned with her and put his arms around her waist. "The police aren't going to be interested in all that, they're with the doc; a heart attack. Anyways, who'd want to kill an already very ill old man?"

Ffi wiped a dirty tear from her eyes with the back of her hand. "I know… but it was murder! Where was he?"

Alun held on tight to his wife. "Up at the circle."

Ffi cried out, "I knew it! He was the hawk, the old spirit of the circle come back again. Oh, and now he's gone. I don't know what to do. I can't do this. I can't protect them on my own."

"Hush, dear."

She spun around in her husband's strong arms. "Where's Ryan?"

"Gone."

"What? When?" The pitch of her voice grew higher as panic set in.

Lowri stood by the door, listening and carefully watching her mother's behaviour. "That's a bummer. Siân'll be gutted."

Alun answered his wife. "He ran off. I ran after him, but my knee went. I couldn't stop him."

"Oh no! He needs to be here. He needs to protect Siân."

Alun let go of his wife and raised his hands in the air. "Isn't he better off out of it if someone's after him?"

"No. You don't get it." More tears were wiped away, smudging the mascara even further.

"Then explain it to me, please."

Ffi took a deep breath. "What I know is that Ryan needs to be here, he needs to protect Siân. She's at the heart of all this." She paced around the room as she talked, stepping over books and papers and knocking them out of sync with the hem of her dress. "It's all about Siân. She's the deer. Then there's two men fighting over her, like the Oak and Holly Kings. The stag, who is meant for her, and the boar, who most certainly is not. Ryan has to win."

"Eh?"

"I'll show you." Ffi picked up her wooden cubes and cast them roughly to the floor. They fell as they had done on the moor, except this time she had included an extra cube. "Every time, they show me this. See the deer, there. She's under both the stag and the boar – they're fighting over her. And look, there's the hawk." She pointed to the extra dice, slightly distant from the others and angled on the carpet so that it was half hidden by shadow. "Now the professor is dead the boar will make his move. I've spent all day trying to work this out. It's the boar who messed up at the circle. If we find him, maybe we can stop him."

"OK, who is he?"

"I don't know, that's the problem. Otherwise I'd have already done something."

"What do you know?" Alun's practical nature kicked in.

"He'll literally behave like a boar. It's a strong personality. He'll be boorish, assertive, abrupt, even rude."

"God, that's most men," Lowri said absentmindedly as she fiddled with her hair.

Ffi did not hear. "His name could be boar-something, torc-something – that's Gaelic for boar – or Baedd-something. He's obsessed with Siân, whoever he is."

Lowri piped up. "What about Huw? He was well-weird with Siân's boyfriend last night. Said some really dumb-arse stuff, I think he was trying to threaten him; just made him sound stupid though."

Ffi's eyes widened. "Huw?" She rolled the idea around in her mind, it did not seem quite right. "Huw? Is he capable of all this? All that negativity and evil? Could he kill? No. He's not the type, surely."

"Who else then?" asked Alun. "Who else do we know of? He's always been sweet on her and if he's been messing with dark magic, who's to say what he's really like?"

Ffi made up her mind. "Let's go find out." She stormed past her husband and daughter out into the corridor.

"Wait," Alun called after her as he moved forward slowly; the painkillers were still getting going. The back door slammed. "Lowri, go round to Siân's and bring her back here. Make something up if you have to. At least if she's here we can keep an eye on her."

Lowri nodded and headed off. "Bollocks," she swore to herself. "I'm never gonna get a boyfriend. When I find one I like, turns out he's some nutter."

Taking the torch from the hall table, she walked out into the night.

CHAPTER THIRTY-SIX

The melody and the monotony of the road drowned out the voices in Ryan's head. Mile after mile of grey and white was a blur. He smacked the steering wheel with the heel of his palms, annoyed by his own behaviour. Although he was overjoyed to be away from Maenddu, he could not shake the feeling that he should have brought Siân away with him. He had not even had the chance to speak to her while he was there, and in a village of that size it would not be long before she found out. He sighed; he had killed that relationship before it had much of a chance to begin. The thought saddened him greatly. He had never felt that way about anyone before. The guilt of being responsible for taking Trevivian into that malevolent, mystical mess, knowing full well how weak the old man was, gnawed deep at his soul. It did not matter that Trevivian had insisted, he should not have done it. Simple as that. What on earth had he been thinking? In one day he had broken two hearts, one physically and one emotionally. Inwardly he screamed and swore vociferously at his own stupidity.

He slumped with the realisation that he had left all his valuable camera equipment behind as well. "Well done," he said aloud, sarcastically. He could not have screwed up more if he had tried. Running his hand through his hair, he considered the mess of the last few days. Stone circles, devil dogs, ghostly women, death and falling in love. Nothing made sense anymore; Ryan had a sneaking suspicion that he was losing his mind. Hearing voices was a major sign of that, wasn't it?

He was nearing Carmarthen when he noticed the street lamps there were working. The light was reassuring; somehow it felt that he was returning to normality. Wanting nothing more than to go home, to go to sleep, Ryan drove on. With every mile his heartache worsened, as the memory of Siân tugged at his heartstrings.

Ffi's comments about the strange shadows and the old Druid at the circle, circled continually in his brain. What was it she had been on about? He remembered the bit about the shadow; he had paid attention to that because he had seen something on that first day, but when she had started to carry on he had sort of switched off. He dragged the memory out, kicking and screaming. "Ryan is here to protect you." Yes, she had definitely said something like that. Ffi had emphasised that point heavily. What was he supposed to protect her from? Had that even been mentioned?

The white and grey of the road was mesmerising. Strange shapes and shadows formed in the road where the headlights struck. A grey crouched figure seemed to hover for a moment. "Go back," it whispered feebly before fading away. Ryan rubbed his dry and tired eyes, one at a time, to keep one hand on the wheel. He knew that he could not protect Siân if he was eighty-odd miles away, and he had to see her again. He could not leave things as they were. Ffi had told him not to go back to Cardiff and someone else had told him that too. He could not think who; perhaps he had dreamt it? His dreams had certainly been weird lately. Being in his own little world, Ryan only noticed the small black car in front, which had halted at the roundabout, just in time. He slammed on the brakes hard and looked ahead, his eyes wide open. The car registration was a sign; there could be no doubt about it. In amongst the letters and numbers was the word 'Siân'. Tapping his fingers erratically on the wheel, Ryan waited impatiently for the car to go. It hovered back, despite the gaps in traffic, as though the driver was overcautious.

"Hurry up, I get the message," Ryan said to no one in particular, and on cue the black car drove away. Ryan did a complete 360 degree tour of the roundabout, then headed back the way he had come, back to Maenddu and back to Siân.

CHAPTER THIRTY-SEVEN

The metal connected with the back of Siân's head; she fell amid falling containers and tins. Reaching out to steady herself, Siân's fingers burned as they slipped against icy, glistening metal. She felt consciousness and awareness ebb away. She tried to fight it, to keep her eyes open, to hold on to the light, but the numb darkness washed over her. She felt herself falling and falling, as though it would never end. Then falling became flight and she was running barefoot across the rough grass and heather of the moors. Their blades and stems tore at the flesh of her feet and legs and the hem of her dress. She grabbed fistfuls of her dress, pulling her hem from the ground away from the mud that was soaking into her dress, making it heavier. The mists closed in, disorientating Morwyna. She kept her eyes ahead, running as fast as she could towards the stone circle, from where she could follow the safe route of the avenue to the village.

Winds buffeted against her, making her work harder in order to progress. She bent her head against the wind and pushed on. The faint sound of hoof beats, steady and strong, chilled her to the core. Morwyna automatically half-looked around and floundered against a high lump of ground, falling on to her hands and knees in the mud. Throwing her hair back out of her way, she pushed herself off the ground and ran for her life. The hoofbeats grew closer, thundering, echoing in the mists. Her own heart pounded harder away in response. The village was too far, she did not have long before the rider would catch her, so she concentrated her efforts doubly to reach the old stone circle. Surely it was not far from here, if only she knew where 'here' was in this mist.

The circle was protected and powerful, Gwalchwen and his ancestors had seen to that. Morwyna felt the circle was near, not much further. She could feel its presence, like the comforting presence of old Gwalchwen. It called to her in the mist, and her soul responded to its call. The horse was almost upon her, she could hear the rider's and the horse's panting breaths above her own. Her lungs ached for air and her heart ached for rest, but she had no desire to let Badden have her, ever. The man was pure evil.

A cold, gnawing sensation hit her hard in the chest, stealing her breath away. Tears welled in her eyes, blurring her vision. "Owein!" she half-screamed and half-sobbed into the night, her heart breaking as she felt him die. The horse and rider were almost upon her now, their shadow visible in the mist.

"Morwyna, stop," Badden commanded from his mount. "You're mine now, my darling."

Closing her eyes, not wanting this to be happening, Morwyna ran on, her legs aching, her feet cut and blistered, but the real pain was in her heart. She could feel the horse's breath on her back; he was almost on top of her now. Morwyna changed direction, planning to head to the shrub. Badden reached down and grabbed her by her long dark hair. Morwyna yelped in pain as he wound his fist tighter into her black knotted hair, pulling her closer to him.

"My wife," he gloated. "You're my wife now."

She caught the tiniest glint of metal in his leather boot. Seizing her chance, Morwyna grabbed it and pulled at it sharply. A small bronze blade came away in her hand and she used it to slice away at his hand, causing him to let go. Now free from his grasp, she bolted off towards the bushes, hoping the horse would not follow her through there. Badden pulled the reins back sharply. The horse reared off after her for a few feet, then stopped harshly. Badden dug his heels into her sides and hit hard to get her going again, but she refused. She paced the ground, nodding her head up and down, neighing softly.

"Aargh! Stupid creature."

Dismounting, Badden then followed on foot. He could see Morwyna's plan; she would use the scrub as cover to get her as close by the circle as possible, then make a final run for it. He knew he was fresher than her; she had already been running for some time, she would be easy to outrun, and he could snatch her on the final stretch. An eerie smile crossed his face; he loved to hunt and this prize made this hunt even more fun than usual.

Morwyna pushed her way through the bushes, the twigs and thorns scratching at her clothes and skin. No longer could she hear the horse; that was some relief, but she knew that Badden would not give up that easily. She crouched down under a gorse bush and listened out for him. Soft footfalls told her he was close, running ahead to intercept her. Morwyna was terrified that he would hear her, hear her heart beating so hard or her gasps for breath. Forcing herself to calm down, and her heart and breathing to slow, she prayed hard to her ancestors, to the Gods and Goddesses and the spirits all around to help her. 'Please don't let him get me', she thought, over and over.

A hawk called in the gloom. It landed on a hawthorn, not far from Morwyna. She looked up from her prayers and smiled. Gwalchwen, the white hawk, was calling to her, speaking to her from the Otherworld. Her courage boosted, she sprinted out of the undergrowth towards the circle.

Badden heard her move, and turning on his heel he saw her running off. He bolted after her, angry at his miscalculation. Her youth held her in good stead, and with her lithe figure she was a natural runner. Badden, however, was much older and had relied on magic for power. It was his magic he now called on to stop Morwyna from slipping away. He called aloud to the dark spirits of the moors, to the souls lost and loathsome.

Wispy, silvery, indistinct forms began to rise from the pools of water that lay on the ground, their figures misshapen and malformed. Several arose close to Morwyna and their presence frightened her, but she ran on, dodging the phantoms as they reached out towards her. The shadows of the stone loomed ahead of her in the gloom. She gave a final effort, straining herself to reach the circle, to pass through the boundary of the circle to safety. A phantom arose before her and blocked her way. The hawk called in the distance, his voice desperate. Morwyna twisted herself away from the phantom, increasingly desperate. The ground gave way beneath her feet; she sank to her waist in the marsh. Thick and sticky, the marsh pulled at her dress and her body, pulling her down further.

The wispy forms grabbed at her; she waved her arms to fend them off. They had no solid structure so her arms cut through their forms, severing wisps from them which then reformed. Her movements only caused her to sink faster. She screamed at the top of her voice in pure terror. She was so close to the circle, only a few feet away. Morwyna tried to kick out or up with her legs to push herself up, while tugging on tufts of grass with her hands and stabbing into the firmer ground with the bronze knife. The grass broke off in her hands and she slipped deeper; the mud was now at her breasts and continuing to creep up.

Badden caught up with her at last, huffing and puffing. "Hold on." He lay on his stomach and edged himself nearer to her. The mud was pulling slowly at him, but his spread weight meant that it did not get a grip. He reached wildly out towards Morwyna. "Take my hand."

"No!" she screamed.

Badden, determined not to lose the woman he desired more than anything else in the world – more than power, more than fame, more than wealth – slid closer. The tip of his longest finger grazed against her hand. Reviled by his touch, reviled by the man who had killed her husband, she struck out at him. The blade connected with his flesh and he pulled his hand back. "Bitch!" he exclaimed. "You're mine, now let me help you."

"I would rather die," spat Morwyna acidly, "and join Owein." She struggled harder against the marsh, knowing that it was bringing her closer to her death, to the Otherworld and to her beloved.

Sensing defeat, Badden's anger and despair erupted. He had to have Morwyna, to possess her as his own. He grabbed for her wrists, still flailing. He tried to hold on tight, to pull at them to stop Morwyna from sinking any more. She struggled from his grasp and pushed her arms deeper. His knees and elbows began to break the surface of the marsh; he could feel its damp through the plaid of his trousers and hear the sucking and squelching as he tried to reposition himself. "Damn you, Morwyna."

The wet mud was now up to Morwyna's pale mouth. She smiled wanly as she tasted the foul mud, bitter and peaty, and ducked herself deeper into the ground.

Badden dug with his hands where Morwyna had been, scraping away the mud in vain. "I damn you, Morwyna, may you never cross to the Otherworld. May you always be here on the marsh, like one of these other damned souls, until you are mine."

CHAPTER THIRTY-EIGHT

Scrunching her way up the gravel track, Lowri regretted not putting a thicker coat on. The cold of the night was cutting through to her bones. She hunched her shoulders higher and lowered her head to conserve heat. She aimed the narrow beam of torchlight carefully ahead to light her way in the darkness. There was no moon tonight and the stars were hidden behind the clouds. Siân's cottage was in darkness. Lowri thumped her fist hard on the old door of Dragon cottage. "Siân, lemme in. It's bloody freezing out here."

No answer came. "Siân. Hellooo?" Lowri thumped again. Flashing the torch around, taking a quick peek to be sure no one was watching her, Lowri reached for the hidey key. Lowri felt guilty about entering without permission, but this was definitely a case of something happening. Reaching up behind the carved dragon, her fingers found the robust key. Letting herself in, Lowri had a nose around as she searched for and called for Siân. Siân had really cleaned the old place up; Lowri was impressed. Gone were all the trinkets and adornments that had cluttered the place up. All the pictures had been taken off the walls, apart from the wedding picture of Siân's parents that hung on the stairs. The stairs creaked as Lowri ascended them.

"Siân, are you here?" she hissed. No one was home. Lowri checked every room, but there was no sign of Siân, or even that she had been home that night. Lowri's first thought was that perhaps she was still at work. She knew Lloyd had made Siân stay ridiculously late before for stock checks; Siân had moaned about it enough at Christmas.

Lowri headed back out; she was about to replace the key when a little thought entered her head. If someone was after Siân, perhaps it was best not to put a copy of the door key less than a foot away from it. Whoever was after her might easily guess and let themselves in. Instead, she pocketed the key and walked on to the shop.

The shop was a mess, wooden boards for windows and for the door. She thumped on that door and the wood nearly gave way. She was shivering now, her teeth chattering in her skull. No longer in the mood for hanging around, Lowri dashed off back home to the warm. She had probably just missed her anyway. Maybe Siân was already sitting in the pub. Oh yeah, she realised, Siân had said she would go there tonight to meet up with Ryan. She was going to be gutted when she found out he had gone back to Cardiff.

CHAPTER THIRTY-NINE

Tyres screeched as Ffi pulled the van up close to Mountain Farm, an old pastoral farm, high up away from the village. She slammed the door shut and stomped up to the front door. Within, she could see the faintest light in the front parlour and another upstairs, so she knew at least one person was home. Repeatedly she hammered the wrought iron knocker on its pad until the door was opened.

"What do you want?" snapped Mrs West, never the friendliest person in the village.

"A word with your son, if I may?"

"No, it's late. Go away." Mrs West pushed on the door to close it.

Ffi stuck her foot in the door, jamming it. "I don't have time for you today, Mrs West," she said, pushing past her.

"How dare you…" the old woman began bitterly, her hand raised to slap Ffi in the face.

"Sorry, this is important." Ffi glowered menacingly at her; it was suspected that she used her hands against her husband and that was why he had left. "Don't you dare."

"I'll call the police!"

Ffi was already bounding up the stairs. "Please do… if your phone is working. Tell them to find Siân Derwyn."

A faint light under the second door suggested Huw was in. Ffi opened the door without bothering to knock. Two stubby candles illuminated the small messy room. Huw was on his bed, curled up, fully dressed, in an old sleeping bag, listening to music on his headphones. When he saw Ffi he pulled the earphones out from his ears and twisted his legs over the side of the bed, pulling at some open books and CD cases in an attempt to tidy up. "Um, hi, Mrs Phillips," he said nervously.

Ffi opened her mouth to speak, to demand to know if it was Huw who was after Siân, and stopped mid-breath. Even by candlelight she could see the red mark on Huw's face, a day or two old but still vivid. It told her clearly that Huw was not the boar she was searching for.

"Huw." She bit her lip. "Who did that to you?"

Huw went a deep red with shame and embarrassment. "It's nothing, I walked into a wall."

"Huw, don't lie to me, please."

"It's nothing, Mrs Phillips."

Ffi changed tack. "Have you seen Siân lately?"

"Not for a while, I think I upset her," he mumbled.

"What did you do, Huw?"

Huw sighed. "I don't want to talk about it."

Ffi pushed for answers. "Please, Huw."

"I followed her home from the pub and told her she could do better than the city boy. I might have had a bit too much to drink and got a bit carried away."

"Is that why you threatened Ryan?" asked Ffi.

"It's not like that. She could do better."

"Like you, you mean."

"Nah, she made it very clear she's not interested in me. We've agreed to be friends. I wanted to warn her off, save her the heartache." He lowered his head. "I wanted to know why she didn't fancy me, cos I needed to know."

Ffi was confused; she sat down on the corner of the bed. "Why do you need to know that?"

"Cos I fancy someone else, *really* fancy someone else, and I want her to like me..."

"Oh, I see." She remembered how complicated young love could be. "Huw, do you know of anyone, anyone who might want to harm dear Siân?"

He shook his head. "Nope, only the city boy."

"He doesn't want to hurt her, he loves her. It's complicated. They're meant to be together."

The young man frowned.

"Listen, dear; someone is trying to hurt Siân. If you think of who it is, you come and tell me straightaway, and if your mother ever hits you again, you tell me about it." Ffi tapped him kindly where she thought his knee was under the quilted sleeping bag.

"It wasn't…" he began.

"I know it was."

"Yeah."

"Good." She stood up to leave and paused. She could not leave without asking. "Who do you fancy?"

Clearing his throat in his usual gawky manner, Huw said, "Doesn't matter".

"Oh, it matters to you, dear, so it does matter." She cast him a soft, friendly smile, knowing inwardly why he had not given her, of all people, the name. "I have to go, take care of yourself, dear."

"Don't tell her," he shouted after her.

Mrs West was waiting at the bottom of the stairs. "How dare you come into my home like this, in the middle of the night."

"The middle of the night? It's not even gone seven." She put her face menacingly close to the other woman's. "Don't you dare lecture me, Mrs West. I know what you are. I know what you did. Don't you ever, ever hit that dear son of yours again, or I will call the police. Is that clear?"

* * *

The mud sucked at the tyres of Lloyd's blue escort until it could go no further. The wheels spun, spraying mud higher up the paintwork. Badden cursed and gave up. All these years, all this technology, yet not much had truly changed. Wheels still got stuck in the mud and people were just the same, weak and spineless. Opening the boot, he hauled Siân's limp body out and flung her over his shoulder. So close, he was so close now. All the years of waiting almost over. The excitement of the moment was like the sweetest wine. Gazing up, he saw the last of the clouds drift away, leaving a crystal clear night, perfect for the ritual. He slunk towards the old circle, the extra weight of Siân pushing him down in the marsh up to his ankles with each step. He swore and cursed at Morwyna, but this was the only way to get her there. He wondered why she always fought him, always simpered after Owein. What was he but brawn and no brain? Some insignificant warrior wannabe. Why could she never see that Badden and she were meant to be? He had power, prowess and could make her a Queen. Why did she reject him when all he wanted was her? The intervening centuries had offered him no answers; only time to obsess over the questions until they consumed his every thought.

Badden looked to his side; he could sense someone watching him and, whoever they were, they were not happy. He squinted in the pale starlight to see who it was. There was only the hawthorn and the gorse. Badden was unnerved, he had the sight, he had trained it long and hard, so why could he not see who it was? "Come to watch your final defeat, old man?" he sneered.

As he walked, the invisible companion seemed to be always at his side. Always out of sight and out of reach, but there and constant. At first Badden simply ignored his shadow, but its continual presence gnawed at his psyche, fuelling his paranoia. "Ooh, think you can scare me by following me; it ain't going to work. Victory's mine, old man, and you're going to know that in every moment as you wander forever in this world. You lost and I won. I was always the better magician, always the better man. I had hopes, ideas, I knew what I could do and you were too weak, too narrow minded to stop me," Badden ranted wildly the whole way to the old circle.

He crossed the threshold of the circle gingerly, putting his hands out before him to test the energies. An invisible force resisted him as he pushed his way forward, making it feel as though he were pushing through yet more mud. The old man's magic and presence, though faint, still lingered. He set Siân's body down on one of the fallen stones, her head closest to the centre of the circle. It would have to do as his altar, though the centre of the circle would have been more fitting; he could not push that far in.

Calling aloud to the ancient powers of darkness, Badden began his ritual to enslave Morwyna's soul to his own.

* * *

Ffi emerged from Mountain Farm no wiser than when she went in. If it was not Huw, then who was it? Who else had a thing for Siân? There were not that many people in this village. Could it have been someone from Cardiff, someone from her college days? No, it had to be someone who knew the old stories about the area, and that meant someone local. Who knew the energies, who knew how to twist and corrupt them? The energies on their own were neutral, neither good nor bad; it was what was done with them, how they were used. Who knew such evil, who had such a black heart filled with obsession for Siân?

Ffi began to mentally run down a list of the local men; most were too old or already married, so she crossed them off mentally. Only a handful of names remained, and, as far as she knew, none of those men had a thing for Siân, and none of them were capable of this type of occultism. One name did disturb her; Lloyd knew Siân well and had access to her day in, day out. Ffi realised that she knew very little about Lloyd, other than the fact that he ran the shop and was not popular with his employees. Come to think of it, had she even met the man? Every time she had gone in the shop, she had been served by either Siân or Mandy, never by a man. He was local – ish – in that he originally came from Nevern, only a few miles away. He had always kept himself to himself and never socialised with the rest of the village. Did she actually know where he lived? He had arrogantly come into the village a decade before, with big ideals, but time and village life had eroded them away.

Ffi remembered the gossip; he had inherited Bayden's old place, some distant nephew or more likely he was his illegitimate son. Bayden's old place, of course! The boar, old Mr Bayden was the most boorish man in the history of creation; perhaps the name had evolved from Baedd, the boar. Ffi floored the van, heading to the shop.

The store was apparently empty, but Ffi was not satisfied to let it go at that. She parked the van so its headlights were aimed into the shop. Using her shoulder, Ffi shoved the door. Once, twice, then on the third strike the board fell away and she stepped through, rubbing her sore shoulder. It was as it appeared; there was no one here. Ffi took hold of an upturned lamp, still flickering with the last remnants of power, and sneaked quietly towards the stockroom. Looking inside, the place was a tip; the shelving units had been knocked over, spilling foodstuffs and housewares everywhere. Holding her hand out, palm to the floor, she closed her eyes and centred herself, feeling for the energies left in the room. She sensed fear, pain, dark clouds and ruby swirls. Siân was hurt. Ffi raised her hand to her mouth; it must be Lloyd. He had woven the dark magic, polluted the area's energies, conjured up the Gwyllgi and the Pwca, killed the old man and now, by the looks of it, he had Siân. Where would he take her?

With dread and fear, she knew the answer; up to the circle. That was what all the energy work was about; he was trying to break down the circle's protection so he could use it for his own means. She prayed wholeheartedly to the Goddess, to the spirits of the land, please could she stop him, please could she save Siân, as she took off in the van.

Gruffly spluttering, the old van accelerated up the High Street to the junction. In amongst her fervent prayers, Ffi had seen but not registered the approach of another vehicle oncoming from the right. The other vehicle, in its own rush, failed to spot the van. Ffi ploughed into the side of the other, bigger vehicle, metal tearing against metal. Ffi felt the force of the blow go through the van and through her own body, shaking her up. Too late, she swerved the van away, propelling it sideways off the road and towards the wall that stood in front of a cluster of stone cottages.

Ryan was also shaking, from the impact and from fear. He pulled at the door catch and shoved at the door. It would not open, too crumpled by the impact. Clambering over the gearstick, he exited instead by the passenger door. "Are you all right?" he called out to the other vehicle.

Ffi, blinded by the headlights, was relieved to hear his voice. "Ryan!" She opened her own car door as far as was possible. There were only a few inches between her and the wall. Breathing in hard to shrink her curvy figure, she eased her way out of the van.

"I'm so sorry, I didn't see you."

"I didn't see you either. We've no time for pleasantries." Seeing how dented and damaged the passenger side of the van was, Ffi guessed it was not going anywhere tonight. She gave the four by four a quick once-over, and although the front driver's side and door were dented, it was in much better condition than her own vehicle, and its engine was still purring.

Waving her hands in small circles to hurry Ryan along, she issued orders. "We've got to get up to the circle. Lloyd's got Siân and he killed your friend."

"Her boss?" A new emotion arose, one of revenge, as he climbed back into the driver's seat. Ffi followed on his heels and plonked herself in the passenger seat. "Yes, I don't know why I didn't see it before. He's Bayden's son, he's the boar. How good are you at offroading?"

"Time to find out."

"That's the spirit! Head for the cemetery and go straight out the back of it. We might be able to cut across from there to the circle."

Silently she thanked the Goddess and the spirits of the area. 'You're good,' she complimented them, 'How about being a teeny bit more gentle next time though?'

CHAPTER FORTY

Siân woke up gradually. First her hearing returned, and she became aware of a low, continuous intonation in no language that she recognised. The flow and sound of it were ancient, like some primal language. On and on it went, irritating every fibre of her being. Then feeling returned and she wished it had not bothered. Her whole body felt bruised and battered, and she was lying uncomfortably on an ice cold stone. Her body heat had melted the ice, some of the liquid had soaked into her clothes, and the rest had run down the sides of the stone to the ground, where it pooled. There was something warm and sticky in her hair and her head throbbed violently. Her groggy brain ran through a form of self-interrogation. 'Who am I?' she asked herself. A dozen names came back all at once, fogging her mind. 'Who am I?' she asked again. She heard the names Siân and Morwyna in unison, spoken by her own internal voice. A third time she asked and again two names came in reply.

She concentrated on checking herself over as quietly as possible. She was in one piece, her hands squashed uncomfortably under her own mass against the stone. Her hands and feet were both bound, no doubt by the cheap twine they stocked in the shop. Panic clawed at her and her breathing quickened. Siân forced herself to be calm, not wanting to give away to Lloyd that she was awake. Opening her eyes narrowly, Siân could only see shapes and shadows; not much use. From the smell and feel of it, she was out at the circle; the moor there had a unique smell of peat and flowers, not that there were many flowers there. She figured it was night from the low temperature and the lack of light, but was it tonight or another night? How long had she been out of it?

Lloyd could be heard not far from her, chanting seemingly random syllables out into the night. He enjoyed the sound of his own voice and the longer he went on, the more chance she had to get away. She knew that her hands often shrank when cold, she had once lost a ring that way, so she manoeuvred herself very slightly to maximise the contact between the cold rock and her hands in the hope that cold hands would be easier to wriggle loose of the twine. Her plan was first hands, then feet. Cramp bit sharply at her hands and feet, but she forced herself to stay still.

* * *

The four by four passed the row of wooden crosses, marking the most recent graves in the cemetery, and carried on along the curving narrow lane. "Speed up," Ffi told Ryan.

Ryan tilted his foot down on the accelerator; the monster increased its speed. "Uh huh."

Ffi put her arms out to brace herself against the car door and ceiling. "Things are going to get a bit bumpy."

Ahead lay a gap in the fencing; one panel had been taken clean out. Large splinters of light-coloured wood lay all around it. "Lloyd must've come this way too. I do hope we're not too late." They zoomed through the gap and flew over a ditch on to the moor. "Now, go that way and keep going." Ffi sliced at the air with her right hand. The uneven ground jolted Ryan and Ffi all around, despite the seat belts.

"What do we do when we get there?"

"We stop him. We deal with it one step at a time. He still has to make her his, and that's some nasty and complicated magic. It takes time and has to be performed correctly, he's got the disadvantage," Ffi said confidently to hide her own worries.

Ryan nodded, reeling the wheel around to avoid a particularly big gorse bush. The further they went on to the moor, the more Ryan struggled with the wheel. They passed the blue Ford; both door and boot were open.

"He can't be that much ahead of us. It's not too far now."

The mud strangled the progress of the four by four, sucking at its great weight. Ryan swerved to get a grip on the grass, which gave way to a large sticky pool. He thumped the wheel with his hands. "We're on foot from here," he said grimly, turning to face his passenger. Ffi was already bounding out of the monster, leaping across the puddle. Her short legs did not take her far and she pulled herself free from the squelching mud. Ryan followed, his longer legs taking him further and away from the dip. Ffi pulled him close as she steadied herself. "Whatever happens, you have to stop him, do you understand? We don't have much time."

Surreptitiously, the odd pair made their way across the moorland and into the cover of the shrubs, their location given away by their footfalls and rustling. Ffi knew they were being watched, she could feel their energies being tracked. "He knows we're coming," she whispered.

"I'm not going to make this easy for him," Ryan replied, his jaw set hard.

Under her breath, Ffi prayed. "Goddess, Gwalchcyfddydd, anyone. Please help us! I don't care how, just help us. Lloyd must not have Elain's beautiful girl. Not now, not ever."

Badden walked around the circle, his arms raised, repeating strange syllables over and over, while Siân lay on a stone on the other side of the circle. Badden stopped, facing Ryan and Ffi, and opened his black eyes. He smiled, his mouth a strange rectangle, his teeth bared, and continued to chant. He dropped his hands to his sides, bowed his head, and then raised his hands to waist height, grasping tightly at something in the palm of each hand.

The pools of water dotted over the moor and the dew on the vegetation began to tremble. Ryan made to sprint forward, but Ffi caught him. "Careful, he's summoning, and it's not the good guys." Wisps of the wraiths broke the surface of the waters. Ffi attempted to counteract his magic. She shoved her hands to her sides, palms down towards the ground, using all her energy to keep the ghastly ghosts down in the bog, where they belonged. "This is your battle, Ryan; Oak King versus the Holly King. I can help keep it even; the rest is down to you two."

Ryan nodded and bolted towards the Ring of Maidens. Badden saw him coming and spun around, bolting around the inside of the circle of stones towards Siân. Badden had the lead by a long way. He reached Siân well before Ryan even reached the circle, and placed his hands over her heart. His voice became louder and clearer, the tone of his spell more urgent and firm. The water around them, in the air and on the ground, whitened and solidified to ice. Siân screamed out in agony as her heart burned cold within her chest, her blood freezing in her veins.

"Get off me!" She squirmed and writhed in pain, still trying to free her wrists from the twine. As she struggled, it cut deeper into her flesh. She focused on the pain, on the heat of the pain and the blood oozing from her head and her wrists; focused on the heat from her heart of her love for Ryan and for her friends and family as the numb coldness crept over. Her heart called out to Ryan, still far away.

Badden closed his eyes, savouring her bloodcurdling screams, savouring his prize. The cold was spreading quickly; with every one of her heartbeats she was becoming his.

Ryan looked on in horror as he ran. He reached the outer edge of the circle, where the air seemed suddenly much thicker. He slowed to a walk as he pushed his way through what felt like an invisible wall. The force pushed his clothes and skin back towards his bones; Ryan did not let it deter him. His heart reached out to Siân's and pulled him onwards. "Siân!" he called out to her. "Hang on."

"Ryan!" she screeched in reply. "Help me!" Her heart felt huge, as though it were growing in her chest, filled with love, anger and an increasing coldness.

Still held in the invisible pressure, Ryan fought with increased desperation as Siân's convulsions became weaker. "I'm coming, love. I love you…"

Siân sobbed with frustration as her limbs deadened with numbness; no longer could she feel her extremities, she could feel her own will dissipating into the numbness of her body; how ironic that he chose to tell her now. "I love you too, Ryan. Now get your arse over here and help me."

The starlight reflected off the frozen water around Siân and the stone. The silvery white light sparkled and rose like particles of dust into the air. Particles collided and exploded to produce more, which spun upwards in an eddy of air. The particles tightened in to form the shape of a woman, with long white hair. As the last particles settled into place, Ryan saw the face of Siân appear, only not Siân but the vision, the Pwca from his nightmare. "Siân!" he yelled at the top of his voice, his muscles tense and straining as he fought harder against the restraining force.

Siân tried to open her eyes; a million tiny, icy needles stabbed at her eyeballs. She saw a blur of her own self, in crystalline form, standing above her. Her feet by her own. Only she knew it was not herself. The face was slightly wrong, not exactly what she remembered from when looking in the mirror. The apparition launched her hands forward over Siân's body and into Badden's. He opened his eyes, staring in disbelief at Siân, then at the Pwca, then down to his own chest. The Pwca's long slender arms stopped at his chest, her hands deep within him, holding on to his heart. A bitter chill spread through his own body. Interrupted, he ceased his enchantments.

"Gwynhwyfar? You can't do this," he gasped. Removing his hands from Siân, he grappled with the ghostly form of the Pwca, but his hands passed right through hers.

Badden's magic faded and Ryan found he could move swiftly and easily again. He rushed to Siân's side and helped to free her from the twine, the wiry threads cutting deep into the tender flesh of his fingers, then dragged her aside from the confrontation. Badden, frozen to the spot, tried to lunge out to stop his rival.

The Phantom watched the young couple with sorrow in her ethereal eyes. Her voice tinkled as she spoke. "Badden, I can do what I like. You agreed to pay my price when the time came."

"No," he screamed, his body racked with pain. "You were to take him." He pointed at Ryan.

"He was… not available."

"Neither am I, tell her, Morwyna. My heart is taken."

Siân gasped for breath and snuggled against Ryan's warmth as he led her away. "I don't want it."

"But it's yours," Badden stammered as he shivered. The veins in his face and arms stood proud from the flesh, the purple green turning to pale blue. His lips and fingers were turning a white blue. "It always was and always will be. I did this for you, Morwyna. I love you. I only wanted to make you love me."

The Pwca looked from Siân and Ryan to Badden. "For so powerful a wizard, you know nothing of magic. Mortals cannot force or command love. A heart offered is not the same as a heart accepted."

The White Phantom sneered as she pulled him closer to her. "You do not know what love is, Badden. You do not love, only desire."

"No, I love you, Morwyna." He called after her as the couple walked away, out of his reach forever. The moisture in Badden's skin and eyes began to crystallise, whitening his grey skin and hair.

Badden fell to his knees, the ice creeping from the ground up his clothes, stiffening and blanching them. The Pwca dropped to her knees and kissed his nose. "Oh, but you have the potential to love, my darling Badden. Come dance with me and I will show you love. You have such a sweet voice, I may even let you sing with me."

Struggling to swallow, his throat now full with ice, he gargled, "No! Gwynhwyfar, no!"

The flesh began to fall away from the Phantom's elegant face, her eyes glowed and her teeth greyed. Inside Badden's chest she squeezed his heart harder with her icicle fingers. Her clothes became torn and ragged, blowing in the breeze. "You promised me a man, Badden. A man that you said shall keep me company for all time, and you will get your dearest desire. You will live forever..."

Badden's heart and body froze solid as the white ice crystals engulfed his form. The starlight reflected against Badden and the Phantom as the particles of frost began to unwrap themselves from their human forms, evaporating into spinning silvery swirls which drifted off into the night. Faint strains of singing echoed into the distance to where two pale flames danced on the surface of the marsh.

EPİLOGUE

Siân took a deep breath; the faint smell of new paint and high summer lingered in the air. She rolled over on the bed and turned off the persistent chirruping of the alarm clock. Lying back, she watched the rainbows that danced on the bed and the wall as a golden beam of morning sunlight passed through the crystals hung from the window. She loved the way the light poured into the cottage since she had got rid of the heavy drapes and lightened the décor. A wide smile formed on her face as she looked over at her sleeping fiancé. Siân stretched happily and placed her hands over Ryan's sleeping eyes. "Good morning, sleepyhead," she whispered huskily in his ear.

"You shouldn't be here."

"Excuse me, this is my family home. Besides, it's only bad luck if you see me, so keep your eyes shut until I'm gone."

"Shouldn't be too difficult," he yawned. "What's the time?"

"Six thirty."

"Huh? Six thirty? In that case I've got plenty of time for more sleep." His eyes still firmly closed, Ryan rolled on to his side and thrust the pillow to his face. "Are you sure you've got enough time to get ready?" he added sarcastically. "I mean, the ceremony starts at twelve thirty; is six hours going to be long enough?"

Siân played along as she climbed out of bed and organised her clothes for the morning. "Well, I dunno. Could be cutting it a bit fine, what with make-up, hair, costume changes, last minute panic, some of the guests getting lost on the way to the Ring of Maidens, then somebody losing something vitally important, like the rings…"

"Don't worry love, Huw has the rings all ready; both your Gran's Welsh gold one and my white gold one. It's all organised and he's been duly threatened."

"And the ring for Lowri, where's that?"

"Huw's given it to Ffi already, so she can hang it in the flowers. Remember to chuck the bouquet at Lowri, and everything will be fine," Ryan mumbled into his pillow.

"That's so romantic! Did Huw really come up with that all by himself?"

"Ha ha, very funny. He had a little help, from most of the village in the end, especially your mate, Mandy. The bloke's got less idea of romance than I have."

Siân laughed. "That's saying something!"

"I don't know what makes Mandy such an expert on romance anyway."

"She has read more romance novels than anyone else I've ever met, and have you noticed how sweet Pete has been to her of late? Ever since she insisted they go to counselling together, he's making such an effort, bless him."

"You'd best be off to Camp Merry Maiden. Don't tell me, the dress will be white velvet if Ffi's making it, and you'll look like Maid Marion," Ryan teased.

"You'll have to wait and see. And don't think I'm going to put up with a little peck on the cheek when the kissing time comes, like during the rehearsal, Mr Ackley."

"No, Mrs Ackley…"

MELROSE BOOKS

If you enjoyed this book you may also like:

A Simple Man
Theresa Baldwinson

A Simple Man is about Piers de Terre, a traveller and herbalist. The story begins with Piers telling us how he travels around the land, using a variety of plants to heal the sick. Piers, a widower whose wife died in childbirth, has two children that he leaves with his mother while he travels, often for up to six months at a time. He sets out in the late spring when the young seedlings are well and he returns home in the autumn, spending the winter months planting and making notes on his observations.

Size: Royal Octavo: 234 mm x 156 mm   Pages: 110
Binding: Hardback   ISBN: 978-1-906050-53-5   £11.99

Fern in a Black Hand
Jessica Farquhar

Fern in a Black Hand is a lively and vivid murder mystery. It is set in Gloucestershire, on the banks of the Severn, in an area centered on the desolate place known as Tomb's Piece, a forgotten stretch of riverside flood plain dominated by an abandoned canal. Our principal character is Cecily: one afternoon, out walking with her husband and their friend John, who is a senior policeman, Cecily discovers the body of a man in the canal. John takes the situation in hand, and later reveals that the man has been murdered. Concealed in his pocket is a small drawing of a fern in a black hand. A few days later, another body turns up in the river, with an identical drawing in its pocket. What is the explanation for these events? Can Cecily and her associates solve the mystery and prevent further misadventures?

Size: B Format: 198 mm x 129 mm   Pages: 144
Binding: Paperback   ISBN: 978-1-906561-94-9   £9.99

St Thomas' Place, Ely, Cambridgeshire CB7 4GG, UK
www.melrosebooks.com sales@melrosebooks.com